TMI

A Chuck Taylor Novel

Novel Written by
I.R. Plummer

In collaboration with
J. Grindstaff

Screen Play Written By
J. Grindstaff
I. R. Plummer

Published by
I.R. Plummer & J. Grindstaff

twomuchinformation.net
irplummer.com

Acknowledgements

Cover model: Courtney Pritchard

Photographer: Erika Boone & Ardis-Blu Photography

Jacket designer: Kimberly Killon – Hot Shots

A very special thanks to Holly Petitt and the Five Sisters Book Club

Holly Petitt, Loveland, CO
Zoey Petitt, Loveland, CO
Sharon Brownlee, Loveland, CO
Diana Schmick, Loveland, CO
Kristen Alexander, Gig Harbor, WA

My good friend and professional comedian Beny Mena

Reviews:

"I thoroughly enjoyed getting to know Chuck in this great Murder Mystery called TMI.

In the beginning of the book I thought he was a shallow punk who was a womanizer. As I got further into it there is a lot more to Chuck than meets the eye. He takes the readers thru his life and it's there that we see that he has a depth that is not readily seen by others.

This book kept me reading to see what was going to happen next, and there is always something happening right to the end. I can't believe this is your first book Joe...you write like you are a seasoned Author...Congratulations, I am looking forward to all the other novels yet to come from you.

"Thanks for letting us be the first to read TMI...I loved it!"

Sharon Brownlee, Loveland, Colorado, Five Sisters Book Club

"Mystery lovers will delight at Joe Grindstaff and I.R Plummer who gives a fresh, new perspective on the sometimes tired genre of mystery we've all come to know. You'll find characters to love, many you'll love to hate, and more that you'll cheer for and hope to see again. With relatable characters, readable suspense, unexpected turns, and lots of drama, you'll find yourself wanting more even after the very last page. Great success!"

Kristen Alexander, Gig Harbor, Washington, Five Sisters Book Club.

"TMI was filled with 'who done it' mystery until the very end. I liked the contrast of being light & airy too. The main character was able to maintain his moral values even though constantly challenged. Good storyline. Joe writes with the ease of an experienced writer. Job well done!

Diana Schmick, Loveland, Colorado, Five Sisters Book Club

Authors I.R. Plummer and Joe Grindstaff team together in TMI to create a fantastic murder mystery and romance novel combined into one that keeps readers in suspense until the very end. Readers quickly fall in love with this novel's rich and complex characters never anticipating all the twists and turns their lives will encounter. First time novelist, Joe Grindstaff, makes a brilliant entrance into these wonderful genres of writing. TMI is a must read for Murder Mystery and Romance novel enthusiasts alike!

TMI Review by Holly Petitt

TMI

Chapter 1

Chuck Taylor rested his tanned arm on the open window frame of a Toyota pickup with faded blue paint.

It was summer. The soggy spring had given birth to a hotter than hell sun that sucked the ground dry and left tempers simmering.

He thought about the meeting he'd just had with Alicia Pointer, his accountant, and wished he could turn the clock back to when life was simple.

But he couldn't, and not wanting to think about the simple, he shutdown the memories.

A billboard advertising insurance pushed his thoughts towards missing supplies, and too many irritating problems that couldn't be answered by shoddy workmanship, errors in shipments, or miscalculations. But he didn't want to think about work, either.

With a snap of his wrist, he twisted the on/off knob on the radio. The black knob fell onto the floorboard and rolled under the seat.

The Beatles song playing on the radio hit a high note, and turned to static. Like a drowning robot the radio sparked, popped, sputtered, and with a final sizzle fell silent.

He wacked the dashboard with his fist.

The speakers screeched to life at full volume. The high pitched hiss, and hair raising static sounded like a rattle snake on speed, or a demented witch breaking the sound barrier.

"Piece of crap," Chuck muttered.

He aimed the second tap just above the radio.

The instant silence was deafening.

Restless, his mind wondered back to the meeting with the accountant, and tapped his fingers against the steering wheel.

His rendition of Paul Jones, I've Been a Bad, Bad Boy, matched the wail of the police siren on the white and black, Texas State patrol car that came out of nowhere, and crept up his bumper.

Chuck swerved.

The tires bounced over the shoulders rumble strip.

Gravel pinged against the trucks back fender.

The driver of a spice red Mustang convertible honked his horn.

In the rear view mirror, Chuck saw the driver's one finger salute. His passenger, a black haired woman with a wide smile, playfully slapped at the man's hand.

The patrol car shot past.

The driver of the Mustang whipped into the traffic lane, tromped the gas pedal and yelled, "Watch where you're going asshole."

"I was," he said to the Mustang's taillights as the driver cut across to the left lane, and hit eighty within seconds.

Ten minutes later, restless and irritated, he took a freeway exit, and pulled into a strip mall parking lot.

A cute brunette, wearing cut-off jeans and a low cut midriff baring blue halter top, popped out from between two parked cars.

The old pickups brakes squealed a protest, and left a strip of rubber on the blistering hot asphalt.

The woman offered a lopsided smile and blew him a kiss.

Chuck parked the truck, hopped out, and picked up a booklet the woman dropped.

His knees popped as he jogged towards the woman.

"Miss you dropped this."

"Thanks." Her green eyes traveled from his sandy brown hair, down his lean well-toned torso, lingered on the bulge in his faded jeans, and traveled back to his smiling brown eyes.

"Next time, keep your hands on the wheel. If you'd been paying attention to the road you wouldn't have almost run me over." Her sweet as honey voice gave his manhood another nudge.

"You look pretty good for being run over."

"And young enough to be your daughter—pervert." She licked her bottom lip, winked, and gave him a nice view of her braless assets as she slid into the seat of a banana yellow Volkswagen bug.

"Yep, that's me."

He was still chuckling when he entered Radio Shack.

The long narrow store smelled like plastic, recycled air, and taco sauce. The merchandise was stacked neat and dusted. But the display units were old and chipped.

The store was in need of a major facelift and a good air conditioner.

A man with salt and pepper hair, and a slight paunch tore himself away from a cluster of men in the back corner of the long rectangular room.

Reaching Chuck he gave a curt nod. Pencils, pens, scissors and a pen light stuck in a pocket protector made him resemble a cross between a pharmacist and an electronics guru. Under the pocket was a dollar bill sized name tag that read, Manager, Todd Shelf.

"Welcome to Radio Shack. May I help you?"

"Maybe."

Chuck studied a cardboard display panel with six buttons and six descriptions of radio features. He pressed the top button and nodded at the clear tone coming from the speakers.

"If you're shopping for a car radio we have several models."

"I see that."

Chuck punched the third button, a less expensive unit according to the sign, and fiddled with a knob to locate Fox 92.3.

"That radio's on sale for only two hundred and thirty nine dollars."

"Only? I can buy a damn good transistor radio for twenty bucks. Do you have something cheaper?"

The manager pushed the bottom button, and selected the same station.

"This model doesn't have a CD player, but for a hundred bucks it's a decent machine."

Chuck winced. "Decent must depend on your hearing."

The manager grinned.

"How hard is it to install a radio in a truck?"

"That depends on the year and model. We have installation and adapter kits for most vehicles. But you'll have to order them online."

"Don't suppose you have a damaged radio with a CD player for a hundred?"

"Don't suppose I do. When my wife has a bad day she buys something that makes a dent in the checkbook."

"Am I having a bad day?"

"It can't be good if you're shopping for a radio."

A man at the other end of the store hollered, "Knock the crap out of him."

"What's going on over there?"

"They're listening to a scanner. The First Century Bank on Executive Street tripped their silent alarm."

"A bank robbery?"

The manager nodded. "Just before you arrived dispatch received a call from someone inside the bank. They confirmed a robbery in progress."

Curious, Chuck headed towards the cluster of men. The manager dogged his steps.

"What happened?" The manager asked a young clerk with a neon green buzz cut, a gold hoop in his nose, and a name tag that read Randy.

"Four guys, with high power rifles, entered the bank. They killed the bank guard. When they left one of the idiots tripped over his feet. The police have him in custody. The other three took off in a white Honda Civic."

The scanner crackled and static filled the air.

"*All units be advised the vehicle has stopped. The*

suspects have fled on foot. Last seen in the area North of Executive and Mesa."

Chuck spread his feet and stuck his hands in the back pockets of his worn jeans.

"That's a pretty cool toy, how much?"

"Scanners aren't toys."

"Does your wife own one?"

"You need to be responsible to own one," Todd Shelf said.

"Are you saying I'm not responsible or did your wife say that to you?"

"I'm…" Todd shook his head and took a breath. "The hand held model you see is top of the line. On sale it's a hundred and thirty nine dollars."

"Spit out the rest."

"What rest?"

"The gadgets that are sold separately."

"It comes with one antenna and a home charger. Batteries sold separately."

Chuck nodded. "Does it work like a radio, with a dial to change frequencies?"

"It does. You'll want to buy a frequency manual for this area."

"Thought you said it was a full meal deal. Do they make a scanner that doesn't need to be programmed?"

"How much are you willing to spend?"

"One thirty nine. Besides the police, what will a scanner pick up?"

"The fire department, airline pilots, the railroad, and truckers CBs. Basically any radio that transmits a signal."

"Is every frequency listed in the manual?"

"That and more," Todd Shelf said. He walked to the cash register, and grabbed an inch thick manual, the size of a phone book, from under the counter.

"You want to be nosey you can listen to cellphone conversations but that would be breaking the law and requires a little reprogramming, but that's TMI."

"TMI?"

"Too much information."

"But you listen to them."

"I didn't say that."

"Sure you did. Box one up and add a package of batteries."

"You want a charger for the car?"

"Do I need one?"

The manager rolled his eyes.

"What the hell; add the car charger to the total."

"Are you going to buy the car radio you looked at?"

"Not today."

Todd rang up the purchases and offered a smug smile. "That will be one hundred sixty nine dollars and thirty eight cents."

That's more than the cheapest radio with the CD player."

"It offers more entertainment than traffic and weather reports."

"Humph." Chuck listened to the police dispatch scream orders while the manger put batteries in the scanner, and programmed the police and fire department radio frequencies.

In the truck, Chuck turned on the scanner. When he

pulled out of the parking lot, he checked the rearview mirror, and made a left hand turn from the right lane. He waved off the irate driver he'd cut off, cut across two lanes and headed the pickup towards the bank.

Half a dozen police cruisers, light bars flashing, were parked along the street.

A block from the bank, a police cruiser blocked the road.

Chuck nodded at the young, clean cut, stern faced officer who pointed towards an alley.

He backed up ten feet and made the turn. On his left was the high-end furniture store that had moved into the old red brick Woolworths building. Butted to its back was an old hotel that had been converted into boutiques.

The Playhouse Theater, purchased by the local theater club and currently being remodeled, was on his right, across from the furniture store. Behind the theater was a restaurant with a long list of reincarnations.

The two story buildings blocked out the light, but trapped the obsessive heat, and shot the temperature into triple digit figures.

Like toys scattered haphazardly down a hallway, blue dented dumpsters and trash littered the alley, and perfumed the stale air with the sour scent of rotting food and human waste.

Chuck crept past the third dumpster in the narrow obstacle course.

A crazed, shirtless man with a dark olive complexion and greasy straight black hair opened the driver's door. The automatic pistol he stuck under Chuck's nose was cold and hard.

"Get the fuck out of the truck."

"You know how to ask nicely?"

"You stupid puto, get out. Stop the fucking truck and get out."

Chuck looked into the kids drug crazed eyes. He'd seen the look before. Even if he got out of the truck the punk's desperation could get him killed.

"You're stoned and stupid," Chuck said, and slapped the horn on the steering wheel with the palm of his hand.

"You're a fucking idiot, man?"

Probably, Chuck thought and stomped on the gas pedal.

With drug fueled adrenaline, the man wrapped his arm around the open window frame and kept pace with the truck.

The muzzle of the pistol was now angled towards Chuck's thigh. Better than his face, he thought, and pressed the horn again.

He dug the thumb of his left hand into the artery on the wrist of the man's left hand. When the gun hit the floorboard Chuck tried to suck air past the breath he'd been holding. His lungs screamed a protest. He coughed and blinked his watering eyes.

Chuck glanced in the rearview mirror. The cop who'd directed him to the alley blocked the entrance.

Chuck gave the punk a shark hungry grin.

"Look behind you shithead, cops will be on your ass in seconds."

The man glanced, and spit out words Chuck didn't understand. But he got the drift; the guy was pissed, scared, and willing to do anything if he thought it would help him escape.

Chuck slammed on the brakes, the tires squealed and

the tang of burnt rubber filled the cab.

The man stumbled.

Chuck gripped the window frame and shoved the door outward.

The man and the door slammed against the edge of a dumpster. The wheels on the dumpster screeched. The rust pocked metal box hit aged red bricks with a sharp slap, and bounced forward.

A cat yowled.

A scrawny black cat, followed by a dingy white cat, darted down the alley.

Like a mushroom cloud of toxic waste, the distinct stench of piss and rotten meat floated through the stirred air.

The man swore, did a half skip, reached his right arm through the open door, grabbed Chuck's left arm and tugged.

"Shit punk, you should've run while you still had a chance to escape."

Chuck pulled his arm out of the man's grip, and twisted his upper torso towards the door. With both hands clasping the window frame he gave the door a slight push, hit the gas pedal and pulled the door towards him.

A sickening snap filled the moment of silent surprise.

The jagged end of a bone poked through the black diamond pattern of a tattoo. Blood dripped off the man's fingers. His brown eyes widened in surprise and darkened to deep pools of pain.

"Fuck man, what the hell?"

Chuck pushed the door open, and tried to slam a fist

into the punk's nose.

The guy tucked his chin.

Chuck's fist connected with his forehead and snapped the guy's head back. Dazed, the robber released his hold, dropped to the ground and landed on the broken arm.

Hollering with pain, he rolled as the trucks back wheels caught the edge of a tennis shoe. "Fuck man, I'm going to kill you."

Chuck grinned and slammed the door shut. With his arm hanging out the window he answered with the flip of a finger.

Stomping on the accelerator he glanced in the rear view mirror.

A white cruiser, the light bar flashing like a Christmas tree, blocked the alley.

Two officers, with guns drawn, stood over the fallen bank robber.

Chuck tapped the garage door opener, parked in the center of the double car garage, and pushed the remote to close the door.

His raspy breathing filled the silence.

Three deep breaths stopped the hyperventilation.

He heaved a sigh and reached for the automatic pistol at his feet. He flipped on the safety, removed the bullets and sniffed the muzzle. The gun hadn't been fired recently. Thank God, he thought, the gun hadn't been the one used to kill the bank guard. He opened the truck door and eased to a stand.

His knees popped.

In the kitchen he stuck the pistol in the waistband of his pants, pulled a bottle of whiskey from a cupboard and chugged three swallows.

His heart stopped then bumped into a rhythm a step above normal.

He placed the whiskey bottle back in the cupboard, pulled a bag of pretzels off the shelf, and grabbed a beer from the refrigerator.

In the living room, he set the pistol, scanner, pretzels, and bottle of beer on a small table in front of the brown leather couch.

He sat, rested his head in his hands and closed his eyes.

"Shit."

His head throbbed.

His hands shook.

The whiskey burned a hole in his empty belly.

Like an instant replay of a defensive end clobbering a quarterback, flashbacks raced through the scene. The punk had been young, mid-twenties at most. Short legs, long torso, and a compact body pumped full of drugs that had glazed the anger in his chocolate colored eyes with a glassy sheen.

The cold hollow barrel of the pistol pointed at his head had shot his reflexes into survival mode with no thought about mortality.

The bitter metallic taste of fear still coated his throat.

The adrenaline high, a buzz similar to booze on an empty stomach, rang in his ears.

He grabbed the beer and chugged half the bottle.

At least five police officers had seen his truck.

Had they written down his license plate number, or

in the confusion had they concentrated on the robber?
    Leaning his head back, he ate pretzels, finished the
beer, and contemplated where to hide the frigging pistol.

Chapter 2

Hours later a feminine voice on the scanner pulled Chuck out of a light sleep.

"Station fourteen and station seven. Pumper fourteen. Pumper seven. Truck four. Truck five. Quint seventeen. Quint seven. Four and Chief two. Structure fire, man trapped. Location - High Point Apartments, one, eight, zero, zero, Christopher Street. Time-out, nineteen twenty hours."

Chuck listened to the fire department and police confirmed they were en-route.

He knew the apartments and Britney Watson, the apartment manager. A feisty brunette, she was a friend who offered sleepovers that satisfied their needs without complicating the arrangement with long term expectations.

He grabbed the scanner and the bag of pretzels on his way to the garage.

Minutes later he rolled to a stop on a side street half a block from the apartment complex.

The fire added a layer to the day's frying pan sizzle of heat that hadn't lessoned.

A gray haze of smoke, that gave the impression of

walking through fog, smelled like burning pine, burnt rubber and the sharp acid of gasoline.

The scanner in his hand fed information—a broken gas line needed to be shut off, a firefighter was down, a call for backup.

He walked towards the yellow ribbon barriers and scanned the clusters of people drawn to the action and those that lived nearby.

He found Britney standing beside a police cruiser with her arm around a woman holding a small child. A girl, if the hairless baby doll the child clutched to her chest was any indication.

"You okay?" He placed his hand on Britney's shoulder and gave a reassuring squeeze.

"No. Yes. Oh crap." She turned and buried her face in his chest.

Chuck felt her sob and the hitch in her breathing. Her shoulders shuddered and a quiver walked down her spine, but she held back the flood of tears.

He rubbed her back until the knot in her shoulders relaxed and her breathing slowed.

"Did your latest dinner experiment blowup?" Chuck asked.

The child in the woman's arms giggled.

Britney shifted in his arms and kissed his cheek.

"Thanks, your shoulder and sense of humor are both appreciated.

"I was headed to my car when I smelled ammonia and something with a pine scent. I've received enough bulletins from the police department to know what it could mean."

"Meth lab?" Chuck asked.

"That was my thought."

"Did you try to figure out which renter was cooking?"

"I probably would have tried, but I got a creepy feeling that someone was watching me and something bad was about to happen. I continued to the car and acted like I couldn't find the car keys. Back at my place I called 911. I was asking dispatch to send cops when the kitchen window shattered, the kitchen door blew open and the building swayed like we were having an earthquake. I ran out the door. The back corner of the building was gone. My car was buried under chunks of concrete."

"How many people are home this time of day?"

"It was dinner time, for most of them. Kid's had been sent outside to run off excess energy. After…" Britney's breath hitched then settled.

"It was utter chaos. Only lasted seconds, but it seemed like a lifetime. One of the women rounded up the kids, and made them stay with her until their parents arrived. Three of us went door to door until the flames stopped us. All but four families were in the head count. If we're lucky they weren't home."

"What about the man reported trapped and the meth cooker?"

Britney shook her head.

"Is there anything I can do to help?"

"Right now I can't think past the present."

Chuck nodded to the grim faced police officer who approached.

"Britney, if you need anything call, and come to the house if you don't want to stay in a motel."

"Thanks." She gave him a bone crushing hug, turned and walked towards a cruiser with the police officer.

Chuck counted three fire trucks, and saw the steady spray of water from a fourth truck behind the building.

The building had been a two story U shaped structure with a swimming pool and playground in the center. Parking had been around the outside of the building. The complex, constructed in the early sixties, had been built on the cheap end of construction standards. Now the lack of firewall material would be the building and firefighters curse.

A woman behind him softly sobbed, but the crowd was somber.

With his hands in his hip pockets, Chuck watched.

Like a gas stove being turned on high, flames shot through the roof.

Windows shattered. Landing on a cruiser the glass fragments sounded like a thousand wind chimes.

As fresh air and gas fueled the flames, the fire churned like a locomotive running at full speed.

Chuck heard the Fire Chief, shout orders. Like an echo in a canyon, half a breath later, the words flowed from the scanner in his breast pocket.

The situation was surreal and exciting.

He'd never been an ambulance chaser. But the scanner offered insight into what was happening, and the calm assurance of trained men doing their job. It was easy to understand why people were drawn to the high risk attraction.

But he'd seen enough.

As he eased through the crowd a deafening explosion drowned out a woman's scream.

Chucked turned.

A second explosion shook the ground.

Walls exploded outward.

Something shrouded in flames, a body Chuck thought, and hoped to hell he was wrong, sailed through the air. With a thump the mass landed on a car.

Glass, wood, red hot metal, and fragments of building material and household possessions created a starburst of sparks.

Mesmerized Chuck watched a piece of metal sail through the air like a shooting star.

The high pitched whistle grew louder.

People ducked.

The woman next to him whimpered.

He turned and shielded her frail body.

A blistering heat singed his hair.

A trickle of warm blood ran down his jaw.

"Damn," he muttered.

He released the woman and wiped his jaw with the sleeve of his sky blue polo shirt.

"You're bleeding. How bad is the cut?" She asked.

"Like I can see it," he said with more calm than he felt.

The elderly woman chuckled.

"Lord, I'm getting senile. Don't you hate it when people ask dumb questions?" She wrapped cool bony fingers around his hand and tugged him through a crowd that parted like the red sea for Moses.

When they reached the back of the waiting ambulance, Chuck bulked.

"You earned my gratitude and respect; don't blow it by acting like a baby. Let the pretty EMT check you out.

If you don't act like a big boob maybe you can weasel a date out of her. If that doesn't work ask for a sucker."

"I'd rather have a date with you."

"Aren't you a charmer, but you don't hold a candle to my Henry."

"If Henry's your husband, he's a lucky man. If he's a boyfriend, I could call him out for a duel at dawn."

Several people turned to look as her bell like laughter filled the air.

"I married Henry the day after Pearl Harbor was attacked."

"How long were you married?"

A spark lit her faded green eyes. A faraway memory brought a wisp of a smile. She held up her hand to show him a simple gold wedding band. "We're still married, but now Henry's a big green bullfrog."

"Have you kissed him?"

"That's what turned him into a frog." She chuckled but didn't share her thought.

"Do you live in the apartments?" Chuck asked.

"Henry and I live in the green house behind us."

She gave him a wink and pushed him towards the EMT who'd listened to their conversation.

"Why didn't you duck?" The EMT aimed a flashlight at the cut. The blue and white name tag pinned to her starched white shirt pocket read, Nancy Padilla. She was fortyish, medium height, with soft brown eyes. Her brown hair was highlighted and swept into a sloppy top knot that would look sexy if she was just stepping out of his shower.

"I needed a tetanus shot. Thought baring my ass to you would be fun."

"You're a charmer and a smartass."

"So I've been told." He winched when she used a Q-tip to swab the cut with disinfectant.

The scanner in his pocket kept them abreast of what was happening.

"You hear about the fire on the scanner?"

"I did, a friend manages the place. I came down to make sure she was alright."

"Did you find her?"

"Yeah, she's fine."

"You don't need stitches, but you do need the shot updated. Next time stay home. Emergency crews don't need the added stress of protecting bystanders."

"Yes, Ma'am," Chuck said.

"Drive to the ER and ask for Maria. You can charm her with your sexy smile and swap phone numbers."

"What about your number?"

"My bullfrog is six-three, two hundred ten pounds. Goes by the name Detective Jim, and he doesn't share his toys."

"I don't blame him, I wouldn't share either."

"The old gal was right, you are a charmer." She said and handed him a grape sucker.

By the time Chuck drove to the hospital and walked into ER, a tom-tom beat a war call against his temples, and his eyes were ready to pop out of their sockets.

As Chuck approached the check-in counter, he heard a child's whimper, and a mothers soothing voice drift down the empty hall.

The male nurse on duty was the color of strong coffee and built like a champion heavy weight fighter. His name tag said, Nurse Peters. He lifted a brow and eyed the blood on Chuck's shirt.

"You're not shot, and the nose isn't busted. You suck someone dry?"

"Everyone's a comic. Nancy Padilla, an EMT, said to ask for Maria. I need a tetanus shot, and something for a hell of a headache."

"You have insurance?"

Chuck nodded.

"You just cost me a buck for the coffee jar."

"You place bets on who has insurance?"

"Nancy called to say that you were on the way. Said you'd be a paying customer, I mouthed off that after dark they were rare creatures."

Chuck scanned the empty waiting room. "Is it always this quiet this time of night?"

"When the place empties like this, it's a bad omen. I hate nights like this. Something's about to happen and when it does all hell will break lose."

"You sound like Radar, the character on Mash who heard helicopters before anyone else."

"So I've been told. I lived through nights like this in Afghanistan, there's a feel to them." He handed Chuck a purple clipboard. A pen with a silk daisy taped to the top end was tied to the clamp. "Go to the first room on the left. While you wait, fill out the forms."

Chuck settled into an ugly green plastic chair three shades darker than the hideous green walls. The color cut the reflection of light, but instead of soothing, Chuck found the room claustrophobic and depressing.

Ten minutes later the insurance forms were signed and the odors, bells, and intercom commands unique to a hospital scratched his nerves raw.

The two year old People magazine rattled when his hand fisted.

He tossed the magazine aside, leaned his head back, and counted the holes in the acoustic ceiling tiles.

When the door opened, he straightened and pasted a smile on his face.

The woman's white nurse's uniform was stretched tight over an ample bosom and wide hips. Her hair was a thin halo of silver and her left eye drifted towards her nose. The stainless steel tray in her hand held two syringes, cotton, a sterile pad and a Band-Aid.

"Unzip your pants and bare you right hip." Her teeth slipped, giving her a slight lisp.

"Do we do introductions after the pillow talk?"

"Honey Bun foreplay is for amateurs. Now drop the pants and bare the ass. When I'm done, if you want, we can swap stories, but right now I'm hot and need satisfaction."

"Military?" Chuck asked as he unbuckled his belt.

"Army, why?"

"You remind me of a nurse I knew."

He hissed when the first needle pierced his skin like a sword. She didn't let him catch his breath before the second needle felt like it kissed his kidneys.

"Was she smart and sexy like me?" Her lemon drop breath caressed his neck. She patted his ass as he zipped up his pants.

He stepped away and turned.

Her sassy smile dared him to comment.

"No Ma'am, you're in a whole different league."

He was halfway down the hall when the silence was broken by the wail of sirens.

At the desk he listened to the intercom as Peter's calm baritone voice called a list of coded numbers for backup.

"What happened?" Chuck asked when Peters hung up the phone.

"Two gangs decided to use semi-automatics to see who would control a street corner. Have nine incoming. Six are headed to the morgue."

Chuck pulled a twenty out of his wallet and handed it to Peters.

"For the coffee jar."

"Thanks," Peter's said as the first ambulance pulled under the portico.

In the pickup, Chuck checked his watch and started the engine.

He entered Radio Shack ten minutes before closing.

"You're back." Todd Shelf lifted a bushy brow and smiled.

"Yeah, you miss me?"

"There's blood on your shirt and you smell like wood smoke, disinfectant, and grilled garlic."

He jerked his thumb towards the scanner on a shelf behind him. "I heard two EMTs talk about a guy who saved an old lady from getting hurt at the apartment fire. Was that you?"

Chuck shrugged.

"I told you a scanner would get you into trouble."

"I remember," Chuck said.

"Did you decide to buy the car radio?"

"No."

"It goes on sale for fifty percent off this weekend. I'll give you the discount now."

"You could have made that offer earlier today."

"I only offer deals to regular customers."

"Likely story! You mentioned cellphone frequencies. How does that work?"

"That's one of the frequencies I mentioned that need to be tweaked. Give me the scanner and I'll fix it for you. Off the record, of course."

"Of course," Chuck said and grinned.

Todd plugged the scanner into a laptop on the counter, hit several keys, unplugged the scanner and handed it back to Chuck.

"That's it? What did you do?"

"TMI."

"Jeez, you sound like an undercover cop." Chuck mumbled.

"Do you have any suggestions on how to clear the reception?"

"For the car or home?" Todd asked.

"Home."

"A stronger antenna would help," Todd turned and pulled a box off a shelf. "With this antenna you'll hear things you never knew existed or were possible."

"Is that good?"

Todd gave him a sly smile. "That's good. And remember…"

"I got it, we never talked."

Chuck sat on the couch.

The wonder drug Maria shot into his system had eliminated the headache, but left him feeling wired.

Without paying attention, he fiddled with the dials on the scanner and thumbed through the manual.

A high pitched beep, then a male voice laced with anger filled the room.

"It doesn't matter, the bitch is dead."

"How much is it worth to you?" A deep, calmer voice asked.

"It's not worth shit, you owe me."

"I paid my debt with the last one."

"Then you fucked up and made this mess. The boss don't like being questioned by a broad. You owe me."

A second beep filled the room and the scanner went silent.

Chuck squinted to read the tiny words under the red flashing light—battery needs charged.

"Shit."

Chapter 3

Chuck parked the truck in the manager's parking space.

Superior Apartments had twenty units. Each two story unit housed six apartments with two or three bedrooms, and two and a half baths. A playground, swimming pool, a recreation center available for parties and the manager's office sat in the center of the twenty-five acre landscaped plot.

At half past eight, the day was already hot. The weatherman had promised it would get hotter.

Chuck had one foot planted on the blistering asphalt when Mr. Kellerman, a retired teacher, approached. The crease in his black slacks was razor sharp. His blue pinstripe shirt was crisp. His Old Spice aftershave drifted between them.

"Are you going to paint my apartment?"

"Not today."

"When?"

"Without looking at the schedule the twelfth of never would be my guess."

"No need to be a smartass."

Chuck bit back a smile.

"I'll check the schedule and let you know."

"Can't you give me an idea?"

"Without being a smartass I could not."

"I'll be out of town next week. I don't want you painting when I'm not home."

"Not a problem. I'll stop by later this morning with a date."

"If you paint this week the place can air out while I'm gone."

"I understand," Chuck said as he walked towards the office.

Hector Gomez, dressed in paint splattered jeans, a well-worn blue and white checkered shirt and a Hooter's baseball cap followed Chuck into the office.

"Morning," Chuck said to the three employees already in the office.

He filled a green mug, and lifted the pink lid on the box in the middle of his desk. The sweet aroma of yeast and sugar made his stomach grumble.

"George, you left a message that you got called to apartment F-6 last night. Why?"

"Mrs. Adams dropped a diamond ring down the bathroom sink drain." George Summerland was a handsome dark haired man who wore a perpetual scowl. Like a round peg forced into a square hole he didn't quite fit with the rest of the crew. Now he leaned against a wall, slurped his coffee and bit into a cinnamon twist.

"Were you able to retrieve the ring?"

"One hundred percent, Boss. Paperwork is filled out and on the clipboard."

Chuck nodded. "I got a call at home last night. I need you to check out a disposal in apartment K-4. If

Mrs. Lark put chicken bones in the disposal again, remove the disposal and tell her she won't get a new one."

"You're the boss," George answered with a hint of disagreement. Chuck knew he resented having a boss. He also resented filling out worksheets and answering simple questions. But more than anything George disliked taking orders.

"Did you hear about the fire at High Points?" George asked.

"The fire killed two men and a teenager." Roberto Sanchez, a five foot seven, good looking Hispanic, had an odd way of looking at life. His short temper, bulging muscles and inability to think before speaking got him into a lot of fist fights. He sat in a straight back chair that put his back to the wall and gave him a full view of the room.

"Damn inferno. Heard an old lady lost a dozen cats. Swear it stunk like cat piss when I drove by this morning." Hector chuckled.

"Thanks for sharing," Chuck muttered, and bit into a raspberry filled donut.

"Families were displaced. With the apartment shortage you might get calls. C-2 is ready to rent. By tomorrow the new carpet will be down in M-5." Frank Hanson was five-ten, lean, with a graying mustache, a full head of wavy black hair, and a slight limp from his time in the gulf war.

"Who will call first, the dead men needing a place to haunt or the live ones looking for a handout?"

"Roberto, you're an ass." Frank said.

"Fuck you."

Chuck watched Frank's eyes cloud over before he sucked in his temper. His pressed lips were a fine line under the mustache. He caught Chuck's look and ducked his eyes to stare at the floor.

"I watched it on the news last night. Did you see the clip, Boss?" Hector asked.

"I caught the morning news. Last night I heard the response on this." Chuck pulled the scanner out of his pants pocket and set it on the desk.

"How much that set you back?" Frank picked up the scanner and turned it on.

"Enough."

"Who talked you into buying that?" Hector asked.

"Yesterday I was at Radio Shack during the bank robbery."

"They're paying you too much if you got money to spend on crap like that," George said.

"Was that cool or what? One of the robbers is my cousin," Hector said.

"Young punk with a snake tattooed on his forearm?" Chuck asked.

"Nah, that's Juan. How'd you know about him?"

"Must have heard something on the scanner," Chuck said.

"Juan's a dumbass. He should have worn something to cover up the tat."

"As opposed to your cousin being a smartass for robbing a bank?" Frank said.

"He got caught because he's clumsy." Hector said and shrugged.

"An idiot and inept," Chuck said.

"He's just trying to make a living," Hector said.

"Having a job is making a living. Robbing a bank is a one-way road to trouble," Chuck answered.

"If they hadn't screwed up they had the opportunity to make good money and set their own hours," George said.

"You think stealing is a better choice than say, punching a timecard and earning the money to buy your next beer?" Chuck's tone was causal, but his eye had narrowed.

"Just saying, being your own boss has perks," George shot back.

"My cousin, he's not good at taking orders," Hector said.

"Not good at bank robbery either." Chuck scanned the list of complaint calls and maintenance requests, and finished his donut.

"What does the scanner pick up?" Frank asked.

"Any equipment that produces a radio wave, including cellphones and cordless phones."

"Cool. I need to borrow the scanner to check out my neighbor." Frank said.

"No," Chuck said, and reached for another donut.

"But I think she's selling drugs."

"Call the cops," Chuck said and bit into a cinnamon swirl.

"More like you're horny and want to check out her ass." Hector said and laughed when Frank flipped him off.

"I just want to know if she talks about me to her girlfriends."

"Oh man, she says, 'you are stupid.'"

"Frank, you're not borrowing the scanner. Roberto

you're out of line. Apologize."

"Sorry, you're stupid Frank," Roberto shot back.

Frank's fists balled but he didn't move.

"Can we get some work done? Frank, are you done with the repairs in the laundry room?" Chuck asked.

The shotgun click of heels grabbed Chuck's attention.

He saved his work on the computer, shutdown the screen and leaned back in his office chair.

Angela Summerland opened the door and stepped inside. Her creamy Latino complexion glowed. A white mini skirt showed off long shapely legs. A hot pink spandex tank didn't quite cover the white lace on a push up bra. Over the spandex top she wore a pale pink gauzy blouse tied in a knot at the waist. Her black hair hung in a thick French braid.

She stood in front of Chuck's desk and placed a hand on a nicely rounded hip. Her deep red lips gave him a sexy pout. Her dark brown eyes danced with mischief and a hint of anger.

"Nice outfit. Did you come to rescue me?" Chuck asked.

"I came to pick up my shithead husband. It's our anniversary. He promised me lunch at the Acapulco."

"That's nice."

"I'd rather have dinner at Armani's or the country club."

"Did you tell him that?"

"Why bother he never listens."

"Maybe a different way of handling him would have gotten you what you wanted."

"Do you think you could handle me?"

"I didn't realize I'd offered. Did you have something in mind?"

The deep vibration of her chuckle was wrapped with sexual overtones and made his body hum and twitch.

"I could handle you." She sat on the edge of his desk and leaned into him.

"No doubt you could."

"If I was single maybe you could tempt me to give up my freedom."

"Marriage isn't a ball and shackle," Chuck said.

"My momma would agree but that's not true for everyone. Can you afford me?"

"Definitely not. You could get a job and pay your own credit card bills."

"My momma has never worked. Daddy gives her anything she wants. I need a man like that, a man who will take me to Europe to shop, and pay someone to do the cooking and cleaning."

Chuck smiled and leaned back in his chair. "Learn to cook like your momma and George might be tempted to pay for a housekeeper. Otherwise my best advice is to do something to make him happy, see where that gets you or start over."

"What about making me happy? George could try."

The office door opened and banged against the door stop.

"Can I go to lunch?" George asked without acknowledging Angela.

Angela slid off the desk and folded her arms across

her chest. Her eyes sparked with defiance and a touch of anger.

"Did you sign off on unit I-6?"

"Not done. It still needs a new disposal and sink. I'll pick them up after lunch."

"Anything else?" Chuck asked.

"Like what else have I done?"

"That would be the question."

"The old disposal and sink are pulled. The pool is cleaned and I checked the toilet handles at Mrs. Cutter's unit. They work fine. I think she calls in complaints just to have someone talk to her."

Chuck nodded.

"I'm hungry. Can I go to lunch now?"

"I won't stop you. By the way, I picked up a gun yesterday. Would you like to do some target practice?"

"Whatever you say, Boss. I have nothing going on at home tonight." He turned and headed out the door.

Chuck heard Angela suck in a breath. At the door she turned. "Guess I'm spending my anniversary with you."

Chapter 4

Chuck stood in front of a wall of cookbooks and rubbed the back of his neck.

"May I help you?" The clerk was fiftyish and looked like the old fashioned grandmother who liked to cook and rock a baby on her bosom.

"I'd like to purchase a gift for a friend who likes to experiment when she cooks. Do you have any suggestions?"

"Do you know what cookbooks she has?"

"None, they were lost."

The woman selected eight books, and set them on an empty narrow table next to the checkout counter.

"The first three are the most popular selling basic cookbooks. Then you have the most popular specialty books for desserts, Italian, Mexican, Southern cooking, and breads."

"Do you have any specialty cookbooks for diabetics?"

She pulled a book off the shelf. "This book covers main courses." She handed Chuck the book and selected another. "This one is desserts for diabetics."

"Okay," Chuck said.

"Okay what?"

"Ring them up, please. Do you have a bag to put them in and maybe an apron?"

"We have a cute bag with a lobster reading a cookbook stenciled on the front. You'll find aprons at the kitchen store two doors down."

Half an hour later he stood in the lobby of the Holiday Inn. Britney wrapped her arms around his waist and laid her head on his chest. He kissed the top of her head and rubbed the small of her back. "Bad day?"

"It couldn't get much worse. Since you called this morning I've spent most of the day talking to police and fire inspectors."

"You want to talk?" He asked as they sat in overstuffed green checked chairs.

"Not much to say. The men who died were brothers and my tenant's seventeen year old son. The uncle arrived two days ago. He'd just been released from a three year stretch at the pen in Susanville, California. According to the police both brothers had a long list of drug related arrests and the kid was headed down the same path."

"You need a place to stay and dinner?"

"The apartment owner paid for a week at the hotel. And I just ate a late lunch with a couple of the tenants, but thanks for the offer."

"In a week one of my units will be empty."

"No offence, but your place is way above my beer budget."

"Brit, you let me worry about the rent. If you need a place don't let pride stop you from asking."

"Thanks, I'll think about it."

"Have you done any research into cooking dinners for people and doing weekend catering?"

She sighed. "I know I said I would, but now...I don't even own a spatula."

He handed her the bag at his feet. "This isn't much but it's a start."

"You can't boil water but you bought me cookbooks." She bit her bottom lip and rubbed her hand over each glossy cover.

Standing, she slipped a black apron over her head and tied the strings in the back. "Cooks are Sexy," she read as she ran her hand over the colorful rhinestone design.

"What's this?" She said when she pulled an envelope from a pocket. She paled and sat when she saw the gift certificate.

"I didn't mean to make you cry." Chuck said as he sat on the arm of the chair, rubbed her back and looked around helplessly.

"Why do you have to be so nice?"

"You deserve nice."

"I'm just not used to having a guy in my life that doesn't want something from me."

"I want something."

"What?"

"The first batch of cookies you make when you're wearing that apron."

Chuck climbed in the truck, plugged the scanner into the cigarette lighter, set it on the passenger seat and headed home.

He was a mile from highway 20 when 911 dispatch called for a fire truck to put out a car fire on the north bound lane just past exit fourteen.

Two miles past the gutted shell of the car Chuck pulled to a stop in front of a gray BMW Roadster parked on the shoulder of the road.

The driver sat on the ground with her back against the driver's door. With one leg bent her hand was braced on her knee, thumb up. Her dark russet colored hair was tucked behind her ears. She wore a sleeveless green dress and black heels.

"Hi, anything I can help with?" Chuck asked as he approached.

She cocked her head and regarded him through blue gray eyes.

"My cellphone's dead. Could you drop me off at the gas station at the next exit?"

He offered a hand to help her stand and resisted the temptation to offer to dust off her nicely rounded ass.

"Do you need gas?"

"The tank's full. The starter's going out, but I don't think that's the problem."

"I'm Chuck Taylor; I'll drive you wherever you need to go."

"I'm Laura Cannon. Thanks for stopping. Do you live around here?"

"I live on Willow Springs."

"Really? I live on the corner of Willow and Colorado."

"Small world. I can drop you at your place and then check out your car."

"That's sweet, but not necessary."

"I don't mind." Chuck nodded at the policeman who rolled to a stopped on the shoulder of the road across from them.

"Is everything alright?" The officer asked.

"The car stalled. I'm taking the lady into town and will come back to see if I can get the car running," Chuck said.

The officer nodded and watched them climb into Chuck's truck.

Laura squirmed, locked her knees together and gave him a half smile. "Your place is closer than mine. Would you mind stopping, I really need a bathroom?"

"Is this where I lecture you on the dangers of going to a stranger's house?"

"You sound like a parent with a daughter. How old is she?"

Chuck smiled. "She's in college."

"You're sweet."

"Sweet doesn't mean harmless. How old are you?" The words came out sharper than he intended.

She shot him a devilish smile. "Older than I look."

"You look around twenty-five."

"Thanks for the compliment. Don't worry; you won't be accused of being a daddy figure."

"More like lecherous old man," Chuck muttered to himself. "Why didn't you lift the car's hood to let the cop's know you had car problems instead of thumbing a ride?"

"Would you believe I didn't think to do that?"

"No."

"Okay, how about I've never hitchhiked and decided

to try a new adventure?"

"Don't buy that one, either."

"How about I'd been sitting there for an hour with the hood up and no one stopped. I decided to see what would happen if lifted my skirt and I stuck my thumb out. Until you talked to the cop that stopped, I had my hand on a can of pepper spray."

"That, I believe."

Chuck pulled into the driveway of a house painted creamy white. The trim was black and the metal roof was gunmetal gray. He pressed the garage door opener and cut the engine.

Laura stepped out of the truck and looked at the freshly mowed lawn. A smile curved her lips when she spotted the red geraniums and white petunias blooming in the flower bed that followed the line of the curving sidewalk.

"Nice place."

"Thanks. The bathroom is straight down the hall. I'll get the tool box and wait here for you."

When she slid into the seat beside him she was smiling.

"It's nice to know some men know how to put down a toilet seat."

"You impress easily."

"Not really, but it's a bench mark I plan to add to my perfect man list."

"What else is on the list?'

"He bathes more than once a season, no tattoos, doesn't fart, belch or scratch his crotch in public and doesn't refer to me as his old lady." She batted her eyes at him. "Think you can pass the test?"

"Tough rules to make a guy live by. How about dinner tonight? I'll impress you with my ability to suck spaghetti off a plate without using my fingers or utensils."

"Tempting but I can't tonight. Another night would be nice."

"I'll be sure to bathe before I call."

"Sounds like a good strategy. Do you always help damsels in distress?"

"Only redheads with great looking legs."

"You're flirting with me."

"I am."

"That's sweet," she said and sighed.

Chuck pulled to a stop in front of the BMW and grabbed the tool box from the bed of the truck. Twenty-five minutes later he dropped the car's hood and tossed a bag with battery cables and his tools into the bed of the truck.

He leaned against the driver's door and kept one eye on the traffic. "You're set. The battery cable was corroded and one of the battery rods is loose. You need to buy a new battery."

Laura nodded. "What do I owe you?"

"A thank you and a promise to never get into a car with a stranger."

"Thank you and yes, Daddy."

Chuck laughed.

"One night soon, dinner will be my treat," Laura said.

"You know where I live."

Chapter 5

The moon was a sliver short of full.

The desert sand was hot, the night air a scant degree cooler.

A small spotlight was fixed on empty cans and bottles set on an eight foot long fence rail.

Past the shadows, coyotes let them know they weren't happy about their evening being interrupted by visitors.

"When did you get this, Boss?" Seated on the tailgate of Chuck's pickup, George frowned as he examined the pistol in his hand.

Chuck leaned against the tailgate.

Sandwiched between them, Angela rubbed the back of Chuck's thigh with the toe of her shoe.

Chuck stepped away.

Angela chuckled. The sound was like rich dark chocolate and hot sex.

"Yesterday," Chuck said.

"You didn't buy this from a dealer; the serial number's filed off," George said.

"Shit. I didn't notice that."

"What did it cost you?"

Chuck thought about the alley, the crazed man sticking the gun in his face, and the nightmare flashbacks he'd had during the night.

"Too much."

"Why in hell would someone carve a horseshoe symbol in the handle of a gun?"

"Good luck?" Chuck said.

"You believe in superstitious bullshit?" George asked.

"Don't believe or disbelieve."

"No such thing as luck," George muttered.

"I helped a lady today. She thought she was lucky."

"Who?" Angela demanded.

"A woman stranded on the highway."

"How much did she appreciate your help?"

Chuck shrugged.

"You get laid for your efforts?" George looked at Chuck, lifted his brows and grinned.

"Can't a man do a good deed without expecting to get laid?" Angela asked.

George snorted. "I would expect to get laid."

"You would!"

"Dinner, she offered me dinner."

George and Angela ignored him.

"Did you get laid last week when you helped my cousin move?" Angela asked.

"Didn't have time, Leona gave me a blow job instead."

"You lie. Leona wouldn't do that to me." Angela hissed.

"Stop bitching. She saved you from giving me one when I got home." He hollered as she stalked off into the darkness.

George removed the magazine and sighted the gun on Angela's ramrod straight back. "You could get me a raise so I could afford a new gun."

"You got a raise three months ago."

"That was an insult not a raise."

"You want to shoot or whine?" Chuck asked.

George handed Chuck his pistol, picked up his gun and headed to the shooting range.

Angela strolled back to the truck, sat on the tailgate and leaned towards Chuck.

"Can you finish what you started?"

"Finish what?" Chuck watched George hit the first target. The can flew into the air and landed twenty feet from the fence.

"What you said in the office, before shithead walked in."

"I said if you were unhappy to move out. Start over, find a man that will be happy to kiss your ass."

"You could be that man."

"Never was good at kissing ass."

"I bet you're just being modest.

"Not going to happen, Sweetheart."

"It almost sounds like you love me."

Were they talking the same language? Chuck wouldn't pass a test on what made a woman tick, but he knew better than to fall into a trap.

"Why did you marry George?"

"George wasn't always an asshole."

"That wasn't what I asked. But let's try this, when did George have a personality transplant?"

"When our son died he built a wall around himself.

Everything made him mad and bitterness grew out of the anger."

Chuck thought that after three years he knew Angela's life story and her moods, but obviously she'd omitted pertinent details.

"I didn't know you had a child."

Angela stared into the darkness. "For a long time the medical bills were a constant reminder of what happened. When George lost his job he snapped."

"You're giving him excuses. Does George blame you for what happened?"

"I blame me. I got the measles a week before our baby was due. I'm the one who failed our son."

"You didn't get sick on purpose."

Angela shrugged one delicate shoulder.

"Tell me, how bad do you want me?"

"You're married!"

"You didn't answer my question?"

"You're a beautiful woman."

"Does that mean you want to kiss my ass?"

"That means you're a beautiful woman."

"Would you kiss the ass of the woman you met today?"

"She hasn't asked."

"Maybe I will give you a little taste." Angela slid closer and leaned into his body.

Chuck shook his head but softened the rejection with a grin. "We've been over this ground before. Unless you're divorced I'm not willing to be more than a friend with flirting privileges."

"George got a blow job from my cousin, why should I care what he thinks."

"What you think doesn't change my stand."

She ran a finger down his arm and looked at him through thick lashes.

"We should run off to Aruba, find a secluded beach and skinny dip in the ocean."

"That's a nice image, but it's not going to happen."

"We could spend a day in your backyard. Spread a blanket, drink a few margaritas. Scratch our itches."

Angela's big brown eyes danced with amusement. Her breath tickled his neck.

His manhood twitched to full attention.

"Then what? You go home and fix George dinner?"

"You should take what's offered and not question." Her bottom lip lowered into a sexy pout.

He thought about Laura, her shy teasing and her tongue-in-cheek wish list for a man with basic social skills. Laura intrigued him, and made him miss the easy give and take of a solid relationship.

Angela could make his blood boil, but she also scared the hell out of him.

"Use your well-honed powers to tease George into a good mood."

"George bores me. I think that if I offered you'd say yes."

"Wrong." And Lord help me if she tried, Chuck thought.

"I think you lie." She purred into his ear then nipped his earlobe.

"If we found a way to be alone I could get you to change your mind."

"Change his mind on what?" George demanded as he walked towards them.

Angela draped her arms around Chuck's waist and smiled at her husband.

"Chuck's thinking about buying an apartment building on the East side. I told him I'd find a way to work for him."

George looked at Chuck and gave a slight shake to his head.

"Angela likes to spend money, and she doesn't care if it's her money to spend. I'd be a better bet as a manager."

Angela, a walking advertisement for every high end name brand on the market, tossed her shiny black hair, but Chuck thought she hadn't tried to deny the truth.

Her ability to manipulate and lie bothered him but he'd been a willing participant in her sexual banter so he wasn't in a position to judge her actions. The teasing had been done in fun and he'd made sure George knew it would never progress further.

Being a willing participant in one of Angela's lies, even if the lie looked like an innocent ploy to cover her invitation was a different matter. There was an undercurrent between the two of them Chuck didn't understand, and probably, like the baby that died, more he'd never know. But that didn't mean he'd be her accomplice.

"The place has been mistreated. If I bought the package I'd invest love and attention to get it back where it should be." Chuck knew Angela understood and could take the statement at face value for how he felt about commitment or twist it anyway she wanted. Either way he wouldn't be caught in her web of deceit.

George grunted.

"Buildings don't need love. Do you want me to check the place out before you make an offer?"

"Not necessary."

"You're the boss. Don't get suckered into buying a cash cow."

Angela gave Chuck a wink.

"Sometimes a little extra time and money are a good investment."

"Not if it means the bottom line suffers," George insisted.

"George, life isn't always about money and possessions." Angela stepped away from Chuck, crossed her arms and glared at her husband.

"Next time you head to town see how far a smile gets you without cash or plastic to back it up."

"With a short term investment wasting money wouldn't be an option. But I'm only interested in long term dividends," Chuck said.

"That doesn't sound like a wise investment," George said.

"You are such a dickhead," Angela muttered.

"Are you still thinking about moving?" Chuck asked to derail the situation that was about to explode.

"I need a career with a future and benefits. As soon as I find the right fit, I'm out of here."

"I don't want to move," Angela said.

"And I don't want to live the rest of my life under someone's thumb. So divorce me," George snapped.

"Maybe I will."

"Fuck you, Angela." George turned and stalked off.

"He's such an asshole."

"I keep hearing that," Chuck said.

"I think he's seeing someone."

"I'm not sure I'm the person you should be talking to," Chuck said.

"He's not fucking me," Angela said as if she hadn't heard him.

Chuck winched.

"Why don't you leave him?"

"In front of you he acts like a big man but if I left he'd retaliate."

"He's threatened or is it more?"

"More."

"Move in with your parents or one of your sisters? Get a restraining order if you have too. Putting up with abuse isn't necessary."

"Been there, done that."

Crap, he thought, it must be the night for disclosing secrets.

Standing, he left Angela at the truck and walked halfway to the shooting range. With his hands in his pockets he watched George fire off nine rounds.

It had been three years since Angela walked up to him at a coffee bar, and asked if she could share his table. They'd met at the coffee bar several mornings a week but she always refused his offers for dinner. Two months after they met he still hadn't figured out what she wanted from him. Then, one morning she mentioned her marriage.

He'd walked away from her a dozen times, but she always managed to walk back into his life. The last time was when she'd convinced him to hire George. She was hot tempered and unpredictable. And she'd sell her soul to get what she wanted, but no matter how self-centered she acted, she didn't deserve to be mistreated.

She stopped beside him, draped an arm through his and leaned her head on his arm.

"Why did you go back to him?"

Angela shrugged.

"You flirt with me to build your ego. You keep saying you're ready to make changes but you don't plan to leave George."

"It's not like that."

"Then explain what it's like."

"I want to leave but I'm not ready. I don't have your courage to face life alone, at least not yet."

"You wouldn't be alone. You have family, friends, people who care."

"Do you care?"

"If I didn't, I wouldn't be standing here. Is the situation different than you've led me to believe?"

"Yes and no."

"Yes, you've lied, or no you haven't?"

"I can't explain."

"If you can't who can?"

Chapter 6

"**H**i, Sweet Pea, the answer is still no. I don't need an ankle nipping yappy dog to keep me company." Chuck said as he continued to scan the invoice on his desk.

"Good to know." The feminine voice ended in a light chuckle.

Chuck laughed.

"Laura. Sorry, my daughter's on a campaign to have me adopt a dog. She's called three times this morning."

"If you're still rescuing damsels in distress I'm in need of a little flirtatious TLC. Are you free to meet me for lunch at Louie V's? I promise not to yap."

"I'll do my best to fill the bill. What time?"

"One o'clock."

"I'll be there."

An hour later Chuck admired Laura's graceful stroll as she weaved between tables. Her black slacks, matching heels, and berry red blouse were professional without being fussy. But the cool cover also held a sexy appeal that drew the eyes of every male in the restaurant.

He stood as she approached and pulled out the chair

next to him.

Laura kissed him on the cheek and sat. "A gentlemen; how refreshing."

"Living up to the Sir Galahad code isn't easy."

"You're doing fine."

They ordered; vegetarian lasagna for her and spaghetti and meatballs in a spicy tomato sauce for him.

When the waitress left they settled back and sipped red wine.

"You have a daughter. Where's her mother?" Laura asked.

"I'm a widower."

Laura grimaced.

"Give me a moment to extract the foot in my mouth and I'll apologize."

"No need. Most people assume I'm a divorce statistic."

"You miss her." She said. It was a statement not a question.

"Once a week my daughter reminds me that living in the past is a waste of time."

"Smart girl. Where's she going to college?"

"She's at the University of Texas in Austin, enrolled in the Speech-Language Pathology program."

"You're proud of her."

"I am. You're not a local. What brought you to El Paso?"

"That was a smooth way to change the subject. I worked my way up to management for, Look at Me Now, a national glamour photography studio. Once a new location was decided and a storefront leased, my job was to set up the studio and hire and train staff."

"How often did you move?"

"I spent a year at each location. But to answer your question I've lived in ten states in nine years."

"One location was a bust?"

"I'd been in New Orleans two months when Katrina blew through town. The company moved me to Kansas City."

"You said was, as in past tense. What happened when you arrived here?"

"One of the business partner's took off with her partner's husband and the company assets. The company folded."

"If there's business potential why not open your own studio?"

"I'm researching the possibility."

"Is that what you meant by choosing a rocky road?"

"That and a commitment not to be sucked back into a dead end situation by lies and flowers."

"Sounds like a solid plan. If a bank wants a business plan call, I'll be happy to help you."

"Who taught you to play the role of Sir Galahad?"

"All the fairy tales I read my daughter left an impression."

"Besides reading fairy tales what kept you busy?"

"College and the military before moving back here."

"You're a local boy?"

"Born and bred."

"The house you live in belonged to your parent's?"

"My grandparent's bought the house. When I was two my folks moved in to help my grandmother."

"You're an only child?"

"I am. And you?"

"I was raised in Virginia by a single mom who spoiled me rotten. After high school I studied art and design at a local college. At the end of my second year Mom died from breast cancer. A month later a cute boy, with a trust fund, a good sense of humor and no common sense, offered to take me with him to see the world. I got a passport and never looked back."

"What happened to the cute boy?"

"He became addicted to the delights offered in the red light district in Amsterdam."

"That could be a fun addiction."

He smiled when she wrinkled her nose.

"Not my idea of fun. My Mom taught me some toys shouldn't be shared with strangers."

"Your mother was a smart woman."

Chapter 7

Chuck set the scanner on the kitchen counter and opened the freezer. A dozen frozen TV dinners and four pot pies were covered with a film of frost. The tub of strawberry ice cream had crystallized.

From the refrigerator he tossed out baloney that had curled around the edges, bacon that looked like it was covered in green plastic wrap, and something in a plastic container that was no longer identifiable.

From a cupboard he grabbed a can of chili and pulled a can opener out of a drawer. He dumped the contents into a blue bowl and set the microwave for two minutes. While the congealed mass heated he grabbed silverware, a sleeve of crackers, butter, and poured a tall glass of iced tea.

He sat at the bar and wolfed down the meal, read the scanner's instruction manual and half listened to sporadic conversations as he fiddled with different settings.

"Ronnie, meet me at my house. We'll load and hit the 7-11 on Red Road."

"Cool. I'm almost out of cash. What time?"

Chuck stuck a napkin between the pages and closed

the book.

"The after work rush will be over by eight. There should be plenty of cash on hand and the shift change isn't until nine. It's an easy mark."

"Cool," Ronnie said again and ended with what could have been a low whistle.

"See you in a few."

"Later."

The first speaker had a slight slur, and a swagger to his voice, like a, know it all, punk with a silver stud pierced in his tongue.

Ronnie sounded like a twelve year old nerd willing to follow his hero into hell.

Chuck looked at the black and white cat shaped clock Carrie had made in a ceramic class at school. There was plenty of time to make the fifteen minute drive.

He picked up his cellphone and headed out the door.

On the way, he dialed 911 and told the dispatch officer that he'd overheard a conversation about a robbery. Before she could ask for a name or trace the call he disconnected.

Across from the convenience store he pulled into an empty parking lot and cut the engine.

Thin rays of milky moonlight poked between bands of clouds, giving the street an eerie Halloween ambiance. The night air was sultry and saturated with the oily flavor of fried chicken and pepperoni pizza.

He should be home reading the stack of brochures his accountant insisted he read or be calculating the dollar value of the losses at the apartments. Instead he watched two drunks stumble out of the Red Door Saloon and head to the Dark Horse Bar half a block away.

He thought back to the first signs of trouble. The twelve unit complex had been stripped down to concrete and support beams. The new floor plan was for six two story units. The two-by-fours marking the new rooms and separating the units were built without a problem. But the day after the wiring was installed a nick in the plastic coating on a wire caused a hot spot. When they opened a door the next morning, the two-by-four studs were smoldering. The fresh air fanned the flames. If not for a handy fire extinguisher the place would have been gone by the time the fire department arrived.

When the fire marshal's report stated that the problem was caused by human error, the loss was covered by the insurance company of the electrical company that did the wiring.

Since then, shorts in supplies, missing tools, and damage to newly completed work had become a common occurrence.

What if the fire hadn't been carelessness, what if it had been sabotage? What if the continued problems had started because the unit hadn't burned to the ground? He hated speculation, but if what he suspected was fact, why?

A white El Paso city cruiser pulled up and parked next to him.

A male officer, five-ten, two hundred pounds, stepped out of the car and walked around the front of Chuck's truck.

He held a hefty, foot long silver flashlight in his left hand. The palm of his right hand rested on the grip of his pistol.

Three feet from the driver's door he stopped and raised the bright yellow beam.

Chuck squinted and raised an arm to shield his eyes.

"Put your hands on the wheel and roll down your window." The glass muffled the man's voice.

"Which do you want, the window rolled down or my hands on the wheel?"

"Place your right hand on the steering wheel. Roll the window down with your left hand, now. Then place your left hand on the steering wheel." As if he were talking to a drunk, the officer meticulously enunciated each word.

"Yes sir." Chuck rolled down the window and nodded at the officer.

"Do you have identification, vehicle registration, and proof of insurance?"

"Yes, sir."

"Would you get them, please?"

"Can't."

"Why not?"

"I have to take my hands off the wheel to get to my wallet. The registration and proof of insurance are in the glove compartment."

The officer scanned the floor and the empty passenger seat with the high powered flashlight. "Move slowly and we'll both get through this unharmed."

"Sounds like a good plan," Chuck said. Slowly he reached for his wallet.

"Have you been drinking tonight?"

"Not yet."

"Do you have weapons or drugs in the car that I should know about?"

"No sir, nothing you should know about."

"Step out of the car please."

"Why?"

"Sir, step out of the car."

"Obviously you don't have a sense of humor." Chuck muttered, opened the door and stepped out of the truck.

"Turn around and place your hands on top of the roof. I'm going to pat you down."

Lucky me! He braced the palms of his hands on the trucks roof and spread his legs shoulder width apart.

The officer touched his right shoulder. "Keep your hands on the roof of the car."

"I already have a girlfriend so let's keep this impersonal."

"You're a dumbass." The officer said. After he'd patted Chuck down he pulled handcuffs out of a hip pocket.

"Am I being arrested?"

"No sir, I'm going to handcuff you for my safety."

"Your safety?"

"Yes sir."

"Then place them on yourself, I'm harmless."

The officer activated the microphone attached to the shoulder of his shirt.

"West 34, I need an additional unit."

Chuck was getting pissed—at himself for letting curiosity bring him to the site of a possible robbery and the officer for having the observations and common sense of a piss ant.

"Officer, what's the problem?"

"Do you mind if I search your vehicle?"

"I mind," Chuck said.

"Are you hiding something you don't want me to see?"

"I'm protecting your innocence. My girlfriend's red panties are under the seat."

"I'm married."

"I know. You have a warrant you can have them."

"Subject to an arrest, I can search your car without a warrant."

"Arrest for what?"

"Suspicious activity."

"Standing on the corner wearing a long trench coat in ninety degree weather would be suspicious."

"What's the police scanner for?"

"I'm a concerned citizen."

"Sir, I am going to ask you again, may I search your truck?"

"And again I decline your request."

A patrol unit pulled into the lot and parked behind Chuck's truck.

A female officer, five-six, one-forty, with dark hair tucked behind her ears, stopped short of kicking distance and placed her hand on the butt of her gun. It was too dark to read her name tag.

"What's the problem?" Her voice, raspy from too many cigarettes was firm and commanding.

"Loitering and a bad attitude. He's refused to let me search the truck."

"Sir, we're going to search your car for drugs and weapons." The female cop said.

"And tomorrow morning a lawsuit will be slapped in your hand."

"You have something to hide?"

"Not at the moment."

"Are you willing to take a breathalyzer test, comedian?" The male officer asked.

"I didn't study for the exam, but I'll do the best I can."

"Regular smartass aren't you," the male officer muttered.

"If you have nothing to hide why refuse to let us do our job?" The female officer asked.

"Your job is to protect the innocent. I have no record and parking here isn't forbidden. The wall behind you isn't covered in fresh graffiti. And I've been physically searched which shows cooperation."

"Are you an attorney?" the female officer asked.

"No, but I know enough about the law not to be pushed around. The worst I'm guilty of is poor judgment and an uncontrollable urge to ask pretty boy for a date."

The female cop wasn't fast enough to swallow her snicker.

"Why did you decide to loiter in a closed stores parking lot after dark?" She asked.

"Finally, a sensible question! On the scanner I overheard two males talk about taking down a Seven-11."

"Did you call it in?" The female officer asked.

"I did."

"Then you decided to play superman?"

"This is Texas. I'd blend better if I dressed as the Lone Ranger."

The female cop chuckled. The deep rich sound rolled through the tension in the air.

The male officer cleared his throat and scowled.

"Are you carrying a weapon?" The female officer asked.

"No, ma'am."

"Did you think about what you would do if they planted a gun in your face?"

"I hadn't planned on confronting them."

"What did you plan to do?"

"Call the friendly dispatcher and give her the license plate number of their car."

"And protect a female clerk if necessary?"

Chuck shrugged.

"Did either of the males mention a time?" The female officer asked.

"Eight."

The officer lifted her left wrist and aimed the beam of the flashlight at a large faced watched rimmed in rhinestones. "It's ten past now. Do us a favor Mr. Taylor, go home and leave the police work to us."

"Yes, ma'am."

The female officer drove over the curb and headed east.

Ten minutes later the male officer was still riding his bumper when the scanner burst to life and the dispatcher reported a robbery in progress at the Seven-11.

Chuck laughed until his side ached.

Chapter 8

"**H**ey, nice surprise. What's up?"

Chuck flipped the latch and opened the screen door.

"I wanted to say thanks."

Laura stepped into the small foyer. Her cream colored slacks were tailored. A stretchy green top skimmed her breasts and small waist. The casual feminine sexuality left him wanting to explore what was underneath.

"For what?"

"The business management officer at First National Bank called me. Thank you for taking the time to help and for telling him you were my character reference."

"It was my pleasure. Are those homemade peanut butter cookies?" He nodded at the plate in her hand.

"They are."

She handed him the paper plate and gave him a kiss that lingered a fraction of a second longer than necessary.

"Can you stay for dinner?"

She eyed the bottle of Tecate beer in his hand.

"Is that dinner?"

"This is the appetizer. Dinner's in the oven, turkey

TV dinner with all the trimmings of a Thanksgiving feast. I'll split it with you."

"That's a generous offer but I'll pass. A beer sounds good."

Chuck headed to the kitchen.

Laura stood beside a table height counter that separated the kitchen from a small dining room. The granite tops looked like a swirl of gold sand dusted with specks of obsidian and sugar crystals. The white glazed birch cabinets had leaded glass doors. The walls were off white, the appliances were stainless steel.

"You can cook?"

"I cook a great chili hotdog."

"You designed a fancy kitchen to boil water and heat a can of chili."

"When we moved in, the place was in need of a full makeover. Carrie scoured hundred's of kitchen and bath magazines before deciding what she thought would work. She was a hard boss to please."

"And you loved every minute."

"I wouldn't go that far, but the process helped us get to know each other while we licked our wounds."

"You were in the service. Did you spend a lot of time away from home?"

"More than I wanted."

Not wanting the conversation to head in that direction Chuck asked, "What's happened since we had lunch?"

"Do you want to hear about the cat with five kittens in my backyard or the former boyfriend who's decided to be difficult?"

He handed her a beer, walked into the living room

and, sat on the couch.

"Tell me about the ex."

"He gave me a television for my birthday. Now he claims the set belongs to him."

"Not if it was a gift."

"That's what I told him, but he claims he needs the set."

"Needs or wants?" Chuck asked.

"Needs or wants, doesn't really matter, he's being difficult," Laura said.

"Did it cross your mind that the television could be stolen merchandise?"

"Sad to say, it did. I called the store where he said it was purchased and made up a story about not understanding how to connect the sound system. When they couldn't find a record of sale they asked for the serial number. They filled out the registration form before answering my questions. If it was stolen you'd think the serial number would have sent up a red flag."

"Sounds logical," but Chuck knew a good hacker could have covered that track.

He followed her gaze to the small television set in a tall chest that at one time had been an armoire filled with his grandmothers dresses.

"Would you like to buy a seventy inch flat screen TV with surround sound?"

"Are you selling his gift to get even or because you're mad at him?"

"Neither. I'd rather read then watch TV."

"The ex knew that when he gave you the gift?"

"He did."

Chucks instincts pinged and itched a warning. The

guy could be clueless in the gift giving department, but chances were the set was stolen, and now he was getting nervous.

"I told him if he paid back the money he borrowed, he could have the TV. He didn't like that deal," Laura said.

"He borrowed money for what?"

"His car needed tires. Since I didn't want to risk being in the car if a tire blew, and I don't allow anyone to drive my BMW, I loaned him the money."

"Did he purchase tires?"

"Let's put it this way, the next day there were new tires on his car."

"You think the tires were stolen?"

"The day after he got the tires there was an article in the paper that B&S tires had been burglarized."

Chuck grinned. Most people called the place BS tires because the two owners had reputations as modern day horse thieves.

"Did you ask him where he got the tires?"

"I did. He sidestepped the question."

"How long ago did this happen?"

"Six weeks before I cut off the relationship." Her audible sigh was heavy with annoyance.

"How long were you together?"

"It wasn't that serious. We dated for six months. Have you ever noticed how logical and clear hindsight can be?"

"I've had an occasion or two to appreciate that fact."

"Before I broke it off, I spent an evening with a bottle of wine and a scalpel. When I finished dissecting our relationship I realize that the week he got the tires, he changed."

"Changed how?"

"He'd never been a big talker, and he seemed comfortable with a weekend relationship. But suddenly he had big plans for our future, and started pushing me to marry him."

"I can see where that would scare the hell out of you."

Laura chuckled. "It did, actually."

"You have something against marriage?"

"Not at all. But he lived in Alamogordo and worked at the Air Force base. We saw each other once or twice a week. The relationship hadn't progressed to leaving a toothbrush in each other's bathroom much less a 'till death do us part,' stage."

"You're smart and pretty. Maybe he fell hard and didn't want to lose you?"

She leaned in and gave him a kiss that tasted like beer and vanilla lip gloss.

"Thank you, that's sweet, but I never thought love had anything to do with the proposal."

"Then what did?"

"I'm not sure," Laura said.

That's a lie, Chuck thought.

"When you told him to pay you or no deal did he threaten you?"

"He mentioned hell freezing and greedy bitches. When he wound down I told him to consider the TV payment for the loan. He made a few more comments, but he didn't threaten me."

"I'll buy the television if you'll let me take you to dinner."

"What about your Thanksgiving feast?"

"It's a sacrifice I'm willing to make."

"That's generous of you. Where are we going?" She asked as she rummaged through an over-sized metallic green purse.

"Some place quiet and romantic."

"That eliminates the Kitchen. I knew there was a reason I liked you."

"What's wrong with the Kitchen?"

"Nothing when you want loud, cheap, and greasy."

"The food's not greasy," Chuck protested.

"The food's greasy, and the waitress's outfits would fit in a shot glass," she snapped.

"Did I miss something?"

"Yeah, my assets didn't pass the test to get hired." Laura said with a huff.

"Your assets look damn good to me."

"You're a sweetie."

"Just being honest," Chuck said, but couldn't imagine Laura fitting in with the type of women that worked at The Kitchen.

"Why did you apply for a job there?"

"I was having a partially lousy week. A friend mentioned how much the waitresses get in tips. I've waitressed before and decided dealing with jerks leaving twenty dollars tips was better than dealing with idiots who think their job titles entitle them to extra perks from the hired help."

"I would have hired you," Chuck said.

"Thanks." Laura leaned in and brushed her lips against his.

"Did I just pass some type of test?"

"Maybe."

She smiled and handed him a business card.

"Call this number when you have time to pick up the television."

"After you kissed the ex goodbye, did you have the locks changed on your house?"

"I never gave him a key, but yes, Daddy I had the locks changed."

Chuck smiled and looked at Laura's business card. Westlake was an upscale, five story high-rise of two and three bedroom units close to downtown.

"How long have you managed the apartments?"

"Two years."

They stepped outside and Chuck locked the door.

"We'll take my truck."

"My car's more comfortable."

"Did you buy a new battery?"

"I haven't had time. What's a battery rod?"

"The negative and positive poles that you see on the top of the battery, extend down the inside the battery."

"A loose connection can cause what?"

"Hot Babes to get stranded on dark deserted roads."

The Mexican restaurant was large and crowded, but the arrangement of tables and booths gave the illusion of intimacy.

The waitress led them to a secluded section of circular booths in the back section of the restaurant. The pumpkin colored leather booths high backs offered privacy. Mustard yellow walls, red tile floors and black and white pictures of Mexico finished the scene.

Laura looked at the hand painted tiles covering the top of the table and smiled. "Look, a bride and groom dancing and a donkey and cart waiting to whisk them away. Add the Mariachi band roaming the room singing love songs and you have romantic and charming."

"Interesting, anyway."

"You don't like the music?"

"I like the company. The music is irrelevant but if it makes you happy I'm pleased."

"You're sweet."

The waiter arrived, placed a wooden bowl filled with chips and a red ceramic bowl of salsa on the table, and took their order for two beef fajitas.

"You were raised in El Paso, but what made you decide to return?"

"After my wife died I retired from the service. The family home was mine and I still knew most of the neighbors. I couldn't think of a better place to raise my daughter."

Laura offered a soft smile and a nod. "Solid reasons to return, but you have to work at blending in with the locals."

Chuck grimaced. He'd worked hard to blend in and thought he'd been successful.

"Like a chameleon you're good at blending," Laura said. "But I've been an outsider half my life, I can recognize a kindred spirit at fifty paces."

"Meaning?"

"Meaning, we observe the locals and adapt to the situation, dialog and customs. I'd bet if you ever talked about your military days, it's how you were taught to survive." If Laura hadn't been watching him she wouldn't have noticed the slight nod.

"Adapting is why I was so successful at building new stores into profitable businesses. And why you were able to take a flea infested piece of property and turn it into an upscale complex without waging a full scale war with the tenants."

"I didn't realize what happened at the apartments fueled the local gossip."

"More than one apartment manager is envious of your success to evict without turning it into a blood bath between the tenant and the law."

"All it took was charm and a big stick."

Laura grinned.

"You can joke, but under your laid back charm and sarcastic sense of humor there's more to you than drinking beer instead of a rum and coke or scotch. You don't wear wife beater t-shirts, think kiss and tell is a bragging right for the male species, and you get your own beer instead of ordering the old lady to do it for you."

"You've been hanging out with the wrong crowd."

"That wasn't the first impression, but you're right. Now satisfy my curiosity, how did you escape the local boys charm school?"

"My grandmother was an old-fashioned school teacher who believed in discipline and obedience. She didn't tolerate improper language or bad manners. You never married?"

"I never met anyone that sparked the kind of interest that led to sharing a closet or a bathroom."

"What about the last boyfriend, if he hadn't pushed

would it have gone further?"

She sighed and broke a corn chip into crumbs.

"I left Virginia when I was twenty, and hadn't lived anyplace more than two years since. When the photography studio folded, I was faced with no real home and no ties. I decided to stay here, and take time to evaluate what I wanted before putting my savings into a pie in the sky dream, and then finding out I hated the ground under my feet."

"That was sensible. You have no family?"

"I do and don't. My aunt died a few months ago. We were close, but she'd been sick for a long time and refused to allow me to help her. I also have two half-brothers but we haven't spoken in years."

"You didn't answer my question. If the ex-boyfriend hadn't pushed would you have eventually married him?"

"He was a nice distraction but nothing more. Which is why I never asked him to spend the night, and never wondered what he was doing when several days stretched between phone calls."

"You mentioned that you dated for six months. When did he introduce you to the wife-beater t-shirt crowd?"

"Memorial Day he took me to a barbeque. The setting was clean and festive but my mother would have labeled the people trailer trash."

"How so?"

"There was a subtle undercurrent that made me believe that what I was being shown was different from the day-to-day normal. The five women were nice, but it was a forced friendly that left a lot of pauses and quick glances towards the men. I got the impression that two of the women were strangers trying to pretend they were long time friends."

"What else?"

"The men treated the women like servants instead of equals."

"Which you wouldn't tolerate," Chuck said with a nod.

"I wouldn't but that wasn't the real problem. There were two men there that everyone treated with a respect that seemed to be fed by fear."

"Did you talk to the men?"

"I was introduced to both but only one man spoke to me. He didn't say anything inappropriate, but I got the impression he thought women were subservient and easily manipulated."

"Then he was a fool. What about the second man?"

"He sat a slight distance from everyone. Only the men spoke to him. The woman stole glances, but even when they served him lunch they never looked directly at him. The whole situation was strange," Laura said.

"Did you tell the boyfriend what you thought?"

"I tried. He walked away and ignored me. When the meal was served he acted like the rest of the men and expected me to serve him."

"I gather you didn't."

"I filled a plate, but oh my, clumsy me, it landed in his lap."

Chuck laughed. "I wish I'd been there to see that. Did he get angry?"

"The man who sat off by himself said something in Spanish. I don't speak the language, but his face turned red. I apologized, blamed my clumsiness on a headache and asked to leave. He refused, said we couldn't insult his friends."

"What happened when you did leave?"

"He wouldn't listen to my concerns, or answer my questions. Over the next week we talked on the phone several times, and I saw a side of him I didn't like. When he suggested we fly to Vegas for a day I told him to ask someone else. End of story." She said with a slight shudder.

"There are good guys out there."

"We've known each other a week and seen each other three times. So far you've been the perfect Sir Galahad. Is that a mask or genuine?"

He thought of Britney and gave a wan smile. "I've been told I fit the nice guy mold. Not all women find it attractive."

"That's their loss. Why haven't you remarried?"

"While my daughter lived at home I didn't date the type of women in the market for a permanent relationship."

"Honesty, I like that," Laura said.

Their meals arrived and talk became general as they ate.

"Would you like the desert menu?" The waitress asked as she removed their dinner plates.

"Bring us a double serving of fried ice cream and two spoons," Chuck said.

Laura gave him a wink. "That's my second favorite dessert."

"What's your first?" He asked before taking a sip of coffee.

Her toe slid under the hem of his slacks and up his

ankle. His breath lodged in his throat. With a gasp drops of coffee spit across the table.

Laura's giggle was seductive and knowing.

"Shit." He wiped his mouth with the napkin and sucked in a breath.

"Are you okay?"

"Just surprised," he said

"Surprises are good."

"Not when I'm swallowing hot coffee. I could have drowned."

"I would have given you mouth-to-mouth resuscitation."

Chuck shook his head, but grinned.

Are you saying you haven't thought about making love to me?"

"Thought yes—discussing the possibility in a restaurant, no."

Laura slid around the booth until her thigh rubbed against his.

"The man across the aisle has his hand up his date's skirt. The couple at the table behind us are married—but not to each other. I seriously doubt anyone is paying attention to us."

"You're enjoying my discomfort."

"I am. It's another indication that you're a good guy."

The waitress set the bowl of ice cream and two spoons on the table.

Laura fed Chuck the first bite.

"Are you teasing me?"

"I don't tease."

Chuck cleared his throat. "Behave."

"That's no fun. Tell me what you thought when you stopped to pick me up."

"I stopped to help a hot looking lady who looked slightly pissed.

"Hot as in, wow look at her, or hot as in wilted from the heat?"

"A lady with great looking legs that would look nice wrapped around my waist. Satisfied?"

"Very. Go on."

"This hot babe with a broken down car, was about to be picked up by the cops. I decided I'd be nice and help her out before she was given a free ride to the police station and strip searched."

"They were going to arrest me, why?"

"Hitchhiking is illegal. The cop that asked if you were okay had been dispatched to your location."

"How do you know that?"

"I was listening to a scanner."

"Wow. I was a person of interest. That could have been exciting."

She rubbed her foot against his calf and winked.

"Then again, the police being more concerned about me hitchhiking then being stuck on the shoulder of the road with a broken down car doesn't make me happy."

"They were looking out for you. Hitchhiking is known for being the first step to heinous crimes."

"You rescued me from the cops, the bad guy and you thought I was a hot babe."

"A lady. The hot babe came after I checked out your legs."

"Sweet. Is there anyone special in your life, besides me?"

"Not really."

"Not really can mean a lot of things, including yes."

"Not really, as in no."

"But?"

"A woman friend has made it clear that she's interested."

"Can men and women be just friends?"

"It can be tricky but it's possible."

"Okay back to this friend, why aren't you interested?"

"She's married."

"Is she talking love or flirting with lust?"

"I suspect neither. She's unhappy and looking for attention."

"That's it."

"It is."

"Then why tell me about her?"

"Because she's possessive and makes remarks that can be taken ten different ways and never touch the truth. If you meet her I don't want you jumping to erroneous conclusions."

"Can I say that makes me happy without sounding desperate or easy?"

"You can."

She fed him the last bite of ice cream and leaned in. Her breath smelled like cinnamon and vanilla ice cream. The light kiss she offered tasted like promises and got his full attention.

"Take me home. You can pick up the television tomorrow. Tonight I want to experience being strip searched."

Chapter 9

"**D**ad."

The front door slammed shut.

Sandals slapped across the hardwood floor.

"Dad?"

Carrie Taylor headed to the dining room where French doors led to a covered redwood deck.

When she opened the door the fresh scent of mowed grass blanketed the early morning heat.

Carrie sneezed.

Hunched over the lawnmower, Chuck turned, and banged his knee on the corner of the large red tool box that had belonged to his father.

"Sweet Pea, what are you doing here?" Pain shot through the knee when he lifted her into a back cracking hug.

Set back on her feet Carrie aimed a light punch at his midriff.

"I'm here to confront you about your lying."

During the accident that killed his wife, Carries vocal cords were severally damaged. Chuck still found it difficult to connect the deep sultry purr that turned grown men's heads with the sweet innocence of his daughter who had sung soprano with the school choir.

"Me?"

"I'm not buying that innocent look. For the last two Monday's you charted five miles instead of your normal three before heading to the downtown businessman's breakfast. And you charted a five mile run for yesterday."

"Your point being?"

"No way, no how, you lied. Yesterday, you didn't run."

Hell, he thought he'd done a better job of covering his ass. "You have proof?"

Liquid warmth spread around Chuck's ankle and down the inside of grass stained tennis shoes. He rolled his lips to suppress a chuckle. The culprit was a dusty brown colored pup with fist size paws. Plopped on his fat rump, he looked at Chuck and yelped.

"I said no dog."

"You said no yappy dog. Runner will produce deep dignified barks."

"Runner?"

"Runner is half Great Dane and half golden lab. He's healthy and has all his shots. All he needs is daily runs and attention. Oh, and he needs to be housebroken."

"Of course he does," Chuck muttered.

"What makes you think I didn't run yesterday morning?"

"You had company."

"You know this how?"

"I called. Laura thought it was her cellphone ringing."

"And you tricked her into giving you her name, and

not telling me?"

"I asked. She answered. We agreed that you didn't need to know we'd talked."

"So, why are you here with a half grown horse named Runner?"

"You went online and logged a five mile run on the chart." The chart had been Carries idea of motivation and a way to count off the days to the Breast Cancer Awareness Marathon in October.

"I might have run after Laura left."

"But you didn't."

"How do you know that?"

"I talked to Leia. She saw you pull out of the driveway in your work cloths at the same time Laura left."

"Humph." The pup tugged on his shoelaces and yelped. Chuck bent and scratched the pup behind an ear to hide his smile.

"You had breakfast?" Chuck asked.

"Runner and I shared a pop tart. I thought we'd make pancakes."

Runner sniffed his way around the house and barked every time the smoke detector wailed. When he settled on the rug under the dining room table a plush yellow duck was clamped in his jaws.

As they consumed pancakes blackened around the edges and soaked in maple syrup and a cube of butter, they kept the conversation general.

Finally Carrie filled their mugs with the last of the coffee and got to the real point of her visit. "Tell me about Laura."

"Not much to tell. She's nice and little off balance

because she understands my jokes."

"Serious?"

"It's far too early to know that."

"How did you meet her?"

"She was hooking."

"Dad, that's disgusting."

"What's disgusting, her car broke down. She was thumbing for a ride."

"Hitching, not hooking."

He gave her a wink.

"How old is she?"

"Have you seen the movie Lolita?"

"Dad, be serious, you're not dating a fourteen year old."

"That's right, Laura's a Mrs. Robinson. She likes younger, vile males with washboard abs and muscle bound arms."

Carrie rolled her eyes. "You could just say I don't know."

"I don't know."

The scanner beeped. *"Medic 12, five, zero, zero, Sun Valley Drive. Male subject with chest pains, caller states; male subject now passed out on the floor. Engine 14 respond with Medic 12, male subject with chest pains, passed out on the floor."*

A second female voice responded, *"Engine 14 and Medic 12 responding from the station."*

"What's up with you and the scanner?" Carrie asked.

"It's entertaining."

"It's weird."

"Different. I don't do weird." He mimicked her eye roll and they both laughed.

"You can thank the scanner for my meeting Laura."

"And for your trip to the hospital for the tetanus shot?"

"Good point. Besides sweet talking Leia into disclosing my secrets what are you doing with your time?"

"You mean besides school, running and yoga classes?"

"That would be the question."

"Last Monday I started volunteer work at the animal shelter where I picked up Runner."

"Any cute boys volunteer at this shelter?"

"Maybe."

"Now we get to why you decided to enroll in summer classes instead of torturing me, and wearing out batteries in the smoke alarms. Is there a boy in particular that caught your attention?"

"No," but a faint blush kissed her checks and she dropped her eyes. "When do I get to meet Laura?"

"You're changing the subject?"

"Did it work?"

"And answering questions with questions, did you learn that trick in psychology class?"

"No, you taught me."

"Humph. Do you plan to tell Laura my deep dark secrets?"

"Of course."

"Then the answer is never."

"Dad!"

"Soon Sweet Pea, but not today, Laura's busy today."

"Where does Laura work?"

The scanner beeped. A male voice broke though the static. *"Good morning. Hilton, reservation desk. This is Rodney, may I help you?"*

The scanner beeped again and fell silent.

"Does Laura approve of you spying on people?"

"I don't spy…" *Hell maybe in a twisted way he did.* Chuck rubbed the back of his neck. "Laura manages the Westlake apartments."

"Whereas you pretend to be an apartment manager so you can rip out walls and play with power tools."

"Power tools are more fun than dealing with people and their problems." Chuck stood and started to clear the table.

"And less personal," Carrie said.

"Don't you need to go somewhere? Visit a girlfriend or buy a new pair of shoes to impress the dogs at the shelter."

"You're stuck with me until tomorrow."

"And you're going to torture me how?"

"We're taking Runner to the pet store to let him choose a bed and squeaky toys. After that I'm going to enjoy watching you sweat through a five mile run. And tonight we're going to test the surround sound and television with a marathon of chick flicks."

"What about this afternoon?" His voice held a hint of humor and resignation.

"Leia is looking forward to meeting Runner. We're invited to a barbeque next door."

"Good, the smoke alarms need a rest."

Chapter 10

Chuck loaded the washing machine and pulled sheets out of the dryer.

The scanner, tuned to the radio frequency officers used to talk between themselves beeped.

"North 12—What was that last call about?"

"North 7—I believe that was a booty call."

"North 12—Is she sweet?"

"North 7—No such luck. I always get the desperate fat chicks."

"North 12—Luck of the draw."

"North 7—Are you going back later?"

"North 12—Ah yeah, welfare check."

"North 7—Do you need a backup?"

"North 12—No, sir, I can handle this on my own." His laugh was cut off.

"North 7—Future ex-wife?"

"North 12—Could happen that way."

"North 7—That was really my call."

"North 12—Whine to dispatch. What was the complaint you answered?"

"North 7—Barking dog."

"North 12—Owners deaf or don't care?"

"North 7—Out of town."

"North 12—You get to deal with Bruce or Jose at Animal Control?"

"North 7—Bruce."

"North 12—No wonder you're grumpy. I'd be…"

The scanner filled with static and beeped twice. A calm female voice announced, *"Engine 17, truck 7, fire alarm five, nine, nine, Murchison. No other reports at this time."*

Male voices answered, *"Engine 17 and truck 7 responding to five, nine, nine, Murchison*

"Time out, 1920 hours. Pumper 12, Medic 19 traffic accident 4th and central, injuries reported, PD on the scene. Pumper 12 in route—Medic 19 in route from Children's, Time out 1920 hours."

The scanner fell silent and remained silent.

He put the folded laundry away and walked into the living room. Without Carrie's clutter and laptop scattered over the coffee table the room looked empty and lifeless.

Restless he headed to the door that led to the garage.

Runner scurried to his side. With his tail wagging he looked at Chuck with big brown eyes filled with hope.

"Okay boy." He reached for the blue retractable leash on the table by the back door and connected it to the pups blue collar. "Let's go."

Runner jumped onto the trucks bench seat, and sat on the passenger side with his nose pressed to the window.

Chuck revved the engine and headed to a strip mall.

At a red light he watched teenagers in the backseat of the car in front of him grope each other. The scene gave him an odd sense of detachment.

Carrie was right it was time to stop using her and remodeling the apartments as excuses to skirt around the edge of life without becoming involved.

It wasn't like he'd become a monk after his wife's death, but he'd been truthful when he'd told Laura that the women he'd dated hadn't been the type he'd introduce to his daughter.

Angela was a different complication. A tease in a well stacked package, her attention had stroked his ego and allowed him to pretend he had a life beyond work and parental responsibilities. But he hadn't allowed her charms or sexual undertones to blind him to her faults.

He pulled into a parking space at Wal-Mart and smiled when Laura's gray BMW pulled into the space next to him.

She rolled down the passenger window and leaned across the seat. "Isn't it past your bedtime?"

"I need a pacifier."

"Bud Lights on sale, aisle twelve."

"That saves me time."

The pup wiggled his way onto Chuck's lap, stuck his head out the window and gave a pitiful whine.

"Who's your friend?"

"Runner. He's Carrie's idea of punishment for lying about my run Friday morning."

"I offered to run with you."

"And I offered to wash your back and we both got sidetracked."

Laura smiled.

"That was politely put. I gather Carrie told you I answered your phone by mistake."

"She did. She wants to meet you. Think you can handle an interrogation?"

Laura's eyes sparkled and the corner of her lips curled into a smile. "I think I could manage that. Did you get the television setup?"

"I did."

"Invite me over and we can snuggle on the couch and watch a movie."

"You name the day."

"Tomorrow evening, eight o'clock."

"I'll supply the popcorn. What are you doing out this late?"

"I was buying you a present."

"You don't need to buy me a present."

She pulled a black negligee out of bag and held it up. "I can model this tomorrow or take it back to the store for a refund."

"I'll buy the wine and order moonlight and roses," Chuck said.

"That makes me feel special." She blew him a kiss and drove off.

Chapter 11

"**Y**eah?" Winded, Chuck braced a hand on his knee and held the phone to his ear.

Runner plopped his rump on the grass and watched a squirrel scamper up a tree.

"Boss, we got a problem." George's voice sounded like a choked up whisper.

"What's wrong?"

"I…just get your ass here fast." The connection was cut.

Runner stood, tugged on the leash, and looked hopefully at Chuck.

The squirrel, sitting on a low limb of the spruce tree, waved his bushy gray tail like a matador waving a cape, and chattered in a high pitched screech.

"Sorry, you two can play later."

George stood outside the office at the apartment complex. His knees were locked, his expression grim. With his arms crossed his fingers cut deep into the flesh of his upper arms.

Chuck slid out of the truck, waited for Runner to exit and released enough leash for him to check out the English boxwood lining the path to the office.

"What happened?"

George eyed the pup.

"Lock him in the office, I'll wait."

Chuck followed George down the driveway and towards unit L, the last of the twenty units to be remodeled. Five paces from the door numbered L-3 he stopped.

"Open the door. Don't step inside," George said.

Chuck twisted the brass plated knob and pushed the door half open. Heat and stale air rushed through the opening. With no air conditioning the inside of the gutted rectangular building matched a sauna set at ninety degrees.

A young girl, curled in a fetal position lay in shaving and wood dust left from the sweet scented pine two-by-fours cut and stacked against a wall.

Chuck resisted the protective urge to step inside and cover her naked body from prying eyes. He didn't question that she was dead. He'd seen more than his share and recognized the signs. But to see the innocent die before they had a chance to live, twisted his gut.

He closed the door and turned.

"Have you called the police?"

George tried to talk, closed his trembling lips and shook his head.

Chuck pulled the cellphone out of the pocket in his running shorts and made the call.

Before he finished giving personal information to dispatch a cream colored Chevy sedan pulled along the sidewalk. The driver rolled down the windows and cut the engine.

The man was six three, and a solid two hundred. His

broad shoulders strained against his gray on gray herringbone sports jacket. His military haircut controlled the curl in his dark hair.

"I'm Detective Padilla. I was half a block away when I got the call." He handed Chuck and George crisp white business cards with black block print.

In the distance the wail of a siren sounded forlorn and disquieting.

"You're Detective Jim. I met your wife during the fire at High Points Apartments. She described you perfectly."

"Are you the guy she sent to meet Maria after she warned you about getting in the way of emergency personnel?"

"That would be me."

"Are you holding a grudge?"

"Compared to a sadistic military nurse I knew, Maria was gentle. I'm Chuck Taylor."

He used his chin to point. "George Summerland, one of my maintenance men. He found the girl and called me."

"Where's the girl?"

"Nine feet inside door number three."

"Did either of you go inside?"

"I didn't, but you'll find my prints on the door knob," Chuck answered.

"I did," George stuttered. "I thought she'd broken in and fallen asleep or passed out. I touched her shoulder…" He closed his eyes and stuffed trembling hands into the back pockets of his jeans.

Two white El Paso police cars pulled to a stop next to Detective Padilla's Chevy.

"Ralph, rope off the perimeter and Miguel you start access control," Padilla said.

"Yes sir, Detective."

"Albert, start gathering PI on everyone in sight. Mr. Taylor, are you the apartment manager?"

Chuck nodded.

"Please take Mr. Summerland with you to the office and wait for me. Don't talk to anyone. If you don't mind, make some coffee, this is going to be a long one."

Chuck turned to leave.

"Before you go," Detective Padilla said, "As far as you can tell, did anything look different or strange?"

Chuck scratched his chin.

"By different I assume you mean besides the girl; nothing that sticks out, why?"

"When was the last time you saw the girl?"

"Detective, she doesn't live here. I didn't get a look at her face, but other than my daughter and her friends, I have very little contact with teenage girls. I don't believe I've seen her before." Chuck held the detective's penetrating stare without blinking.

"Okay," Detective Padilla said in a resigned grunt.

"I'm going to take a brief walk through. I'll be up to the office shortly." Padilla said as he removed a small jar of Vicks from his jacket pocket.

"You won't need that. She hasn't been dead that long," Chuck said and headed to the office.

At the brown door marked with a black number three Padilla pulled on latex gloves, turned the knob, and stepped inside.

He turned on a voice activated recorder and set to work.

"Naked female, mid-to-late teens. Long dark hair pulled into a tail at the nape of her neck, olive complexion. No obvious trauma to the back of the head. No sign of bleeding or injury. Female is lying in fetal position on her right side."

Making sure not to step into the sawdust he walked around the body. "Bruising around neck. No other visible signs of trauma. No sign of jewelry. No visible tattoos or birthmarks."

Padilla looked around the open space. "No clothing visible on the main floor of premise."

The phone was ringing when Chuck entered the office.

George slumped in a chair, and stared at nothing.

"Superior Apartments, may I help you?" Chuck asked.

"This is Sebastian Torch with the El Paso Times." Chuck unplugged the phone. With his cellphone he called the answer service and told them not to pick up the calls.

"George."

He didn't move or blink.

"George," Chuck said louder.

Like a dog getting out of a pond George shook.

"Why don't you take Runner for a walk? While outside, clear your head, and try to pull yourself together before the detective arrives."

"Who stuck you with the dog?"

"My daughter."

George talked quietly to Runner and scratched behind his ears while he attached the leash. Eager to please, Runner led George out the door and towards the nearest trees.

Chuck showered in the bathroom off the storage room, and dressed in a clean set of clothes he kept in a closet in case he decided to drive downtown after work.

Half an hour later, from the office window, Chuck watched two cops search the ground around the swimming pool. Like ants looking for a crumb of food another dozen police combed the parking lot and bushes bordering the property.

"George, do you remember when we were in that unit last?"

George stopped the insistent pacing that was wearing on Chucks nerves. Standing next to Chuck he cleared his throat.

"Not really. Last week we dealt with the mess from the kitchen fire in A-2. The week before, we dug up the sprinkler system and replaced the leaking pipes. Two weeks, maybe a few days longer."

"Was the door locked when you got there," Chuck asked.

"Yes sir, everything was one hundred percent secure."

"Would you check the key box and see if the apartment key is there?"

"Don't need to, Boss."

"Why not?"

"I got the key out of the box when I arrived. It's in my pocket."

"Did you sign the key out."

"No, I thought since the whole unit is gutted there wasn't any reason to sign the log."

"Dammit George, sign the sheet before the detective starts poking around the files."

The steady stream of tenants demanding answers had trickled out.

Chuck sat at his desk staring at his computer screen, but couldn't get his mind to concentrate on the spread sheet he'd pulled up.

He looked up when the door opened and a man wearing tan slacks and a brown sports coat entered.

"I'm Detective Bill Nelson. Which one of you is George Summerland?"

"I am." George seemed to find his spine. He straightened his shoulders and looked the detective in the eye.

"Mind if I ask you some questions?"

"What happened to Detective Padilla," Chuck asked.

"He's talking to a tenant."

"If you want coffee or bottled water help yourself," Chuck said.

"Thanks." The detective filled a Styrofoam cup and sat.

"What time did you clock in for work, Mr. Summerland?"

"Ah, my wife dropped me off at six forty-five."

"You don't drive?"

"No sir. I got a DUI six months ago."

"The city suspended your license?"

"No, it was voluntary. Our insurance company agreed not to cancel our insurance if I stopped driving until I finished a counseling program."

"You haven't finished the program?"

"I'm working on it," George said.

"What did you do after you arrived?"

"I made a pot of coffee and filled a travel mug. After that I grabbed a key to the unit and headed there."

"Why did you pick the key to door number three?"

"It's the closest door to where the table saw's set up."

"Did you see anyone on your way over there?"

"No sir," He paused and rubbed the palms of his hands on his knees.

"Mr. Kellerman was pulling out when I arrived. I heard an engine turn over as I walked to the unit, but I didn't see a car. Probably someone headed to work, but I couldn't tell you who."

"Take me step-by-step through what happened when you arrived at the unit."

"I unlocked the door and pocketed the key."

"Are you sure the door was locked?"

"Yes, sir. The lock on that door is stubborn. I had to set the coffee mug down and play with the key to get the lock to release."

Detective Nelson nodded.

"I pushed the door open and as I bent to pick up the mug I saw the girl. I said something, I can't remember what, but she didn't move. I left the mug and walked over and..." He paused and sucked in air. "I poked her on the shoulder with my finger. Her body didn't respond."

"What do you mean respond?" Detective Nelson asked.

"I can't explain it. Her skin or her form, it felt off, different. I looked at her side and counted to thirty. She didn't move. She didn't breathe. For a minute it was like I'd gone to a different time and place…I can't explain it."

"Okay. What did you do next?"

"I looked around the floor. There was a set of footprints in the sawdust that led to door number two. Without moving my feet I looked around to make sure no one else was in the unit. Then I retraced my steps. When I closed the door I kicked over the travel mug. I used my cellphone to call Chuck, picked up the mug, walked back here, and waited for him."

"When you were in the building, what made you think to retrace your steps?"

"Instinct and training, I spent four years in the Army as an MP."

"Did you see combat?"

"No sir, but I spent time overseas."

Chuck was dumping a fourth spoonful of coffee grinds into the coffeepot when his cellphone vibrated. He checked the ID.

"Hi, Laura," his voice was hoarse and strained.

"I just heard the news report on the radio. You okay?" Concern etched her voice and soothed the raw edges of Chuck's senses.

"I'll be fine." Which didn't answer the question or

maybe it did.

"Do you want to cancel this evening?"

Did he? He stood at the office window and watched Detective Padilla cut across the playground and past the pool.

"No, let's meet like we planned."

"Okay. Do you want me to bring dinner?"

He glanced at the clock. It was half past eleven. Since entering the office he'd consumed a month's worth of caffeine and a stale donut. There was a good chance he wouldn't get lunch.

"That sounds good. I'll see you at eight."

By the time the detective opened the office door Chuck had poured two cups of coffee.

"If you don't take your coffee black there's cream in the refrigerator. Sugar and spoons are on the counter."

"Black is fine." Padilla sat and rubbed a spot behind Runner's ear.

"Pups going to be the size of a bear by the time he grows into those paws." The simple action eased the firm set to his mouth and relaxed his broad shoulders.

Chuck set Padilla's mug on the desk and walked around to his chair.

"Thanks."

"Have you identified the girl?" Chuck asked.

"We have a possible. Anna Marie Collins, age fifteen, was reported missing two hours ago. She lied to her mother about spending the night at a girlfriend's house."

"Did she live around here?"

"She lived with her folks in San Eli."

"That's twenty miles from here." Chuck said. "What

the hell? Do you know why her body was dumped here?"

"How do you know she didn't die on that floor?"

"I've had a lot of time to review what I saw. There were no signs of body fluids. One set of foot prints enter from the door for unit number two, and one set leaves the same way. From the tread I'd say the guy was wearing tennis shoes. There was no sign of a struggle. The person laid the girl on her side and pulled her legs up to her chest, as if trying to offer some modesty. George entered from door number three. His work boots have a smooth sole. His steps go directly to her back. When he left his steps went over his first set of tracks."

"Why a male?"

"Anna Marie wasn't petite. Couldn't guess a height, but I'd put her at one-fifty. Unless a female had training as a firefighter or military special ops she would have been forced to drag the body. The shoe treads in the sawdust were larger than my size ten. That eliminates most of the female population."

Not bad conclusions Padilla thought, and wrote a mental note to check Taylor's background.

"Was she raped?" Chuck asked.

"I don't have a pathology report yet."

"How long you been a detective?"

"Fifteen years."

"How long were you a cop before that?"

"I spent six years in the service and four years with the sheriff's department."

"You don't need a pathology report to form an educated opinion, and nothing you say will be repeated."

"My educated guess is possible consensual sex,

maybe autoerotic asphyxiation."

"What the hell does that mean?" Chuck demanded.

"It's a choking game that supposedly heightens a climax and offers a high that's similar to taking drugs, but there's a lot more details that I need to know first."

"Jeez." Chuck rubbed the back of his neck.

"Now tell me the bad. You aren't being this generous with information because I'm a nice guy and you want to chat."

"Rigor mortis was just beginning to set in."

Chuck took a sip of coffee. "With the heat that means she'd been dead two hours or less. Tell me the rest."

Padilla realized there was more to Taylor than the laidback, charming, old school, polite, fair, hard worker and thorough descriptions he'd heard tenants use to portray their apartment manager.

He sipped his coffee and watched the pup curl into a ball on a round green plaid dog bed set in the corner beside the desk.

"There's no sign of breaking and entering. Whoever brought her here picked this place because they had a key or knew someone who had a key. It was a fast drop, and they weren't concerned about someone making a call to the police. That says the vehicle or the driver was familiar to the residents. They weren't worried about someone paying close attention to them if seen.

"You have a security pad. Did anyone deactivate it before George Summerland entered the office?"

Chuck picked up his cellphone and punched in a number. "Deanne, this is Chuck at Superior, what time did George use his code to deactivate the alarm? Six, forty seven, thanks. Was the system turned off at any other time after I left last night? Okay, thanks." He paused, "No continue to let calls go to voice mail."

Chuck stood, walked into the backroom and reappeared with a clipboard.

"The system wasn't turned off between six-eleven last night, when I set the alarm, and George's arrival. You can't have a master key to all the apartments, or at least shouldn't have," Chuck said.

"Why not?" Padilla asked.

"If a master key was lost or stolen you'd have to rekey the whole complex. That's why we have individual keys to each apartment and apartment owners are required by HUD to have a key control system."

Chuck pushed a clipboard across his desk. "That's the key control log."

"Where are the keys kept?"

"They're locked in a key safe," Chuck jerked a thumb towards a cupboard above the coffeepot.

"How many people have the code?"

"Every employee has access to the keys. It's necessary because we rotate who's on night call."

"Unit L is gutted. Why would they need unlimited access to the keys?"

"I don't make the guys punch a time clock. If they need to leave early they come in early to make up the time. George needed to leave at three today, so he came in at seven to make up the time. As you said, the unit's gutted; there was plenty of work to do. George grabbed a key and headed over."

"Any of the employees take advantage of the system?"

"Probably, but they're reliable workers who don't whine if a job keeps them here past five. In the long run everything evens out, and I don't have to play babysitter or listen to excuses as to why someone was twenty minutes late."

"Who knew George would be coming in two hours early?"

"He's playing in a golf tournament this afternoon. For the last month he's spent most of his waking hours talking about his chance to play a round of golf with the pros."

"How many copies of those keys do you figure are floating around?"

"There could be dozens or hundreds." Chuck said with a shrug. "Before I arrived the locks weren't changed when a tenant moved out. I haven't changed the locks on the empty units. But since I took over the locks are changed every time a tenant moves out."

Shit, Padilla thought. "Do you have a list of previous tenants?"

"Only for the last two years, but I can give you the names of two tenants who've lived here for over ten years. They might be able to provide you with names."

Padilla looked at his notes.

"Tell me about George Summerland."

"Tell you what?" Chuck countered.

"Your impressions, how long he's worked here, what type of worker he is," Padilla said.

"George has been here two years. He's a hard worker, who knows his way around a construction site. His help with remodeling the units has been invaluable. He spent four years in the Army. Married, no kids."

Hector Gomez," Padilla said as he made notes.

"He was hired the same week I hired George. Damn good mechanic, prefers to do the outside jobs. Married, with three kids."

"Frank Hanson," Padilla said with a nod.

"Frank's only been here two weeks. He's retired military, and more reserved then the rest the crew. He's a good handyman and a fast learner. He's divorced and chases women. From what little I've heard he likes them closer to his own age."

"How did he apply for the job?" Padilla asked.

"Hector recommended him."

"Why?"

"George is looking for a job with a future. Hector's known Frank for a while, and thought he would fit in. I didn't really need a fourth man, but George's leaving is just a matter of time. Reliable helps hard to find. So far, I have no complaints."

"Roberto Sanchez."

"Roberto started a year ago. His dad taught him construction and concrete work. He's damn good. He's twenty-two, single, and flirts with every female between the age of two and a hundred."

"Why doesn't he get a job on a crew with better pay?" Padilla asked.

"He's got a smart mouth and hasn't learned when to keep it shut. After he got fired a few times no one would hire him."

"Does he have a temper?"

"He can. But he's not your guy."

"What makes you so sure?"

"Like I said, Roberto likes to flirt, but for the last

couple of months a tall, stacked, blonde has kept him too tired to do anything but look."

Chapter 12

Courtesy of the local deli, a vegetable tray of munchies, dip, cheese and crackers, sat on the dining room table.

Two bottles of wine sat in an old galvanized bucket full of ice.

Chuck was filling the pup's water dish and Runner was nosing his empty food dish across the floor when the conversation on the scanner caught Chuck's attention.

"You're going to do it? You said you'd eliminate her. If you back out I'm screwed." The voice was male, deep with anxiety and held the sharp edge of a 'don't screw with me' challenge.

"Maybe it's not gonna happen like you want but it will happen." The second voice was also male, and if Chuck had to guess Hispanic.

"Well get it done. I got things I need to do."

"What's the big rush?"

"None of your business."

"How do I know you're not setting me up?"

"You don't, but setting you up gains me nothing but more trouble."

"Damn straight!"

The doorbell rang.

Chuck turned off the scanner and headed to the door.

Runner sat by the door with the plush yellow duck firmly clamped between his teeth. His body wiggled with excitement and his long tail polished the floor.

"Good boy. Stay."

Chuck took the bag of food Laura held out and closed the door.

Runner stood, dropped his toy and ran his cold nose up Laura's leg and under her raincoat.

"I didn't realize it was raining," Chuck said.

"It's not," Laura said. She knelt and lavished Runner with attention until he lost interest, picked up the yellow duck and half skidded and half ran towards a chocolate brown cedar filled bed set next to the oversized chair and ottoman in the living room.

Laura stood, slowly slid buttons through their openings and let the royal blue raincoat slide off her shoulders and puddle on the floor around black stiletto's that added a mile to her legs.

"Do you like?" She asked.

The black piece of temptation was a filmy concoction that laced up the front like a corset. One lace shoulder strap drooped down her arm. Black silk stocking stopped mid-thigh, leaving a creamy expanse of skin begging to be caressed.

"Isn't that obvious?"

Her eyes slowly traveled down his body. When she reached his crotch she chuckled.

"I guess it is."

She stepped around him and entered the living room.

"Nice television. Is it new?"

"I purchased it from a lady in distress."

"Took advantage of her, did you?"

"Not yet."

"Then you better get started."

Two hours later, Chuck leaned a hip against the counter and sipped a beer.

Wrapped in one of his daughter's robes, Laura sipped a glass of wine and hummed as she reheated the Chinese food she'd bought for dinner.

"You look happy."

"I am happy." She said and leaned in to give him a kiss.

"Thanks."

"My pleasure."

She gave him a dreamy smile.

"That too, but I meant thanks for your help. The loan officer called this afternoon. I have thirty days to submit a business plan. As long as the plan is solid and the board feels the proposal is doable, my loan has been approved for twice what I thought they'd allow."

"That will give you a nice buffer if it takes longer to start showing a profit."

"That's what the loan officer said. With the additional operating capital available I put my money into a three year CD. They should earn enough interest for a down payment on a house when I'm ready. And I made an appointment with a realtor to start looking at business locations."

"You had a busy afternoon."

"Thanks to you it was more satisfying than busy."

He gave her a hug and kissed her hair.

"You find a place to rent I'll help you do the remodel."

"Thanks, I'll take you up on that offer."

Chapter 13

Chuck plugged the scanner into the charger set on the small kitchen counter in the corner of the office, and filled his coffee mug.

At his desk he glanced at the worksheet. Empty. In two years that was a first. Considering the reason for the lull, he'd rather have a two page list of grievances.

"Last night, the news said there weren't any leads on the girl's murder." Roberto said from the seat he'd tilted back on two legs.

"I heard it was a group gang bang. I wouldn't mind being part of that initiation." Hector grinned like a jack-o-lantern.

"You live in the neighborhood where Anna Marie lived?" Chuck asked.

Hector shrugged. "It's a large neighborhood, but yeah the general area."

"You know her?"

"Shit no, man, too young for me. But I'd seen her and her girlfriends hang at the corner looking for action."

"Drugs?" Chuck asked.

"Drugs, booze, boys, a party, you want to have fun you stand at the corner and wait to see what invites you get."

"You said gang, you know that for certain?" Chuck asked.

"Nothing's for certain. I heard a rumor that's all." The corner of Hector's left eye twitched.

Bullshit, what he knew didn't come from a rumor Chuck thought, but when he realized Hector was waiting for an answer he nodded.

"You hear anything about the murder on the scanner, Boss?" George leaned his shoulder against the wall and sipped his coffee.

"No, but I might have overheard two men plotting to kill someone."

"You shitin' us?" Roberto asked.

"Never thought murder was something to joke about."

"If you met the men would you recognize their voices?" Hector asked.

Chuck shook his head.

"The scanner distorts voices. I'm not sure I'd recognize my own mother," Chuck said.

"Lots of crazies out there. Can't trust anyone to be telling the truth," Hector said.

"You'd know," Roberto said.

"Someone needs to give you a lesson on how to keep your mouth shut," Hector shot back.

"Just making a friendly observation," Roberto said. "Are you going to call the cops, Boss?"

"Would you?" Chuck threw back.

"Not without names."

"Maybe what you're hearing is that movie being filmed outside of town," Hector said.

"Get real, the movie's a science fiction about UFO's." Frank growled over the rim of his coffee mug.

"Maybe you should go to the police," Hector said.

"I call the cops and admit I'm illegally listening to cellphone conversations and happen to hear some dumbass ordering someone to eliminate her—no name, just her. How many females do you think live within the city limits? Do you have any other bright ideas?"

Hector gave a loose jointed shrug. "You ever hear any perverted or sexy talk on there?"

"Dumb shit, the words mean the same thing," Roberto chimed in.

"Only in your sick world dickhead," Hector said and curled his fingers into a tight fist.

"Frank, stick Hector's head under a faucet to cool him off, then take him with you to pick up the pool supplies. When you're done head to the plumbing supplier and pick up the bathroom sinks and toilets for unit-L."

"How long before they remove the crime screen tape?" Frank asked.

"I don't know. Roberto set your ass on the mower. If heat stroke doesn't kill you, think of the last time you ate a fist for mouthing off instead of keeping your mouth shut."

"What happened to the lawn service?"

"They quit. My Spanish is limited but I think he said something about dead bodies, angry ghosts or both."

When they left, Chuck leaned back in the chair and looked at George slumped in a chair, glassy eyed and disheveled.

"You look like hell."

"Feel worse," George mumbled.

"Did you ditch the golf tournament and drink yourself into a stupor?"

"My father-in-law used some choice words when I tried to back out. I played three over par. Best game I've ever played and I don't remember any of it."

"Did you drink all night?"

George ran a fat hand down his face. "There was a party at the club house after the game. I had a couple drinks but cut myself off. When I got home I finished off a six pack."

"Did it kill the ghosts?"

"How'd you know?" George shook his head. "Never does," he said quietly.

"Call Angela and tell her to pick you up. Get some sleep or call your brother-in-law and slap a few more golf balls. But stay away from the booze."

"I can't afford to lose eight hours pay."

"It's covered."

At the door George turned. "Thanks."

Chuck's cellphone rang. He glanced at the caller ID and smiled.

"Morning, Sunshine. Are you having a nice morning?"

"Lovely. Thank you. You didn't need to buy me flowers, but thank you. They're beautiful."

"It was my pleasure. What are your plans for the day?"

"I need to catch up on paperwork." She paused. Chuck could feel her hesitation through the phone.

"What's wrong?"

"You have enough going on, you don't need more."

"If it concerns you, I want to know."

"Someone was at my place last night."

"Did they break in?"

"No they were in the backyard. The...The mother cat and the kittens that were abandoned at the apartment were killed."

"Are you sure it wasn't a skunk or a coyote?"

"They weren't eaten. Whoever did it broke their necks, put them back in the box and moved the box from under a shade tree to the backdoor step."

"Have you called the police?"

"I did. They took a report over the phone."

"Would you like me to come over and take a look around?"

"Thanks, but there isn't anything to see. You're busy, I should let you go."

"Do you think the ex did this?"

"I hate to think my gut instincts about him were that off, but it's a possibility."

"Call me if you see anyone suspicious or get nervous."

"I will."

Detective Padilla stepped off the elevator.

The sunshine yellow walls couldn't compensate for the lack of windows in the long sterile hall.

Nor could the room freshener, that shot a vanilla scented mist into the air every five minutes, mask the heavier scent of death.

Padilla opened the double doors to the morgue and stepped inside.

The air vibrated with the blast of drums, guitars, and piano that was unique to the sound of the Grateful Dead.

Lang Yin, a petite oriental woman of undeterminable age, stood on a custom made, stainless steel platform that circled one of four examining tables. The upper half of her heart shape face was hidden behind large pink goggles.

When she saw him standing a foot inside the door she peeled off a bloody latex glove and slipped her hand inside the pocket of a hot pink smock smeared in blood and body fluids.

The instant silence was as deafening as the volume of the music.

As his eyes adjusted to the bright lights Padilla scanned the room and the three empty autopsy tables that glistened under the lights. "Slow day?"

"Sometimes we get lucky. You got my call?"

"I did." He waited.

"Your vic died from strangulation." She tilted her head towards the girl's head. "The bruise pattern on the neck, the damage to the trachea and esophagus, and the conjunctive of the eyes, are consistent with strangulation, or what kids call the choking high. The act probably happened during sex."

He hadn't thought they'd get that lucky.

"The guy didn't suit up?"

"It's more complex than that. I've isolated five DNA's."

"She was gang raped?"

"I see no signs to indicate rape. I called you because there's another complication. Anna Marie was pregnant. Twelve to thirteen weeks along."

Shit.

"Is it possible she didn't know?"

"It's possible she was in denial but chances are she knew."

"Any of the DNA collected match the baby?"

"You didn't get that lucky."

Chapter 14

Chuck stood at the counter at Radio Shack and waited for Todd Shelf to finish helping a customer.

"How do you like the scanner?" Todd asked.

"I like it fine, but periodically the scanner jumps from one conversation to another. Is that normal?"

"Are you listening to cellphones or radio transmissions?"

"The police frequency."

"The radio transmission is being trunked."

"Trunked means what?" Chuck asked.

"The calls are being switched between several frequencies based on use."

"Why do they do that?"

"It eliminates radio traffic from the busier channels used for emergencies."

"Okay, that makes sense. What about a cellphone?"

"A phone is bounced off the nearest cell tower. As the caller progresses to a different area the caller is switched to a different tower."

Chuck frowned. "Is the scanner picking up the tower or the caller?"

"That depends on the type of phone, the frequency of

the scanner and how close you are to a tower."

"That's as clear as mud. You're saying the scanner isn't broken."

"It's not broken," Todd said with a nod.

"Is it possible to record a conversation?" Chuck asked.

"Sure, all you need to do is plug a recorder into the earphone jack."

Todd gave him a shit eating grin but didn't budge.

"Do I beg or are you going to get me what's needed to make that happen?"

"You plan to keep hauling this around like it's an IPod you should purchase a carrying case. A recharge stand for your house would be good idea too."

"What will I do with the charger I already purchased?"

"Put it in another room or at your office."

Like a bee attracted to a bright flower Runner headed to the front porch and tried to bite the red balloons secured to a plastic cupcake holder by thin strips of white ribbon.

The attached sheet of pink paper was covered in childlike hearts and a lipstick kiss. *"Don't eat all of them for dinner or at least share one with Runner. I'll meet both of you in the park tomorrow and we can run off the calories, Laura."*

He ate a chicken pot pie, diluted the salty aftertaste with iced tea, and played with the tape recorder and microphone he'd purchased.

Satisfied that it worked, he slid the scanner into the new charging base, turned it on and settled in to watch the Texas Rangers play the Cardinals.

He was half asleep when a man's words caught his attention.

"I'm one hundred percent sure. I don't love her. I don't want to see her fucking face again."

Before he could turn on the recorder the scanner beeped.

A sultry female voice said, *"Come on sugar, tell your wife you need a pack of smokes. I need you to come over and take care of me."*

Disgusted with the turn of events he switched the scanner to the police frequency and leaned back to watch the end of the game.

He only half listened to the scanner until dispatch called out the address across the street from him.

"Do you have any further information?" The officer en-route asked.

"Negative. Male child called, said his father is hitting his mother."

"Shit," Chuck muttered.

The kid was a cute six year old who'd just learned how to ride a two wheeler.

The mother was the youngest sister of a childhood friend. She and her husband had moved into the house only two weeks ago.

He slipped into his shoes and headed across the street.

Until he'd done the remodel on his place, the floor plan of the pale yellow house was a duplicate of his place.

The front door was ajar.

The kid sobbed. With snot running down his chin begged his dad to stop hitting his mom.

Rosie stood in the middle of the living room. With deadly calm, she stared at her husband as she told Conner to go to his room.

Her lower lip was cut. Her blouse was missing several buttons and one sleeve was torn at a shoulder. Her face tensed when the boy touched her left arm.

Rosie never took her eyes off the man with his back to the door, but from the brush of fear in her eyes, Chuck knew she'd seen him.

The door opened further when Chuck knocked.

The man spun towards the sound.

His eyes, glazed with anger were dilated and blood shot.

The kid grabbed his mother's hand and tugged her towards the dining room where a door led to the garage.

"What the hell do you want?" The guy was built like a Sherman tank. Rage contorted his features. The muscles in his biceps bulged as he flexed a fist.

Chuck kept silent until Rosie and the boy stepped into the garage and closed the door.

"I heard yelling. Is everything okay?"

"Mind your own fucking business."

Before the last word faded a fist connected with Chuck's face. His head snapped and he staggered back. A black metal hand rail stopped him from tumbling off the side of the small two foot high landing.

The door slammed shut and the deadbolt clicked into place.

Chuck pressed the sides of his nose with his fingers.

It hurt like hell but it didn't feel broken.

He walked to the garage and lifted the door.

Conner and Rosie were pressed into the back far corner trying to hide behind a black trashcan.

"The cops will be here any second. I'm going to stand at the curb. If he comes out I'll hear him."

"He'll kill you," Rosie said.

"He can try. Rosie, even if you don't press charges I will."

Chuck sat on the curb, bent forward and wiped blood off his chin. A foot from where he sat, a white patrol car pulled to a stop.

"You okay?" The officer was half Chuck's size. His partner was a tall lanky female.

"I'm fine."

"You need an ambulance?"

"No," Chuck answered. "Rosie and the boy, Conner, are crouched in the right back corner of the garage. I think Rosie's arm is busted. Watch yourself, the guys the size of an ox and has the disposition and speed of a ball busting rodeo bull. He's also drunk or on drugs. Tell Rosie if she needs a place to stay to knock on my door."

"And you are?" The female cop asked.

"Don't twist an offer into something more. I live in the white house across the street." Chuck swiped his dripping nose and stood.

"When you're ready I'll sign the papers to press assault charges."

Runner met him at the door, braced his front paws on his thigh and whimpered.

"It's okay boy, I'm fine." The pup stayed by his side as he dumped ice into a zip lock bag and wrapped the bag in a kitchen towel.

The scanner beeped.

"*Northeast 23—check out the face of the guy who lives in the white house across the street.*"

"*27—Pretty bad?*"

"*23—Solid punch to the face. Bleed like a pig, could have a broken nose.*"

"*27—Doesn't the idiot know domestics are worse than facing a bank robber with a gun?*"

Chuck snorted at the comparison.

"*Do you want me to go over and obtain his PI?*"

"*Thanks, saves me time and paperwork. He said he'd sign assault charges.*"

Chuck turned off the scanner, clipped the leash on Runner who danced around his feet, and headed to the door.

Chapter 15

The sun was an orange-yellow globe on the horizon of a turquoise-blue sky.

At the park Runner wiggled and whined with anticipation when he spotted Laura or more precisely, the large dog biscuit in her hand.

"Ouch," Laura said when she saw Chuck's face. Gingerly, she kissed the side of his mouth. "How bad does it hurt?"

"Painless unless I breathe." The bruising spread across his left cheek, around his eye, and across the bridge of his nose.

"Who'd you fight?"

"No fighting involved. The neighborhood bully objected to my stopping by for a friendly chat. He swung and I didn't duck."

"Did the cops arrest him?"

"They did, and that held a load of satisfaction."

"Was he beating a wife or child?"

"Wife, they just came to town and moved into her parents place."

"Is she okay?"

"She has a broken arm and two cracked ribs. I called

her oldest brother and clued him in. Ralph and her two other brothers arrived within minutes. They talked Rosie into pressing charges and getting a restraining order."

"Then the bruises and pain are worth the price to get her away from him." She gave him another kiss and a smile.

"You really are Sir Galahad."

"I don't feel like a hero and it's probably not over."

"Why not?"

"When he gets out of jail Rosie's brothers will beat the shit out of him. Because I'm the one that called them, he'll be looking for revenge."

"You're not worried about him coming after you, tell me the rest."

"If Rosie refuses to follow through with the charges he'll still live across the street. He'll beat her just to prove that he has more power than me."

"If you have to rescue her again carry a big stick," Laura said.

"There's a thought."

"You should have called me last night. As your girlfriend I would have brought you dessert, kissed your wounds and shared my makeup to cover the worst of the bruising."

"Cookies would have been nice. Wait you said girlfriend, I don't remember promoting you to girlfriend."

"I am a girl and your friend right, right?"

"I don't remember. I'll have to check." Chuck leaned in and placed a hand on her lower abdomen.

"Hey, I reserve that for my boyfriend, do you happen to know where he went."

"I'm a boy, and you're a friend, right?"

"Right," she said and laughed. "Are we jogging or going to negotiate a different type of exercise?"

"Your choice," Chuck said.

"I'm hungry."

"For food?"

"And other things. But first I want French fries," Laura said.

"For breakfast?"

Laura slid her arms around his waist and did a little boggy dance.

"You have a problem with that?"

"None at all," Chuck said.

At ten, Kelly Lutz strutted into Superior's office. Her red denim skirt barely covered a well-padded ass. Stacked red heels added five inches to her lean six foot frame.

"Morning, Kelly. What can I do for you?" Chuck asked.

"You look like hell."

"Thank you, I really needed to hear that. What do you want?"

"Get me a new refrigerator."

"You got a brand new one last week."

"It doesn't work. This time get me a white side-by-side."

"Unless you're buying, you don't get to choose the appliances."

"I'm telling you the refrigerator doesn't work."

"Then I'll have it repaired."

"Send George."

Chuck glanced at Frank who sat in a chair with a shit eating grin.

"I want George," Kelly whined.

"Then call him during off hours. Right now he's busy."

Hector walked into the office, stepped out of Kelly's path and gave a low whistle when she swept past him.

"Sweet piece of tail. What does she want?"

"Trouble. Frank check out the refrigerator," Chuck said.

"If I don't surface by five, call the paramedics," Frank called over his shoulder.

"Why didn't you send me?" Hector slouched into a chair.

"You're a pervert. You would have been there all day. I need you to get the pool hose working."

"Didn't you take her out?"

"Officially, no." Unofficially, it was a half hour of insanity that he'd regretted before it was over.

"What did she look like naked?" Hector used his hands to create his own version of Kelly naked.

Chuck offered a half smile that didn't meet his eyes. "I can't believe you haven't gone down that path."

"She thinks she's too good for me."

"Kelly likes a challenge. Offer her a buck a minute. Ten bucks will get you a first rate view of her assets and time to scream hallelujah. But do it on your time not mine."

Hector pulled a wad of bills out of his wallet, peeled off ten singles and kissed them before he stuffed them into a front pocket.

"Last night I overheard the same two men talk about killing the guy's wife. It sounded like they plan to kill the woman soon."

"Call the police," Hector said.

"You said that yesterday. Don't you have any other suggestions?"

"It's the only one that won't get you killed. What happened to your face?"

"I walked into Kelly's breast implants."

Hector snickered and left.

Chuck pulled the phone book from a desk drawer and found the number for the local police quarters.

"This is Officer Wallace." The voice was clipped and bored.

"I need to report a possible crime." Chuck couldn't believe he'd stammered like a nervous kid on a first date.

"It's either a crime or it isn't."

"It's not a crime yet, but it will be a crime," Chuck said.

"Who is this?"

"A concerned citizen. I heard two men discuss killing a woman."

"Where?"

"On a radio."

"On the radio? Sir, are you're talking to me about a radio program?"

"Not a radio program, a police radio."

"What are you doing with a police radio?"

"It's not a police radio so to speak."

"Sir, is this an emergency?"

"Yes, no, not yet, but someone is going to be killed."

"Are you going to kill someone"?

"Not me."

"Sir, who is going to be killed?"

"I don't know."

"But you heard it on the police radio?"

"Not a police radio, a scanner."

"You heard police officers talking about killing someone on a police radio?"

"They weren't police officers."

"Sir, if they weren't police officers, then who were they and how did they get a police radio?"

"It wasn't a police radio; I heard the conversation on a scanner."

"A scanner that picks up conversations on radio's like a police calls?"

"Yes."

"Then it was a police officer."

"No. The scanner picks up all radio frequencies."

"Then who is trying to kill whom?"

"I don't know."

"When is this crime supposed to be committed?"

"I don't know."

"Call back when you know. Better yet, when you know, file a complaint online."

The dial tone buzzed in Chuck's ear. Brilliant idea! If they'd traced the call, within an hour he'd be arrested for stupidity.

Chuck set the phone down. The immediate ring made his heart rate spike.

"Superior Apartments, may I help you?"

"Give me thirty minutes. I have to stop by my house

and…Shit, that's not what I meant."

Chuck hung up the phone and watched Frank walk into the office and plop into a chair.

"What was wrong with the refrigerator?"

"Kelly turned it off when she wiped off the shelves. I turned it back on, end of problem."

"That took an hour to fix?"

Frank grinned. "Who gave you the shiner?"

"A bull-frog."

"You're losing it."

Chapter 16

Chuck parked the truck in the garage and let Runner into the backyard.

After Angela entered the garage he pressed the remote to close the door.

"You don't have to pick George up from work?"

"I told him I needed to visit family. What happened to your face?"

"I wrestled a nightmare and lost."

At the kitchen bar Angela lifted the tinfoil on a tray.

"How can you burn a TV dinner?"

"I fell asleep. I'll be right back."

When he returned Angela was in the living room picking up the scattered newspaper.

"You need a keeper."

"Are you applying for the job?"

"If I applied it would include more than mopping floors."

"Have you learned to cook?"

"I'm a worse cook than you."

"I've heard that rumor."

"Is something bothering you?" Angela asked.

She hadn't asked about the dead girl. But George

had probably told her what they knew. And he couldn't very well tell her he'd heard two men discuss killing a woman.

"Nothing I want to discuss."

"Is it me?"

"Why would you think that?"

"You weren't happy about meeting me here."

Chuck sat on the couch and refrained from saying he wasn't given a choice.

"When I called I hoped you would suggest we'd meet here."

"I didn't suggest; you pushed the issue."

She looked through her false eyelashes and gave him a sly smile.

"Maybe I want to hook up with you."

"You're married. Do I need to list the reasons our being here alone falls under the heading of ill-advised risks?"

Angela's fingers ran up his thigh. By the time she reached his crotch his breath was lodged in his throat.

"It feels good to me. Do you love me?"

"Like a sister."

"I think you love me like a woman. We can discuss the problems later."

"Why did you call me?"

Angela shrugged, offered a coy smile, pressed in and drew her tongue against his lips.

He could push her away, but hell he was a healthy male and after years of her teasing he was curious.

Her tongue parted his lips, darted in and teased. Her finger tips made light circular motions until they reached his crotch. Then she stroked and petted and cupped his balls.

His body responded but his mind had tripped the bullshit meter.

Angela's moves were precise, as if designed to elicit specific responses set to a timetable only she understood.

The buttons on her blouse magically popped open and she'd managed to unbutton his shirt without him realizing it until the feel of lace and pebble hard tits rubbed against his bare chest.

Her body was soft and curvy. She fit against him like a hand in a glove and squirmed and sighed and made deep throaty cooing hums.

The sounds reminded him of a dancer at a local strip joint who sold lap dances to guys willing to sit on the stage and become part of her act.

Her lack of emotional attachment kept the palms of his hands rooted to the couch.

He thought about the kids he'd seen groping in the back of the car and knew they had more emotion packed in their inexperienced necking than Angela added to her choreographed foreplay.

For a fleeting second he wondered how good she was at faking an orgasm but knew he wouldn't pay the price of admission to watch the show.

Angela pulled back, licked her lips and gave him a satisfied smile.

"Passion, you and I have passion. Is that not enough?"

He couldn't think of a polite way to tell her an hour of passion could be bought with a hundred dollar bill.

Chuck eased her into a sitting position.

Standing he buttoned his shirt and headed to the

kitchen.

"Where are you going?"

"I need a beer."

"What about me?"

"I'll bring you one."

"You know that isn't what I meant."

"Deal with it."

He stood at the kitchen window, watched Runner chase a butterfly, and took a long pull on the beer.

What game was she playing?

Angela was a good woman but she was a tease and not right for him. Hell, until she got her mind straight she wasn't right for anyone.

She didn't love him and possibly didn't know the meaning of the word, but at the moment she'd convinced herself that he was the answer to whatever fantasy she'd created.

He hadn't realized she'd followed him until she slid her arms around his waist and placed a kiss between his shoulder blades.

"I want to be with you, at least for a little while."

"Thanks for the clarification."

"I'm sorry. I'm not ready to make a long term commitment."

"You wear a rock on your finger that states otherwise."

Before he said something he'd regret he stepped out of the embrace, picked up her purse and handed it to her.

"I don't want to go home. Don't you want to be with me?"

Chuck ran his fingers through his hair and begged the devil for patience.

"Let's go."

"Where are we going?"

Hell, he didn't know, but he had to get her out of the house.

"For a drive."

He headed out of town and took several back roads before realizing where he was. Maybe he'd been headed here all along and just hadn't realized it.

He turned onto a dirt road and parked under a shade tree.

"Is that the end of the airport runway?" Angela shifted in the seat to look out the side window.

"It is."

He turned on the scanner and adjusted the frequency.

"What are we doing here?"

"You didn't want to return home."

"You have a strange idea for a date."

"This isn't a date."

"Have dates changed since I've been married?"

"This isn't a date. But yeah, now married women are chasing single men," Chuck muttered.

"Be nice to me."

The breathy pout that turned men's heads and made them believe she was a helpless sex kitten had been amusing, now it annoyed him.

The scanner buzzed. "*Southwest you've been cleared for departure, runway Twenty Nine.*"

"At the house, I wanted to live up to your fantasy." Angela placed a hand on his thigh and gave a squeeze.

"Angela, it's been a long time since my fantasies involve screwing on the couch."

"I wanted to show you that we'd be good together."

The roar of the plane taking off rattled the trucks windows and the canopy of leaves above them.

Chuck smiled, and said a silent 'thank you' to the pilot for cutting off the uncomfortable conversation.

"Ohmigod," Angela screamed and laughed.

They watched planes land and take off and fell silent into their thoughts.

A comfortable hour passed before Chuck's warning system kicked in.

He looked around the clearing. Not even a jackrabbit could hide in the dry golden grass mowed down to stubble, but the unease persisted.

"We need to head back," Chuck said into the silence.

"I know. Thanks for this, it was a nice date."

Chuck buckled his seat belt and looked in the rear view mirror.

"Shit."

Angela turned and giggled.

A white El Paso police car stirred a cloud of dust as it raced over potholes towards them.

Chuck rolled down the window and waited.

"Afternoon folks. May I see your driver's license, registration and proof of insurance?" The cops silver nametag said, Coffer.

"Is there a problem?" Chuck asked as he pulled his license out of the wallet and popped open the glove compartment.

"No problem," the officer said.

Chuck handed over the papers and waited while the officer checked the dates.

"What are you folks doing out here?"

"We're watching the planes take off and land,"

Angela said.

Coffer ducked and leveled his eyes at Angela's chest.

"Miss, I need your driver's license or another form of identification."

"Sure you do," Chuck muttered.

Angela dumped the contents of her oversized orange bag on the floorboard and scattered the pile until she found a black leather card case.

The officer looked at the pictures on both licenses.

"Who tried to break your nose?" Coffer asked Chuck.

"The playground bully."

"I'll be right back," Coffer said.

Chuck waited until the officer was in his car to look at Angela. "You realize there will be a report stating that we were necking like sex crazed teenagers."

"We're fully dressed."

"Angela, fully dressed is not your style."

She giggled and buttoned one of the white pearl buttons on her knit top. Adjusting the handkerchief size skirt was a waste of time but he watched her wiggle it down an inch.

"Now I look like a nun."

Some nun, Chuck thought.

"I'd like to see you try to sell that line to the officer," Chuck said.

Again, she giggled.

"Do you think they'll call George?"

"You aren't fifteen and out after curfew."

He watched her play with a lock of black hair. She was nervous about something, but what? George knew he wouldn't touch Angela so that couldn't be the problem.

When she called she'd said she needed to talk to him. But she hadn't mentioned anything of importance. Then again, talk and sex could be interchangeable code words in a game she thought he understood.

The officer stepped up to the window and handed Chuck both driver's licenses. Coffer's smile matched the, I know what you were up to, look in his eyes.

"Mr. Taylor, your name came up on a report. The bully made bail. Watch your back."

"Thanks for the warning," Chuck said.

"Guys, you need to move on. This is private property."

"I thought the city owned this property." Chuck said.

"They tried to purchase the land but the owner wanted too much money."

"Why isn't it fenced and posted as private?" Chuck asked.

"Ask the owner."

Chuck nodded.

"Did you file a report?"

"This time you get a warning and a word of advice, get a motel room."

"Yes sir."

Chuck rolled up the window, turned the engine over and pulled out.

The cop rode his bumper until they reached the highway.

"You realize if a report had been filed our names would have been listed on a public record that is available to the local newspaper."

"Would that bother you?" Angela's voice was defiant but she still twilled a lock of hair around her index finger.

"Angela you're married. I happen to like your husband. Hell yes, it would bother me."

"Our names mean nothing. The newspaper wouldn't have been interested in our tryst."

"Your father is a well-known and liked figure in this town. If a reporter connected the dots between you and him they'd twist a dull police report into a sexual tryst that would be talked about clear to San Antonio."

"The attraction between us is too strong to leave alone."

To make her point Angela crossed her arms and jutted out her chin.

"Speak for yourself."

"You want me. I proved that this afternoon."

"What you proved is that I'm a heterosexual male with a normal reaction to a beautiful woman."

"You think I'm beautiful?"

Chuck took the cowards route, he didn't answer.

Chapter 17

Chuck glanced up from the computer screen when Detective Padilla stepped into the office.

"Let me finish this then we can talk without interruptions."

Padilla sat.

Runner, always hopeful for a game partner picked up a clump of damp socks tied in a knot and sat in front of Padilla. They were deep into a friendly game of tug-of-war when Chuck finished the weekly report and sent it off to the accountant.

"You'll tire before Runner does." Chuck said and pulled open the bottom drawer of the desk.

Runner dropped his end of the sock, caught the tossed dog biscuit like a seasoned first baseman catching a fly-ball and settled on his dog bed to enjoy his reward.

"Did you stop by with questions or answers?" Chuck asked.

"It'll be on the evening news so thought I'd warn you that you'll receive more calls. Anna Marie died of strangulation."

"As you suspected, does that make her death accidental or a homicide?" Chuck asked.

"It's not that simple."

"It never is," Chuck murmured.

"Anna Marie was three months pregnant."

"Jeez, I hadn't expected that. You know the name of her boyfriend?"

"Again, it's not that simple. None of the DNA found on her matches the baby."

"None, meaning there was more than one sexual partner?"

Padilla didn't comment, but like a man drowning in personal demons, his eyes stared at nothing.

"Are you off duty?" Chuck asked.

"Yeah. How'd you get the shiner?"

"Ask the police officer who looks like Wonder Woman and has the body of Popeye's girlfriend Olive Oil. She answered the domestic at the house across the street from mine."

Chuck walked to the refrigerator and pulled out two bottles of beer. Settled back in his chair, he twisted off the cap and took a long pull. "Hector Gomez mentioned a rumor that Anna Marie might have died during a gang initiation."

"Two hours ago a girlfriend of Anna's told us the same."

"Did she give you the name of a possible father?"

"No need. Juan Rodriquez, age sixteen, died at 0700 hundred this morning at Saint Luke's Hospital of a self-inflected gunshot wound. He left a note for his mother and his blood type matched the baby."

"Is the case open as a double murder?"

"Murder suicide, maybe, but we're still missing some details."

"What are the chances you'll identify the gang members?"

"Not for sure about the gang ties, without more information that's just speculations."

"Are you always this cautious about saying what you really think?"

"Always. Otherwise you slip in front of the wrong person; the comment becomes the header for the next day's news and your back on the street writing parking tickets."

"Any tats or markings on the boy?" Chuck asked after taking a pull of beer.

"A few."

"And that means?"

"Nothing. Our best bet of finding who did this was to talk to the baby's father. He's dead. Now the best I can hope is that at some point the five males involved will be arrested for something else and their DNA put on file."

"D you have any positive news to share?" Chuck said.

"It's not my job to dig up good news. Anna Marie being placed in the unit was a possible inside job or someone with keys, but you already knew that."

"Are you looking seriously at any of my employees?"

"Hector Gomez knows more than he's saying, but so did every kid I talked to today. What do you know about him?"

"He's got a temper, and a mean left hook. Several months ago I overheard part of a conversation he had with a man named Josh."

"What were they talking about?"

"Hector mentioned making good on a delivery and getting paid. There were no specifics."

"Do you have your employees submit to random drug tests?"

"I do, he's always been clean."

"Do you meet your employees at a bar after work for a beer?"

"No. But most evenings Hector heads to a place called, El Congo's to shoot a few rounds of pool."

"What about Roberto and Frank?"

"Roberto comes from a large close knit family. He plays in two leagues. Likes his beer, but he doesn't frequent the bars. Frank has mentioned a place called The Diva. He keeps his mouth shut so can't tell you more."

Padilla finished his beer and stood.

"I'll have someone come by in the morning and remove the crime scene tape."

Britney Wilson strolled into the office at four, gave him a hug and sat in a chair she moved next to the desk.

"I heard you had some trouble left in one of your units."

"That's one way of looking at it, what else did you hear?"

"The girl's boyfriend, the one who committed suicide was related to one of the apartment tenants. The boy was following an older cousin's path into trouble, but he didn't have the necessary survival instincts. The aunt said one of the boy's brother's knew the girl was pregnant. The kids were hoping the whole thing would go away."

Chuck stewed on that as he poured them coffee. "Do you think they could have been trying their own form of abortion when she died?"

"They were scared kids. Who knows what they were thinking. But yeah, the thought crossed my mind when the aunt told me the story."

"How are you doing?" Chuck asked.

"When I was a social worker I did a crash and burn after ten years of beating my head against laws that made no sense. Swore I'd never play that role again. Now I realize I transferred my mothering instincts to the tenants."

"You got involved in tenant's lives?"

"No excuse, but I thought I was being helpful. Since the fire I've realized some of them depend on me to solve all their problems. I've managed to locate housing for everyone who didn't have family to help out, now there are no rooms left at the inns. Is your offer for an apartment still open?"

"It is."

"As soon as I find a job I'll move out."

"Don't worry about that. You want to move in today?"

"I need to shop for furniture. If they can deliver immediately, tomorrow will work."

"You need help financially?"

"You're too good. Why couldn't I be hot for you on every level?"

"The arrangement worked for us."

"But not now," Britney said.

"Why do you say that?"

"There's something different about the way you hold me. I'd like to meet her. Make sure she's worthy of you."

"She bakes good cookies, you'll like her. Now answer my question, do you need help?"

"No. The insurance company came through. With replacement value added to the renter's policy I'll be able to replace what I had without buying recycled junk."

"Good. Let me show you the apartment and introduce you to your neighbor.

The television was tuned to a rerun of Law and Order.

He looked at the caller ID when the phone rang and answered.

"Hi Ralph, how's your sister and Conner?"

"Conner is thriving. We got Rosie to agree to counseling. They say it will take time but she'll be okay. I called to let you know the bastard she married skipped bail."

"Before or after you and your brother's had a talk with him?"

Ralph chuckled. "After he was persuaded to sign divorce papers. Rosie and Conner will stay with me for the next month. If he doesn't cause any problems she'll move back to the house after that."

"I'll keep an eye on the house. Let me know if you

need anything else."

"Thanks, appreciate your help," Ralph said.

Chuck turned on the scanner and headed to the kitchen.

The scanner beeped and he listened to a woman offer instructions on how to bake a chicken.

He set a TV dinner on top of a magazine on the coffee table. The macaroni and cheese and fish sticks looked as unappealing as it tasted. He should learn to cook, or beg Leia to make meals, like she did before Carrie left for college.

The scanner beeped and a different voice filled the quiet.

"I can't talk long; the man is picking me up shortly."

Chuck put down his fork and paid attention to the woman's voice that held a liberal amount of disgust.

"It could be worse, girlfriend." A second female, with a slight southern drawl said.

"You're not the one screwing the fat pig."

"True, but he's more generous than most with the money. And you got yourself some nice ass on the side so stop whining."

"Speaking of nice ass, you want to do me a favor?"

"Who do you want screwed that you think would interest me?"

"My landlord."

"I've seen him. Not bad. Now tell me why you're being so generous."

"I need to buy some silence insurance."

"Do you want pictures or is my word good enough?"

"Pictures would be good, but he might be too smart

to fall for that trap."

"I can talk men into anything," the woman said and they both laughed.

The scanner beeped and fell silent.

Chuck took a long pull on his beer and leaned back on the couch cushions.

Should he feel flattered that Kelly Lutz, his pain in the ass tenant, was setting him up, or pissed that she thought he was fool enough to get into a position to be photographed in a compromising position?

He grinned.

Knowing Kelly the girlfriend would be a knockout that catered to sugar daddies and high rollers in Vegas.

The next few days could be interesting, but the underlying question was why did Kelly need to silence him?

What did he know or what did she think he knew that had her worried?

The scanner beeped and familiar voices filled the room. Chuck started the recorder.

"Here's the deal. When it goes down I'll pry the safe open."

"Do I take the money?"

"It will be empty dickhead. Shut up and listen. At exactly ten-thirty break the glass on the back door. Reach through the opening to unlock the door. The phone line you need to cut is next to the dryer vent."

"Where's the woman?"

"In bed asleep."

"When I hear you take the steps I'll head to the bathroom. That's your cue to run into the room and make a lot of noise."

"*Shouldn't I be quiet?*"

"*She needs to wake up and scream. Then you shoot her. She has to be one-hundred percent dead.*"

"*Dead. Got it, when will I get my money?*"

"*In three weeks I'll deposit cash where we agreed.*"

The scanner beeped.

The echo of two females laughing filled the static void.

"*Do you have a better idea on how to potty-train him?*" One of the women asked.

Chuck shut off the recorder, rewound the tape and listened to the conversation.

He didn't like where his thoughts were headed.

Chapter 18

"Hi Laura, there's been a slight change in plans. Do you mind driving to my place?"

"Is everything okay?"

"Peachy."

"I'm on my way."

Minutes later Chuck opened the driver's door of Laura's BMW and helped her out.

"You look like a man torn between murder and amusement."

"Good comparison."

He ushered her into the house and shut the door.

The two females sized each other up and eyed each other's outfits.

Both of their royal blue dresses showed off long slim legs and well-toned bodies. Both wore cream colored heels and carried matching hand clutches.

The major difference was Chuck wanted to strip one woman naked and sink into her. The other female he wanted to wrap in a nun's black habit and lock in a room until she was thirty.

"Laura, meet Carrie. I made the mistake of

mentioning our date. Carried decided we needed a chaperone."

"Love your shoes and the dress. Where did you buy them?" Carrie asked.

"Go online and search Macy's clearance sales," Laura said.

"I'll check that out. Dad's wrong, Uncle Beny called and invited me to the show. But messing up Dad's plans is a nice bonus," Carrie giggled, and gave them a wink.

"You're underage, Beny knows that," Chuck said for the tenth time.

"Uncle Beny said he cleared it with the owner."

"Chuck, in that dress and with that voice, no one is going to believe Carrie is under age."

"You think?"

Laura gave him a sympatric smile, and handed him the keys to the BMW.

"You drive."

"Nice diversion but it won't work. Unless you and Carrie want to share a bucket seat, we're taking Carrie's Subaru."

They pulled to a stop under the portico at the Comedy Club, and Chuck handed the keys to an attendant.

They entered a cool, high ceiling foyer. The walls were covered with framed posters of well-known comedians who had performed at the theater.

"You called the comedian Uncle Beny?" Laura said to Carrie.

"He's an honorary uncle. After the accident he spent a lot of time at the hospital making a billion animal balloons. Without his teasing, the first weeks of therapy would have been unbearable."

"But you knew him before that," she looked at Chuck.

"We've been friends a long time. That's all you need to know."

Carrie rolled her eyes.

"Carrie," Chuck warned.

"One night Uncle Beny talked Dad into standing on stage to do a comic routine."

"End of story," Chuck said in a well-oiled voice full of fatherly sternness.

"You made it." The man walking towards them was medium height, lean and bald. His skin was tanned and his sense of humor put a spark in his brown eyes.

The men did the manly slap on the back as they hugged.

Carrie was swept into a bear hug before being held at arm's length.

"The little girl who laughed at my knock-knock jokes is all grown up. When the boys get a look at you in that dress they'll be fighting for a seat at your table."

Carrie beamed.

Chuck scowled.

"And you're the lovely Laura." Beny kissed her cheek. "I'll triple whatever Chuck's paying you to pretend you're his date if you promise to run away with me," was said in a stage whisper.

"Laura this is Beny Zima."

"Nice to meet you. There's a conspiracy to keep me from hearing about Chuck's attempt at comedy," Laura said.

Beny snagged an arm around Carrie's waist and

offered an arm to Laura. He led the women to a small round table, second row, center of the stage.

"Chuck, the bars open. I'll take a scotch on the rocks."

"How mad was your dad when you horned in on his date?" Beny asked.

"He acted all huffy but his eyes danced with laughter. I think he might have been warned." She tipped her head and waited.

"Not by me," Beny protested.

"Really? Then explain the stack of Sandra Bullock movies on the coffee table and the six pack of diet Dr. Pepper I found in a sack with a receipt dated today."

"You're busted Beny. Admit your sins graciously," Chuck said as he joined them.

A waitress placed a scotch, beer, a glass of white wine and a Shirley Temple on the table.

"As the military says admit nothing but name, rank and serial number. You're drinking beer?" Beny asked.

"The last time I drank scotch with you I got talked into joining you on the stage."

"Are you serious?" Laura asked.

"Dad and Uncle Beny were at a comedy club on amateur night. Uncle Beny talked Dad into getting on stage with him to help him with a skit Uncle Beny had been practicing. After they were on the stage Uncle Beny told the audience Dad was going to do the routine. Dad stuttered and had to start over. Then he flubbed the punch line. If you want to see his comic debut, I have the tape at home."

"Laura, you don't want to see that tape."

"Oh, but I do."

"That was a good night. I got a lot of laughs," Beny said.

"I got the laughs," Chuck said.

"You were my act, I got the laughs."

"Who got offered free drinks for the night?"

"What I remember is the hangover," Beny said.

"Why do you think I stopped drinking scotch?"

"How did you two meet?" Beny asked.

"I'd decided to live dangerously and let him pick me after my car broke down," Laura said.

"I must not be living right, the last woman I helped had a husband who took exception to my jokes," Beny said.

"Imagine that!" Chuck said.

"And on that happy note I'm headed backstage." Beny stood, kissed both women and headed to the stairs at the edge of the stage.

Hours later wrapped in Carries robe, Laura lay asleep with her head resting on Chuck's thigh.

Carrie and Runner shared the oversized chair.

"I like her," Beny said.

"Me too."

"Serious?"

"Could go that way, but we're a long ways from taking that step."

"Carrie likes her, what's standing in your way?"

"Laura wants to start a business. I've offered to help but she needs to do this on her own."

"Is she recently divorced?"

"No, a bad date that lasted a few months. When the guy thought he had her on the hook, he pulled a one-eighty personality switch. I have the feeling she needs to build back her confidence, and prove that she isn't a poor judge of character before she can fully step into another relationship."

"You okay with that?" Beny asked.

"I've been alone for seven years. I have no problem with slow."

"Does she know your full story?"

"No."

"You might want to share that before she finds out accidently and thinks you've been playing the same game the last guy played."

"Good point," Chuck said.

Chapter 19

Chuck drank half a pot of coffee before the crew arrived.

"Anybody know where George is?"

Hector, Frank and Roberto, answered with sharp negatives and who cares shrugs.

"Listen to this."

Chuck pressed the play button on the recorder set on his desk.

"When you going to be ready to set up the kill?"

"We have a little time. Don't want to rush and leave a trail to our doorstep."

"I don't like the wait. It makes me nervous."

"Then find a broad to take your mind off the time."
The guy chuckled at his joke.

"It's not funny."

"You created the problem. Shut up and deal with it."

"When did you record that?" Roberto asked.

"Last night, about ten o'clock."

"Now you can take the information to the police." Roberto said.

"Without names and dates all they'll do is read me the riot act for listening to cellphone conversations."

"Maybe the police aren't such a good idea," Hector said.

"Last time we talked you suggested I call them."

Hector shrugged. "Today I change my mind. What are you going to do with the tape?"

"I don't know," Chuck said.

"It's hard to believe that listening to a scanner could land you in the middle of a mess." Frank refilled his coffee mug and topped Chuck's mug.

"When I purchased the scanner I was warned not to listen to phone conversations."

"You should have taken the advice," Hector said. "Maybe you should wait, see if you learn more tonight, or stop listening and forget what you've heard."

"And if a woman's murdered, do I ignore the fact that I might have been able to prevent her death?"

"Relax, Boss, you can't save the world or a woman without more information. And you sure as hell can't blame yourself unless you pull the trigger."

Frank was right, but it didn't stop the sense of helplessness that ate at his gut.

Chuck picked up the list of calls the answering service logged during the night.

"Hector, Kelly reported a clogged bathroom sink."

"Don't sniff her panties if she's not there." Roberto elbowed Hector in the side.

"If she's there, call me and we can both sniff her panties." Frank said over the ruckus.

"You guys are sick," Chuck said.

"Can I go with Hector?" Frank asked.

"You're needed at Mrs. Wilson's. She has a mouse cornered under her kitchen sink."

"Where's a stick I can use to club it to death?"

"Being a wise woman she didn't believe me when I said we wouldn't kill the pest. She wants the mouse caught and put in a jar. She's going to drive out of town and release it in a field."

"You have got to be kidding!" Frank grumbled.

Half an hour later George arrived and headed straight to the coffee pot.

"Sorry I'm late, Boss. Someone didn't fill the gas tank."

"It's my fault." Angela sounded resigned and didn't meet Chuck's eyes.

He hadn't seen her since the day they'd watched the airplanes. She looked tired, she'd lost weight, and dark circles were visible under her makeup.

"What's on the list for today?" George asked.

"Roberto needs help with the new roof on building C."

"I'm on it, Boss."

When George closed the office door Angela sank into a chair.

"I told him last night that I needed to fill the tank but he was more concerned about being at the house when my father arrived to pick him up for a golf date. After that I simply forgot."

"It happens."

"George is going to work through lunch to make up for this morning. Can we meet for lunch?"

"Where did you have in mind?"

"Your house."

Chuck leaned against the opening between the dining room and living room and studied Angela.

Her dress was low cut, clung to her like tape and stopped several inches short of decent. She looked seductive hot, and her hip swinging strut made the most of the outfit.

He'd have to be dead to not react, and stupid to not know what she planned or hoped to achieve. What he didn't know was why he'd agreed to bring her to his place.

"Make love to me." She purred as she strolled towards him.

"Not going to happen, Sweetheart."

It's been months since George made love to me." Her lower lip quivered in a seductive pout.

Chuck didn't believe her.

Maybe George wasn't being attentive but his gut said someone was taking care of her needs.

"You're married."

"I love you."

He swallowed a snort.

His eyes traced the hand print on her upper arm. He wasn't in love with her, but he cared and it bothered him to see bruises on both of her arms.

"You need to get your life on the right track."

"You could help me."

"Not by screwing you. You need to make decisions about your future."

"If, and I do mean *if* I left George, where would I go?" She looked at him and then towards the hallway and the two bedrooms.

"I thought your house was a wedding gift from your parents."

"It was but I wouldn't want to live there alone."

"I'll rent you an apartment."

"If I lived at Superior you would have to fire George."

Every time he thought he had Angela figured out she threw a curve ball. She was generous, caring and everyone genuinely liked her. She was smart, but she downplayed that truth under childish pouts and a helpless female demeanor. She was also selfish, self-centered and spoiled. Her relationship with George had him stumped.

"Why would your living in an apartment interfere with George's work?"

"It would be awkward?"

"For you or for George?"

She shrugged and her cheeks flushed with color.

George had arrived at work with a bruised cheek, swelling at his jaw and a red knot just below his ear. He claimed he'd fallen. Had he? Angela had a temper. Domestic violence against men wasn't rare, but was rarely reported. The bruises Angela wore had always been on her arms. Had George been trying to subdue her? Or did they both lash out when riled?

"Has someone fired George because of something you said or did?'

"How can you think that of me?"

The conclusion was easy, Chuck thought.

"You told me George worked for H & G electrics and lost his job when the business closed. Was that a lie?"

"George worked for my dad."

"George was a contractor?"

"My brother manages the offices being built. George managed the subdivision and custom home side of Daddy's business. He also helped with the design and construction of the golf course."

That explained George's resentment at working for an hourly wage and his tendency to give orders, Chuck thought.

"What happened?"

"George and I had a fight. When Dad saw the handprint he left on my face and arm George was lucky my dad didn't kill him."

"Why did you lie to me?"

"You wouldn't have hired him if I'd told the truth."

"So you lied to get what you wanted."

"I told a harmless fib. Before we married, George had a small business remodeling homes. He's a good worker. If it hadn't been for our fight he would still be managing the construction company. Daddy's forgiven him, but George has too much pride. He refuses to take his job back. Instead he works for you, like a common laborer."

And there was the constant rub, Chuck thought.

"I need to get back to work."

"You're the boss. Can't you be gone a little longer? You know what I want." Her voice held the same sultry purr she'd used to lure him in when they first met at the coffee house. But he was no longer the lust struck innocent who was twisted around her little finger.

He opened the door.

"You don't always get what you want."

Chuck knocked on the door and stepped in when Britney hollered that the door was unlocked.

"You've been busy," he said and followed the tempting aromas into the kitchen.

"I like your apron," Chuck said and kissed her cheek.

"I feel like a little girl playing with a dollhouse. I've moved the furniture around so often my back is sore."

"You could have called, I would have helped."

"At three in the morning, I don't think so. Besides I'm having fun. When I watched the apartment's burn I couldn't think of any good that would come from losing everything I owned and my job at the same time."

Chuck took the warm chocolate chip cookie offered and watched her open the refrigerator, pour milk into a glass and set the glass on the counter next to his elbow.

"And now?" He prompted after eating the cookie.

"I realize that without being forced I never would have risked making a change. You put me next to Mr. Kellerman for a reason?"

"That depends, are the two of you getting along?"

"We are."

"Then I'll take credit for making a wise decision."

"Did you know he taught economics and business courses at the University of Texas?"

"I've heard that rumor."

"He was one of your professors?"

"He was, and he doesn't let me forget that making C's in his classes was below my potential."

"He's hired me to cook dinners for him."

"Is that bad?"

"Not at all. Like me, he's a diabetic. Cooking for two is easier than single meals. He eats here and we talk. His sense of humor reminds me of my father."

"He has a sense of humor?"

Britney chuckled.

"I can't wait to watch the two of you interact. He's gotten me two customers who are also diabetics and he set up an appointment for me to talk to a friend who hosts a monthly dinner for a travel group. Is his background why you made a point of introducing us?"

Chuck took a second cookie and watched her put a cookie sheet in the oven.

"His background and his knack for knowing if a business has potential were my primary reasons. But if he hadn't liked you my scheme would have backfired."

"He could have hated my cooking."

"Not a chance. Does the idea of your dream becoming a reality scare you?"

"You know me too well. I'm excited but at three in the morning the doubts and fear creep in, and I question my ability to cook for anyone other than friends who wouldn't hurt my feeling with criticism."

"Mr. Kellerman was a tough teacher. He doesn't give praise freely, and he doesn't mince words when he's disappointed. If you listen to him you'll get a darn good education, and build a business at the same time."

"You really put me next door to him instead of in the empty apartment next to the cute single guy so I'd have a tutor to help me build a business?"

"I did. Besides, Brad Cutlet isn't your type."

"What's my type?"

"The same as Brad's—a bad boy with an attitude and a Harley."

"Oh my" she giggled. "I didn't see that. Maybe I should concentrate on cooking and put bad boys on hold."

"Not a bad idea."

"**P**erfect timing." Chuck said and grabbed a sack ready to slide off the top of a stack of books Laura carried.

The kiss he offered lingered a little longer than intended.

"You taste like bubble gum."

"It's a new chap stick. You like?"

"I like. What are all the books for?"

"Books on how to write a business plan."

"Sweetheart, I have a Master's in Business Management."

"You could have told me that before I spent an hour at the library."

He set the books on the coffee table and drew her into an embrace.

"You're cute when you're flustered."

Laura looked into his eyes and smiled. "And you're full of pretty compliments that make a gal feel special." She said, and gave him a hello kiss that left them both short of breath.

"Don't get me sidetracked," Chuck said, "dinner is ready."

"It smells too good to be a TV dinner or a chilidog." Laura said as they walked into the kitchen.

"The chef prepared lasagna, and a green salad. For dessert we have lemon pound cake and vanilla ice cream."

"You hired Stouffers, Green Giant, Sara Lee, and Ben and Jerry?"

"I'm impressed."

"Don't be, you left the evidence for the main course on the counter. And I'm well acquainted with your freezer."

The round antique oak table was set with bone china with a gold band around the edge, crystal wine and water goblets, and white linen napkins. Two pale yellow taper candles in star shaped holders were lit, and a bowl held three yellow roses clipped from a rosebush she could see in the backyard.

"Now I'm impressed," Laura said.

"You should be."

"How many calls to Carrie did it take to create this masterpiece?"

Chuck laughed.

"Five. If you don't count Carrie's three calls to make sure I set the oven timer, added cheese, tomatoes, and croutons to the salad greens, and took the tub of whipped cream out of the freezer." He'd cut his tongue out before admitting that Carrie asked if he had a supply of condoms.

He handed her a glass of red wine.

"I picked out the wine by myself."

She took a sip. "Good choice."

He leaned in for a kiss and a taste.

"Yes, it was. Can you spend the night?"

"I can."

"Then let's eat and get the business plan mapped out and a rough draft typed. Then we have the rest of the night to play."

"I like your strategy."

"Me too."

She opened the oven when the timer went off.

"You made garlic bread."

"It wasn't difficult," Chuck said.

"Do tell?" She said as she set the hot cookie sheet on top of the stove.

"A cube of soft butter and pressed garlic, it was simple."

"You pressed garlic?"

"Can we change the subject?"

She leaned a hip against the counter and smothered a grin.

"Not a chance."

"Leia, my next door neighbor, came over when I was using a hammer to pound the garlic cloves."

Laura laughed until tears rolled down her cheeks.

"I wish I'd been here to hear that conversation. While Leia made the garlic bread did she tell you we met last week when I dropped off the cupcakes?"

"Why do you think Leia made the garlic bread?"

"Please don't insult my intelligence."

Chuck grinned.

"Yes, she told me. Thank you for being kind to her."

"It wasn't a hardship, she's a nice woman."

"I agree."

They set the food on the table and Chuck topped off

their wine glasses.

"Have you heard any more about the girl found at the apartments?"

"No."

"Have you thought about who would have placed her body there?"

"It's hard not to think about that."

"You have a conclusion?"

"Theory or fear, take your pick."

"You think someone working or living at the apartments is involved."

"It's the only logical answer."

"How far along is the renovation?" Laura asked.

"The open stairways that led to the second floor apartments were removed six months ago. The new siding, roof, and windows were done at the same time. Basically, the exterior has looked like the remodeled units for five months. The inside renovations aren't past the new wiring and insulation stage."

"Why did you evict paying tenants before you were ready to remodel the inside?"

"I'll go back to the beginning. When I started I was told there were a handful of problem tenants."

"Gee imagine that," Laura said.

"The plan was to evict the problems, renovate those apartments and slowly work with the remaining tenants to upgrade the inside of the apartments."

"That makes sense. What went wrong?"

"Everything. Like a runaway train headed to a crossing with no crossing guard, the truth collided with the lies the day I walked into the office."

"Didn't the owner check the place out before

purchasing?"

Chuck nodded.

"The grounds were well maintained. The two empty apartments he inspected were outdated and in need of minor repairs but clean. The books passed two IRS audits and a yearly independent audit."

"Who was the owner?"

"It was a conglomerate of investors that were tied together by a financial investment firm."

"The owner couldn't sue the company for…I don't know what. But surly there was something the law could do."

"The two advisers and a third man acting as an independent accountant vanished without a trace."

Did the investors lose their money?"

"They did."

"What about the former manager of the apartments?"

"Either in hiding with the other men, or he was paid to disappear."

"Maybe an investor is mad because they lost their money but the buyer still got the apartments?"

"Anything's possible, but the complex was just one of five pieces of property the financial firm sold with the same closing date. And it was the smallest of the transactions."

"That was a convenient maneuver for the firm."

"Very," Chuck agreed.

"Why did the owner decide to convert the apartments into two story townhouses?"

"It's a desirable upper scale neighborhood that can command a higher rent. From a financial viewpoint, renovating the apartments to townhouses made more sense than pouring almost the same amount of money into remodeling lower rent apartments."

"And the theory would be that with half the tenants you have half the headaches," Laura said.

"True," Chuck agreed.

"Was there a method to the madness?"

Chuck chuckled.

"You ever pour water down a hole and wait to see the varmints scurry out?"

"Can't say I have but I get the visual. What type of poison did you use?"

"A rent increase to be determined by the number of unregistered permanent houseguests."

"That would work. How many left before the next rent payment was due?"

"After they received an official notice, eighty percent left."

"That leaves a lot of displaced renters. Did any of them get testy?"

"Some people moved out during the night without saying goodbye."

"Which leaves disgruntled employees?"

"I haven't had to fire anyone."

"What about the current employees?"

"I can't think of a motive that would make any of them take that kind of risk.

Chapter 20

Chuck rubbed the back of his neck and thought, *why me*.

A toddler had stuck a bobby pin in a socket while the grandmother was changing the younger brother's diaper. The child walked away unscathed but the hairpin caused a short that melted wiring and plastic and filled the apartment with smoke.

The fire department that answered the call was still parked in front of the apartment when a five year old boy jumped out of a swing and busted his arm. The parents, in Las Vegas for a fun filled day of gambling, called the hospital and gave permission for Chuck to stand in as guardian. The boy cried more over getting in trouble for leaving the apartment to check out the fire engines than having his arm set.

And—Chuck put his mental list of grievances on pause when Detective Padilla climb out of his city issued Ford and entered the office. His dark gray slacks, light gray sports jacket and gray and red tie butted tight against his Adam's apple didn't hint that the temperature was an airless ninety-eight degrees.

"Homicide must be having a slow day if they sent

you over to handle a vandalism report," Chuck said.

The detective slouched into the solid oak chair opposite his desk, and offered Runner a giant dog biscuit.

"Saw your name on two reports. Since I was headed this way I decided to stop."

Padilla braced an ankle on his knee and pulled out a notepad.

"You know the couple that left their son," he glanced at his notes, "Five year old, Robbie Shanks, locked in their apartment while they drank free booze and played keno?"

"I do. The situation isn't as bad as it sounds."

"You ever leave a kid alone?"

"Hell no."

Chuck took a breath and reigned in his anger.

"The parents hired a woman highly recommended by Mr. Shank's boss, who had used the woman's services several times. She arrived shortly before they left for the airport."

"Okay," Padilla's nod said he understood the reasoning. "Why did Mary Poppins lock the kid in the house and leave?"

"When the woman arrived back at the apartment she told me a gentleman invited her to lunch. She saw no harm in leaving the boy alone for a couple of hours. Robbie confided that she offered him two candy bars if he kept their secret. Since candy isn't on the mothers list of food choices Robbie readily agreed."

"It would have worked if the fire department hadn't arrived," Padilla mussed.

"For the record, the parents caught the next flight

home. They arrived half an hour ago. The mother took one look at her son's neon blue cast and burst into tears. The father's threatening to file charges against the babysitter."

Chuck stood and poured two mugs of steaming black coffee and set one mug on the desk in front of the detective.

"You didn't come here just to question me about a kid left with an incompetent babysitter." Chuck sat and used Kleenex to mop up the coffee that slopped over the rim of his mug.

"I had a few more questions."

"About what?" Chuck asked.

"When did the vandalism start?"

"Best guess is a week after the unit was gutted."

"Best guess? You manage a multi-million dollar apartment complex and you don't keep records?"

Chuck let the detective stew while he sucked on his coffee.

"Have you ever done any remodeling?"

"Enough to know when to call in a professional," Padilla answered.

"Good enough. When you remove stairs, move walls and replace windows you have to figure on running into minor snags."

"What's your description of minor?"

"Pipes and windows that leaked and caused mold to build up, work that wasn't done properly when the building was built needs to be corrected. Building inspectors who thought they could blackmail me into paying for their signoffs. Basically irritating crap that cost time but not a major outlay of money."

"You pay off the inspectors?"

"Hell no, I called their bosses and threatened to call the newspaper."

Padilla nodded.

"Two months ago I ripped out the walls in unit L. It's the last unit to be remodel."

"You personally ripped out the walls or your crew?"

"Combination, but I spent several evenings alone striping the place of old wiring and pipes. From the beginning there were minor problems. Tools moved, supply shortages and wire that was installed one day having foot long strips cut out the next morning. Newspaper and toilet paper stuffed down pipes and then the pipes filled with water."

"Any sign of forcible entry or graffiti?"

"That was the problem; no evidence to support the problem being caused by outside forces."

"Until now," Padilla prompted.

"The night the crime scene tape came down a water pipe was loosened and the water valve to the unit was turned on. Since the unit is gutted the only harm done was the waste of time to vacuum up two inches of water."

"Any sign of forcible entry?"

"Yesterday we installed new locks on all the doors. Someone used a glass cutter to cut the glass out of all the first floor windows at the back of the unit."

"Handy trick to keep down noise," Padilla said.

"Inside they shutdown the circuit breakers and cut all the electrical wires. Five rolls of insulation were cut to ribbons."

"You piss off any of your tenants?"

"Not sure pissed is the right word but a tenant's not happy that I've turned down her invitations."

"You get a lot of that?" Padilla asked.

"It happens but no not often."

"You think the woman would be vindictive?"

Chuck thought about the phone conversation he'd overheard and nodded.

"Yeah, she's the type but trying to set me up for blackmail is more her style."

"Is that something I need to know?"

"Past history. If something else comes up that I can't handle, I'll let you know."

"Fair enough. The rent on an apartment is more than my mortgage. Someone could think the owner's ripping them off."

"The tenants are willing to pay for upscale accommodations, without any of the headaches and work that come with ownership."

"You talk to any of the tenants that live at that end of the complex?" Padilla asked.

"I did and no one heard anything."

"What about the surveillance cameras?"

Chuck pulled two tapes from a drawer and pushed them across the desk.

"The tapes show a shadow, nothing more."

"Who knew you had the new camera's installed?"

"Any tenant who saw the logo on the side of company truck. Then add my employees and every person at First Response Security. After that, add spouses, friends, neighbors and people stuck in grocery store lines listening to someone give intimate details about their life."

"Half the town," Padilla muttered. "You said the unit is the last to need remodeling. When the unit is finished will you lay off any employees?"

"The club house still needs to be remodeled. After that, the plan is to convert the carports into garages and add storage units to the backside of the garages. There's plenty of work to keep everyone busy for a long time."

Padilla rose. "I'll pass the information on."

Chuck's phone rang as the door shut.

"Is it a full moon?" Laura sounded tired.

"That bad?"

"I swear one of the tenants is a vampire or is it werewolves that change with the moon?"

"I'll have to research that. Are you home?"

"I'm just getting ready to leave my office."

"Want me to come over and give you a massage?"

"That's tempting but I'm exhausted. I'll have to ask for a rain check."

He heard her sigh and the slight hesitation.

"Have you eaten?"

"I thought I'd have a bowl of soup."

"How about we meet at The Kitchen? I can fill my arteries with greasy food and tell you all the reasons you're better looking than the waitresses. After that you can go home and rest, or not."

"I'll meet you there in fifteen minutes," Laura said.

"How old is that pickup?" Laura asked after Chuck gave her a hug and quick kiss.

"Henry Ford was the designer."

"That I believe. You like driving around in a rattling tin can or does the truck hold sentimental value?"

"It might not look pretty but it doesn't rattle. No sentimental attachment, just a big aversion to car salesmen."

"I didn't take you for a coward," Laura teased as they were led to a tall metal table with an oak top and two bar height stools.

"I'm a pushover for a classy chassis with a nice rear and great wheels."

"Are we talking cars?"

"What do you think?"

"I think you're a dangerous flirt."

"I'm a pussy cat."

"Are we talking a tiger?"

"That could be, but not when facing a car salesman looking for his next victim."

"You take control and negotiate, like you did so smoothly to get me to come to dinner instead of heading home and collapsing."

"With you I have an alternative motive. How about this next weekend I kick tires and you negotiate the deal."

"Chuck, I wasn't insinuating that you should trade in the truck."

"No trade involved. I'll use the truck for work."

"Chuck."

"Don't. Since we had to drive Carrie's car to the comedy club it's something I've been thinking about. Helping you climb into a monster truck will be fun."

"How about something more sedate, like a silver Volvo with four doors and comfortable bucket seats?"

"We'll see," he said as the waitress arrived.

They ordered drinks and dinner and took a moment to allow their beers to smooth out the rough edges of the day.

"Tell me about your day."

"It was…different. The guy who keeps the grounds arrived drunk and broke his leg when he drove the mower into a tree. As they were wheeling him into the ambulance he was threatening to sue. A kid flushed a plastic toy down the toilet. That backed up the sewer to two apartments. The owner arrived unannounced and looked over my shoulder for three hours. Tomorrow morning, at the crack of dawn, he's returning with the accountant to install a new computer program."

"Except for the owner it sounds like my day. If you'd like, after we check out cars we could run away for the rest of the weekend. Find someplace quiet to relax."

"That sounds like heaven."

"Then plan on spending Saturday night at swanky Hotel Fireside."

"Never heard of that?"

"It's the name of my tent."

"Are you serious?"

"Yes, on the tent. But no I don't want to spend time wrestling with the tent and have an invisible rock poke me in the back all night. I'll make reservations and we'll spend the night and Sunday in Las Vegas."

"Will you win me a stuffed animal at Circus Circus?"

"It would be cheaper to buy you one."

"But not as much fun," Laura said.

TMI   Grindstaff & Plummer

The waitress arrived with their hamburgers, a dinner platter stacked high with onion rings and a bottle of fry sauce. As they ate talk became general.

"I almost forgot," Laura said as they were leaving. "I got the business plan typed and dropped it off at the bank. They said I'd have an answer within two weeks."

"Have you found a location you like?"

"Two actually, but they both need work. I'd like your opinion before I decide."

"When you have time, we can look them over," Chuck said.

"What are you going to do the rest of this evening?"

"I'm going to take a shower, head to bed and read until I fall asleep."

"Are you sure you don't want company?"

"It's tempting but along with one of your massages I'm going to need a rain check on the morning run."

"Call me after your boss leaves. If it isn't too late we'll go out to dinner or you can come over and I'll give you a backrub."

"That's a date." She wrapped her arms around his waist and leaned in for a kiss.

"Night," she said as he watched her drive away.

Chuck was ready to call it a night when the scanner beeped. A familiar muffled male voice that held an edge of defiance filled the living room.

"This is it. Tonight. Eleven, sharp. Are you one hundred percent on this?"

"I'm in," The second man responded.

"Don't be late."

The scanner beeped and static filled the room.

Chuck glanced at his watch and punched a number into the phone. A generic message told him to leave a message and number.

He tossed the portable phone onto the couch and grabbed the car keys off the kitchen table.

The truck took the turn into the apartment complex on two wheels.

He was out of the cab before the pickup came to a full stop.

Long seconds later he was back in the truck, and the pistol the bank robber had dropped was loaded and tucked under the truck seat.

Two blocks from the apartments a pedestrian entered a crosswalk. Chuck honked the horn. The man made a mad dash and Chuck swerved.

He ran the next intersection on a yellow light.

A mile later he took his foot off the accelerator, looked both directions and ran a red light. He was halfway through the intersection when a black Corvette came out of nowhere. The driver slammed on his horn and Chuck heard brakes squeal but he didn't slow down.

A patrol car, with lights flashing, headed towards him. Chuck pulled over and swore. He didn't have time to waste talking and didn't know if the cop would believe the truth. The cruiser sped past, hit his siren at the intersection behind Chuck and kept going.

An eternity later, he slowed and turned into a subdivision that snaked around a golf course. The two story pastel colored houses sat in formation on small perfectly manicured lots.

In front of a tan house with a lush landscaped yard he pulled to a stop, unlatched the seatbelt and reached for the pistol.

Headlights shot through the interior of the truck and rolled past. A dark colored car parked at the curb at the next house.

A man, dressed in black, like the villain in an old silent movie strolled up the driveway.

Chuck checked the safety on the pistol, and watched the man disappear between the two houses.

He opened the truck's door and swore when the interior light, that hadn't worked in months, blinked on. A barking dog covered the sound of the truck's door closing.

At a half crouch he ran up the driveway. Hearing a noise he dove behind an evergreen and landed on a rose bush.

"Damn," he muttered.

He sucked blood off his thumb and watched the man dragged two trashcans down the driveway and set them behind his car.

Chucks knees ached and blood from a thorn sticking his thigh stained his jeans, but if he moved the man would see him.

At the side door the man fumbled in his pants for keys, unlocked the door, flipped a light on and entered a mustard yellow mudroom.

Chuck pressed the button on his watch to illuminate the face. It was eleven-ten.

"Shit. Shit. Shit."

The door beside him opened. Angela stood in a pool of golden light.

"Chuck, I saw you park and creep towards the house like a burglar. Why are you trampling my roses?"

Chuck flipped the safety and tucked the pistol in the waistband at the small of his back. "Where's George?"

"He stormed out around eight."

"He drove?"

"No, he doesn't have car keys. After he left he would have called my brother-in-law or my brother to pick him up. If he's not at the country club, then he's at Gracie's Tavern shooting pool. Why?"

"What does your neighbor do for a living?"

"He's the speech and theater teacher at the high school. His wife's a lawyer. Why are you here?"

Chuck swallowed a laugh. "I'm drunk on stupidity. I'll talk to you tomorrow."

In the car he turned off the scanner and tossed it behind the seat.

Chapter 21

Detective Jim Padilla pulled the unmarked police issued Ford to the curb and shut off the engine. He stepped out of the car and with his arms resting on the door frame he scanned the scene.

It was a nice older middle class neighborhood. Lawns were mowed and curtains drawn. A few cars sat in driveways but most were tucked into garages for the night.

Six police vehicles lined the street. Their red and blue light bars flooded the area with an eerie glow that could put the fear of God into the most honest citizen.

The heat of the day had cooled but the night was warm, the air still as death.

A half-moon within a yellow halo hung to the left of the big dipper, the only constellation Padilla recognized by sight.

He counted a dozen people huddled in a cluster behind a patrol car. A female officer was writing down names and phones numbers.

As he walked the street he saw nothing out of the ordinary and the sense that someone was hiding in the shadows never set off his, watch your back, antenna.

A uniformed officer stood guard at the front door to the crime scene.

Padilla nodded hello and signed in on the clipboard he was handed.

"Mary Beth said you had lunch at the diner. Not going to lose those five pounds you've been whining about if you keep eating hamburgers and fries." Andy Carrillo said after he put his initials next to Padilla's illegible signature.

"Rumor mill must have missed the post-it note. I lost ten and passed the physical. Now I get to eat what I want for another year. How's your mother?" Before a two pack a day habit turned his lungs into a feeding ground for cancer, Andy's father had been a close friend and partner.

"She's in Nebraska visiting her sister. If it weren't for the snow I think she'd move there."

"I see CSUs already here."

"Inside."

"Who called this in?" Jim pointed his finger towards the door.

"Mrs. Walter's, lives in the brown-on-brown across the street. She's on her way downtown with Detective Hodge."

"Is there any signs of forced entry?"

"No."

"What about witnesses?" Padilla asked.

"Neighbor to the north, a Mrs. Perez says she saw a truck pull out of the driveway."

"Got a description or time?"

"Just getting dark, no exact time but sunset's around

eight. Mrs. Perez claims cars and trucks no longer have any class. All copycats with no personality. But she did volunteer that it was a normal size truck, no monster wheels, no fancy chrome hubcaps and no sound system that vibrated her windows. The lady is eight-four years old. She's had cataract surgery so her eye sight is damn near perfect. She's deaf as a stone but she's good at reading lips."

"Caught you muttering something you shouldn't?" Andy grinned.

"Along with her teeth she's lost her sense of humor. Another neighbor," he glanced at his notes. "A Mrs. Ward volunteered that the victim used to have a gentleman caller who drove a dark colored pickup. She said he hasn't been around for several weeks."

"A gentleman caller? How old is Mrs. Ward?"

"Older than God. One of those granny albums stuffed with pictures of her twenty grandkids, ten great grandkids and three great-great grandkids is surgically attached to her hand. Before she'd answer questions I had to smile my way through the stack."

"Great," Padilla wrote the name on his notepad and wrote, send Dick, next to the name.

"After I escaped Mrs. Ward's clutches I went back to Mrs. Perez's house and asked if the truck could have been the boyfriends. She said it was possible but not being nosy she didn't stand at her window and take notes," Andy said.

"Terrific, we've got two old ladies who know more than the CIA and they're going to make us stroke their egos to get answers. When did Mrs. Walter's call this in?"

Andy glanced at his notes. "According to the digital readout on her security system she arrived home at eight-eleven. When she pulled into the driveway she noticed that the front door was open. An hour later she looked out her kitchen window and saw all the lights on and the front door still open."

"Did she come over and knock before calling 911?"

"She called it in with an apologetic, maybe this is nothing but, opening."

Padilla looked at the empty driveway.

"Did the victim have a car?"

"There's an unattached garage in the back. The car's parked inside."

Jim dug latex gloves out of his back pocket, stretched the thin white rubber down his fingers and tugged them over his wrists. Two steps inside the front door he stopped to look at the alarm system.

The green light on the alarm pad blinked at him. Whoever the killer was, they knew the code or knew the victim and had been invited inside. If the alarm was set at all, he thought, and made a mental note to check with the alarm company.

He turned his back to the wall, closed his eyes and took a deep breath. The fresh scent of mint tickled his senses.

He opened his eyes. A six foot long, chest high piece of furniture separated the living room from the small entry. A row of five fat spring green candles lined the foot deep top. He placed a gloved finger next to the wick of each candle. Only the candle closest to the door was soft. When he sniffed the soft wax clinging to the glove it smelled like spearmint gum.

He closed his eyes and took a second deep breath. Under the mint he smelled…what …disinfectant, toilet bowl cleaner, furniture polish? The aroma was familiar but he couldn't put a name to it—yet.

He looked over the divider and scanned the upper portion of the living room. The house, built in the nineteen twenties had high coved ceiling and arched doorways.

He stepped into the square living room and glanced to his right, the divider was a bookcase with four glass paned doors. The shelves were lined with paperback books with creased spines and what might be a full collection of Nancy Drew novels.

The room was neat and clean.

Too neat, too clean, he thought. The victim could have been a perfectionist but the cleaner masked by the mint candle gave credibility to a different story.

Hung over a long narrow table was a large framed and matted black and white print. The picture was a beach scene, sand dunes, surf, the corner of a weathered porch in the right corner. He wasn't an expert but he didn't think the picture was a professional print. More like a blowup of a place that had meaning to the victim.

Two old square oak tables, possibly family hand-me-downs, bookended a cream colored couch covered in an array of square and oblong pastel pillows. An old wood rocking chair with a cane seat and an overstuffed chair covered in dusty rose velvet finished the décor.

No fussy knickknacks cluttered the table tops, or collections, like the elephants his wife collected, said this interests me.

He wondered through the wide arched doorway into

a small square dining room. The wood on the square oak table and four matching chairs shone from years of being rubbed with furniture polish laced with wax.

He stepped into the kitchen. Small, was the first thought, tidy was the second.

Three bananas draped over a mound of red apples filled a large white bowl. A twelve cup coffee machine sat next to a small white microwave. A black metal wine rack held five bottles of wine. A brown teddy bear cookie jar was tucked into a corner. Until the forensics team checked for fingerprints he resisted the urge to lift the lid and look inside.

The sink and a teakwood dish drain were empty and dry.

There was no dishwasher.

With the tip of a pen he opened the cupboards. The service for four, white bone china dishes weren't fancy, but like the furniture good quality. Crystal glassware for water, wine and beer were hung upside down by their green stems. The sets were for four each, but one wine glass was missing.

Dish towels, silverware, and pans, were where you'd expect to find them.

The freezer held a selection of pint tubs of Ben and Jerry ice cream and a blue plastic tray of ice cubes. The refrigerator was stocked with the usual condiments, a carton of eggs, a quart of vanilla flavored Greek yogurt, a half used stalk of celery, an open bag of carrots and enough ingredients to make a decent salad.

He walked back to the living room.

A burglary was usually messy, a fast in and out with the valuables.

Domestics could also be messy if the killer thought he had a solid alibi.

This felt different and he'd learned not to like different.

The hallway was short. Two doors opened to the right, one left.

It was easier to retrace steps and protect evidence by sticking to a straight line just off center of a room, so being careful not to brush the wall with his shoulder he hugged the right wall.

He stopped at the first door to his right. White lace curtains covered a small window that faced the backyard. Under the window was a six foot sturdy table, like the ones he'd expect to see in a public library. A chair, that matched the ones in the dining room, was pushed flush against the table.

A dark green plastic trashcan sat in the corner. He edged around the side of the room until he could lean over the trashcan. Like the tabletop it was empty.

Three framed black and white pictures hung on one wall. One was of a Victorian style two story house. One was of a young girl sitting on a woman's lap. Mother and daughter, he thought. The third was of a silver haired man and the woman holding the child. The photographer had captured the adults at a moment when their feelings for each other where tangible, as if the love that bound them electrified the aura surrounding them.

He ignored the voices coming from the door on the left to look in the second door on the right. The row of lights above the mirror shot light off the bathroom's white tiles. The glare was almost blinding. No shower curtain closed off the tub. Pale pink and green towels were neatly folded and hung on two towel racks. A silk bouquet of flowers and a white china dish with balls of green soap were on the counter. A white lace curtain covered a small window.

With the tip of the pen he opened two drawers and the cupboard under the sink. All were empty and immaculately clean.

Padilla walked to the second bedroom and stood at the threshold.

"Bill, what do you have?"

Bill Nelson was pushing fifty. A buzz cut kept you from noticing that only a fringe of brown hair circled a bald dome. He was a good cop, with good instincts. Right now his golden brown eyes were flat and his voice was void of emotions.

"White female, driver's license says she's thirty-eight, but she looks younger. She's on the bathroom floor, strangled by a towel when she got out of the shower."

"How do you know she wasn't getting into the shower?"

"Her hair's still damp."

"How do you know she was strangled with a towel?"

"The towel's still around her neck."

"Could have been placed there after death?"

Bill tilted his head and narrowed his brown eyes. "I'm not the prosecuting attorney or a reporter so cut the politically correct crap. She was in the shower or getting out when it happened."

"Any signs of rape?"

"Nothing obvious," Bill answered.

Padilla nodded and surveyed the bedroom. Like the

living room the space was spotless and clutter free.

The décor was feminine. Not fussy with lace and ruffles like his daughter's bedroom. It was what his wife would call sensual. Silk and velvet in deep rose and soft greens blended with cream colored walls, dark stained furniture and off white carpet.

A short white cotton night shirt was draped across the foot of the bed.

He stepped to a hamper and lifted the lid. Black panties, a white lace bra, cream colored blouse, running shorts and pale blue T-shirt filled the bottom.

The closet door stood open. Dresses and blouses hung from padded hangers. Slacks were draped over pant hangers. Again money had been spent on quality not quantity.

The air conditioner kicked on and sent a soft rumble and a rush of cold air through the room.

The snap, zip and whirl of the department's new digital camera echoed from the bathroom. Padilla knew that meant the technician had already taken a full set of Polaroid pictures and tucked them into a zip-lock bag for backup in case the digital camera failed.

He walked to the bathroom and stood in the doorway.

Sid Purser, the crime scene technician, was young but competent. Padilla watched him place a paper bag over the victim's left hand.

At the top left of the body was an evidence marker, the only one in the room. Not good, since a homicide scene is usually littered with markers.

Too clean, too neat. What was the killer trying to hide?

"Find anything?" Jim asked as Sid pulled out a tape measure, placed it next to the body and picked the camera up.

"Nothing yet, but I haven't been here long," Sid answered.

Jim turned and faced the bedroom.

On the dresser a large green metallic purse was tipped on its side. He glanced back at the open closet and saw three purses hung from pegs.

Out of place, out of character, he thought.

With hands in his pockets he stood by the dresser and studied the purse. Draped over the teeth of the zipper mouth were several bills. Under the coiled shoulder strap he saw a tip of white that looked like the corner of an envelope.

"Bill did you open the purse to retrieve the driver's license?"

"No need, one of those clear plastic cases that hold credit cards was on top of the purse. The case held the driver's license, a health insurance card, and a Visa credit card. It's already been photographed and bagged."

Padilla used a pen to reach in and separate the bills. "Eighty bucks," he whispered. "Whoever did this didn't need the money."

He paused and looked at the way the contents slid out of the purse. Or they decided to make it look like the kill wasn't about money, he thought.

He lifted the corner of the purse with a gloved finger, pressed his pen into the corner of the paper and pulled an envelope out from under the purse. The long sleeve style envelope was marked with advertisements from hotels, car rentals, and off airport parking lots.

Using the pen, he pushed the envelope flap open. The top half of a one-way ticket to Richmond, Virginia, with a departure date in early September, was tucked inside.

"What was waiting for you in Virginia, Laura Cannon?" He asked as if she'd answer.

Padilla walked back to the bathroom door.

Like the bedroom the color scheme was shades of rose and green. A plush green terry bath towel hung from the rack next to the tub. The towel rack above the toilet held a set of matching hand towels.

The terry towel around the vic's neck was sky blue. Not a match, not part of the coordinated décor. Maybe they'd get lucky and maybe not, but it was a mistake, and it only took one to bring a killer down.

Padilla leaned over the white porcelain john and sniffed the towels on the rack.

"You ready to remove the towel from around her neck?" He asked.

"Yeah, I've got all the pictures I need," Sid answered.

"Mind if I do it?"

Sid handed Padilla a stainless steel clamp that was identical to the salad tongs his wife used.

"It doesn't look like the towel is under her head but go slow. I need to take pictures of the neck once the towel is removed."

Padilla lifted the towel; it wasn't wound around the neck or head.

He sniffed the towel, then stood and sniffed the towels over the toilet.

"What's wrong?" Sid asked.

"The towels smell different."

"The towels on the rack don't look like they're used. They could have hung there for weeks or months. The towel around her neck probably came from a linen closet or a drawer filled with potpourri," Sid offered.

"You fill your drawers with potpourri?" Padilla asked.

Sid ducked his head. "My grandmother makes these things that look like bean bags with a loop on one end. They're filled with herbs and dried flowers. My mother and wife stick them in every drawer in the house and hang them in the closets."

"Guess that could be one answer," Padilla said.

"What's the other answer?"

"Different fabric softeners or detergent," Padilla said.

He studied the body then stepped towards Bill who stood at the door.

"You were wrong," he said.

"About what?" Bill asked.

"Cause of death wasn't strangulation."

Padilla headed down the hall and made his way to the kitchen.

He opened doors to a coat closet and a small pantry before he found the laundry room. He sniffed the liquid fabric softener and a box of dryer sheets and walked back to the bathroom.

"Sid, before you leave go into the laundry room and bag the dryer sheets and liquid softener."

"Yes, sir.

Chapter 22

Chuck entered the office and inhaled the tempting scents of sugar, yeast, chocolate and fresh coffee that saturated the air conditioned room.

Runner, with his tail beating the air with enthusiasm, accepted his share of donut chunks as if they were his due and finally settled on his bed with his yellow duck and a chew bone.

"What's the occasion?"

"At four we're leaving to watch Roberto strike out at the softball tournament. We'll work through the lunch hour to make up the time. The sugar high should sustain us until we stuff our faces with hotdogs," Frank said.

"Gotcha." Chuck filled his mug, grabbed a glazed donut and settled into his office chair.

Roberto stuffed half a donut into his mouth and talked around the gooey glob. "I got a call last night from the alarm company."

"Why didn't they call me?"

"Jessie said your code was used to deactivate the alarm. Because it was past ten she called you. You didn't answer so she called me." Roberto finished, bounced on the toes of his tennis shoes and stuffed the last of the donut in his mouth.

Chuck thought back to the frenzied panic that had gripped him during the ride to Angela's. It didn't surprise him that he'd forgotten to reset the alarm but it was a stupid mistake.

"Did you drive over and set the alarm?" Chuck asked.

"Yeah," he answered as he snatched a cinnamon twist donut from the pastry box.

"Thanks. I owe you one," Chuck said.

"What brought you back to the office?" Hector asked in a tone that to Chuck sounded off but he couldn't say why.

"Nothing important. Has anyone seen George?"

"I'm here." George answered as he opened the office door.

Angela entered behind her husband, took a chair by the door and crossed her legs. Every male took a second to appreciate her white shorts and a pink and white striped tank top that showed a lot of creamy skin.

"Was the nothing important connected to what you've heard on the scanner?" Roberto asked.

"Sometimes it's best to mind your own business."

"I told ya' that last week, Boss." Hector hissed under a rumble of crude remarks about minding one's own business.

Chuck delegated a list of jobs and waited for the room to clear.

Angela sat studying the red nail polish on her toes.

He poured two cups of coffee, added two packets of Sweet and Low to one cup and handed her the sweetened coffee.

Settled in his chair Chuck took a sip and looked at her over the rim of his mug. Dark smudges under her eyes had been expertly masked with makeup, but under the harsh florescent lights they were noticeable.

"Did you tell George about my visit last night?"

"There was no reason. What were you doing last night?" She sipped the coffee and looked at him with big brown eyes filled with unease.

"I'd heard some conversations on the scanner. From a phrase repeated several times I thought one of the men was George and jumped to a wrong conclusion. No harm done, forget it happened."

"You thought George was going to hurt me?"

"It was a possibility I couldn't ignore."

"Why didn't you call the police?"

"And tell them what?"

She blinked and took another sip of coffee. A second sip bought her more time to decided how much or how little to say. Chuck wondered what she thought needed to be hidden but knew if asked she deny the accusation.

"George crawled up the stairs after the bar closed. This morning there was blood on his shoes. He claimed it was tomato juice from a Bloody Mary. I don't believe him."

"What do you think happened?"

She shrugged.

"Could be he got into a fight and didn't want to talk about it."

"Not talking is his way to deal with everything."

She finished the coffee and threw the paper cup in the wastepaper basket.

At the door she paused.

"Thanks for trying to be my hero."

Her voice held the same seductive purr but instead of the sexual tug she liked to add with a flick of her eyes or a toss of her hair, he watched her shutdown and draw away.

Chuck heard the door open and thought Angela had forgotten something, but when he entered the office from the storage area, a cute blonde stood by the door.

"Hi, may I help you?"

"Are you Chuck Taylor?"

"I am."

He stepped behind his desk and waited for the woman to sit before he took his seat.

"I'm Jenna Jean Jones. My friends call me JJ."

I bet they do, Chuck thought. Plastic surgery had been kind and shaved a good ten to fifteen years off her age, but the wisdom held in her eyes said she been around the block several times. The soft southern drawl would turn a guy's heads. Blonde hair, blue eyes, and an hour glass figure set on a petite frame would hold the guys interest. And the name, it rolled off the tip of her tongue like the sexy enticement it was meant to be.

"What can I do for you Jenna?"

"Oh please do call me JJ. A girl can never have too many friends."

She sat, crossed her legs, and smiled when she caught him enjoying the show.

"Do you remember Mitzi Garrison?"

He dusted off the mental file and read the notes; bottle blonde, legs to her shoulders, store bought chest and, sea blue eyes, and a weight lifter boyfriend who looked like he ate alligators for breakfast.

"I remember."

"Mitzi and I were neighbors in Houston. When I told her I was moving to El Paso she told me to stop here first. She said if I asked nicely you'd show me around town."

Chuck smiled.

"What made you decide to move here?"

"Hmm," she hummed as she filled her lungs and expanded the impressive cleavage. "I'm in the entertainment business. It was time for a change of scenery."

"Where did you work?" Chuck was toying with her but it was a slow morning and he was curious.

"I'm a singer," JJ said and didn't elaborate.

"How long you expect to be in town?"

"That depends on who I meet and getting a job."

"I'm sure you'll have no trouble finding work or meeting people." Chuck said and meant it.

"Maybe," she said and shrugged a shoulder as if it didn't matter.

"I know I'm being pushy but would you give me a tour of town today. I've booked a room at the Ramada for two weeks, but time flies and I'd like your opinion of where to live."

"You want a house or an apartment?"

"Not a dingy little apartment. Something upscale, like the townhouses you rent."

Now we're getting down to business Chuck thought.

"I have a unit that will be vacant in a week and ready to move into the following week."

"How lovely," JJ purred. "May I see the inside?"

"Not with the tenants still in residence."

"Couldn't you give me just a tiny peek? I won't tell anyone if you won't."

Chuck stood, looked out the window behind his desk, and smiled.

Walking to the door he opened it before turning to face Jenna and her charms.

"Follow me, I have an idea."

"Where are we going," Jenna asked as she tried to keep up with his long stride.

"Not far," Chuck said.

He tapped on a black door and tried to smother the smile that tugged at his humor.

When the door open the women looked at each other, blinked, and looked at Chuck.

"Jenna Jean Jones, meet Kelly Lutz. Kelly, Jenna says her friends call her JJ. She's interested in renting a townhouse and has some questions."

"You brought her here, why?"

"She's new in town and needs a friend to show her around. She reminds me of you. Now please excuse me ladies I have work to do."

Jenna placed her hand on Chuck's arm. "But I thought you were going to show me one of the townhouses."

"I never said that. Nice meeting you Jenna. Besides Mitzi Garrison, I'm sure the two of you will find you have a lot in common."

Chuck glanced at his watch. If Laura didn't call within the hour he'd order a pizza that could be baked after he gave her the promised backrub.

He grabbed a bag of chips, a jar of spicy hot salsa and a beer.

At the kitchen table he read the comics, then the sports section, and tossed the entertainment section aside.

Thirty minutes later he glanced at his watch and frowned.

He threw the chip bag away, put the salsa jar in the refrigerator, grabbed a second beer and let Runner out the French doors to run off energy chasing grasshoppers.

At the table he flipped the front section of the newspaper over.

The headlines jumped off the page, grabbed him by the gut and stopped his heart cold.

He forced himself to breathe. One breath, a second breath and a third.

His heart rate kicked down a notch and then skipped several beats.

He swallowed the sour bile at the back of his throat that threatened to drown him.

This couldn't be happening. Not now, not again.

But the silence of his phone said differently.

His eyes drifted back to the headlines.

He should have gone to her place, spent the night, given her that backrub.

He should have…known.

What seemed like an eternity later, he stood at the window in a room filled with scarred metal desks. The pale blue walls were stained with cigarette smoke and God knew what else.

The clash of aftershave, perfume, sweat and fear that

saturated the stale air brought back memories he'd fought hard to beat into a box and nail shut.

He stood at a window, but a part of him stood outside himself watching and comparing the past with the present.

From the windows ghostly reflection Chuck watched a detective hunt and peck, his way over a keyboard. Next to him sat a plump woman dressed in frayed jeans, a dingy white tank-top and yellow flip-flops. She looked pissed and nervous as she picked at the nail polish on her thumb and popped gum.

He turned when the reflection of Detective Padilla stepping into the room floated across the glass.

Padilla looked crumpled and tired, Chuck thought, beaten down from too little sleep and too many cups of bad coffee.

"Can we talk in private?" Chuck asked.

"Follow me." Padilla nodded at the woman in the chair as he passed and used a thumb to signal to the man at the desk where he was headed.

They entered a small office with walls the color of desert sand and a small window that was placed too high to make an easy exit for a desperate criminal, or offer a view of anything but the sky when one was seated. The pine desk was ancient. The straight back chairs, that weren't made for comfort, creaked when they sat.

"What can I do for you Mr. Taylor?"

"Call me Chuck. A few minutes ago I read about Laura Cannon's death."

Padilla's gut had told him there was a connection to be found, but God forbid he hadn't expected the connection to be Chuck Taylor.

"Do you have information to help us out?"

"I don't know."

"Then why are you here?"

"Laura and I have been seeing each other," Chuck said.

"How long have you known her?"

"Two months ago Laura was stranded on highway 54. The battery in her car was dead. I stopped to help."

"Casual or serious?" Padilla asked.

"Somewhere in between. We were taking it slow and easy." *A lie*, Chuck thought. *He'd fallen; he just hadn't realized the truth.*

"When was the last time you saw her?"

"Last night. We went to dinner at The Kitchen."

"What time was that?"

"We got there around six and left around seven fifteen."

"You follow her home?"

"No. We'd both had rotten days. We made plans to meet this evening."

"Her place or yours?"

"Mine."

"Why?"

"Why what?"

"Why your place instead of hers?" Padilla clarified.

"You've met Runner. For a pup he's well behaved, but he's a pup and not fully house broken. Also, he needs space to run. Laura's backyard wasn't fenced."

"Why didn't you extend dinner to a sleepover?"

"She'd had two stress filled days that were similar to mine with maintenance and tenant problems. Her boss was in town. She needed to be at work early. It was easier for her to go home then to make extra stops in the morning."

"When was the last time you talked to her?"

"Laura called when she arrived home."

"What time was that?"

Chuck sighed and closed his eyes. "I was just pulling into the parking lot at the grocery store. Best guess would be half past seven."

That, Padilla thought, fit the timetable in his head.

"Why did she call you when she got home?"

"Just to say goodnight and say she'd be happy when today was over."

"Why?"

"The owner of the apartments she manages was in town. The accountant was installing new computer software today and doing an audit."

"Was she worried about the audit?" Padilla asked.

"I don't believe so. She'd told me the manager before her skimmed rent money. So the owner erred on the cautious side by doing an audit every six months. She also emailed the accountant a daily expense and payment ledger."

"Did she say anything else?"

"Over dinner or on the phone?" Chuck asked.

"On the phone?"

"Nothing really. She said she was undressing as we spoke and wanted to know if she should pack a fancy dress for Saturday night. I heard the shower turn on. She was going to read until she fell asleep."

Padilla pictured the mystery novel on the nightstand, it fit. "What was the plan for Saturday night?"

"We were going to fly to Vegas and relax. I made

the reservations this morning."

"How far do you live from Laura's house?"

"About two miles, 5432 Willow Springs."

"Did she have any enemies?" Padilla asked.

"I don't know that enemy would be the right word but she'd had words with her former boyfriend."

"She told you she was fighting with her ex-husband?"

"Ex-boyfriend, Laura was never married."

"What is the guy's name?"

"I didn't ask and she never said."

"You didn't think to ask?"

"Did you ask your wife for the names of her former boyfriends?"

One corner of Padilla's firm mouth lifted.

"Good point." He pulled a pad and pen out of a drawer and pushed them across the desk.

"If you would, please write down what you just told me. Include your address, phone number, and where you work for the record. Also, hand me your identification."

"Why do you need identification?"

"I need to make a copy for the file."

When Padilla returned he sat on the edge of the desk.

"Chuck, how much time did you spend at Laura's house?"

"None. When I picked her up for a date I never went past the foyer."

Padilla cocked his head. His expression didn't change but Chuck felt his interest shift.

"Then explain how a set of fingerprints found in the victims living room match yours?"

Chuck mumbled, "Shit," and rubbed the back of his

neck. "I purchased a television from her and…"

"Were you in the house or not?"

"In. The television was on a sofa table."

"Where was the table located?"

"It was set along the wall that ran down the hallway."

"Did you go anyplace else in the house?"

"I needed a screwdriver and wrench to disconnect wires. When I started to head to the truck to get my tools Laura told me to get the tool kit in the spare bedroom."

Chuck saw the spark of interest that Padilla couldn't quite hide.

"What was in the room?"

"A table and chair. Three, no four baskets lined with a checked pink and white material were on the table. Three pictures were on the wall but I only half glanced at them."

"Where was the tool box?"

"It wasn't a box. It was a clear plastic bag with a zipper. It held a hammer, a couple of screwdrivers that had different size tips at each end and pliers. The set is marketed for women. These had green handles covered in white daisies. The bag was inside one of the baskets."

"What was inside the other baskets?"

"The baskets graduated in size. The smallest held pens and pencils and other odds and ends." He rubbed the back of his neck and for a second closed his eyes.

"There was one of those clear plastic balls that hold paperclips and I think I remember seeing a roll of stamps. The next basket held the tool kit and a bottle of white glue. The third held envelopes and the largest basket held pink file folders."

"Did you look at the files?"

"No, but the first envelope in the other basket had the power company's logo on the front."

"Why would you remember that?"

"Because I'd just received the electric bill for the apartments and jokingly offered to trade bills."

"Besides the tool kit did you touch anything in the room?"

"The bottle of glue tipped over when I picked up the kit. I set it back up. That's it."

"What about her bedroom?"

"I never saw Laura's bedroom. I doubt I spent an hour total in the place."

"Are you telling me you never spent time in bed with her?"

"No, I'm saying we never spent time in her bed. One night after a dinner date we spent time against the front door."

"Shit, you nailed the gal against the front door and forgot?"

"I…crap it didn't get that out of hand…in the scheme of things they were two short stops that didn't amount to anything. Do I need a lawyer?"

"Are you going to say something that will land you in jail?"

"I hadn't planned on doing that."

"What scheme are you talking about?"

"I didn't mean scheme, I meant in perspective. We spent time together but we didn't crowd each other."

"Look, this might or might not have anything to do with Laura but it needs to be said. I've recorded several conversations from a scanner. The two men in the conversations talk about killing the man's wife. I called the station and tried to report what I'd heard but the officer on duty treated the call like a kid's prank."

"Do you have the tape with you?"

"The recorder's at my house."

Padilla stood.

"I'll get back to you when I get a chance. If you think of anything, anything at all, call me."

Chuck stood and started towards the door.

"Chuck, you didn't ask how Laura was murdered, why?"

"Not tonight, Padilla. Not tonight."

Chapter 23

"You look like hell," Angela said.

The drumsticks beating against Chuck's temples matched the slap of sandals against the floor.

"Ask me if I care." Chuck leaned his head against the back of the office chair and closed his eyes.

"You have a hangover?"

Chuck opened his eyes to slits.

"There's a good possibility that there are enough fumes in me to fail a breathalyzer test."

"You're drunk? I've never seen you this way. Is your daughter okay?"

"She is. Whisper, please. I can't handle yelling."

"I'm not yelling."

Each word rose in volume and drove a laser beam of pain through his skull. He winced and closed his bloodshot eyes.

He heard water running.

A cold wet towel was laid on his forehead.

Angela used a paper towel to dab at a piece of blood crusted tissue on his chin.

"You're lucky you didn't slit your throat when you shaved."

"Can't slit your throat with a safety razor," Chuck mumbled.

Angela shifted and pressed the wet paper towel on a spot just below his ear lobe.

"What happened to make you try to drown your thoughts in liquor?"

"I don't want to talk. When you leave please don't slam the door."

He opened one eye and watched her toss the paper towel in the trash. She knelt beside his chair and placed a hand over his.

"I'm selfish, and spoiled, and I've done a lot of foolish things, but I don't walk away when a friend needs help."

Her voice softened.

"Beth has been gone a long time. This isn't about her and you say it's not Carrie. Tell me what happened to put the pain and sadness in your eyes."

He sucked in a breath and let the words tumble out in a rush as if saying the words quickly would lessen the pain. "I knew the woman found murdered."

"Laura, she was the woman you've been seeing?"

Chuck nodded.

"I'm sorry, so sorry. You're a good man, you don't deserve this pain."

Chuck's jaw clinched. The sharp bite and suspicions in Padilla's voice he could handle. But the kindness and distress in Angela's voice shredded the paper thin emotional block the alcohol had built.

"Have you talked to the police?"

"Last night."

"Do you know what happened?"

"Does it matter? She's dead, knowing how won't change that."

"Are you a suspect?"

Was he? Hell, anyone who knew her would be checked out. Having a relationship would label him with probable cause or was it person of interest?

"They'll question everyone that knew Laura. Her former boyfriend was giving her problems. Chances are that's where they'll find their murderer."

"For your sake I hope it's that easy."

"There's nothing easy about murder."

"Do you know the man?"

"No."

"Good that means you won't be fool enough to hunt him down."

"Humph."

"What time was she murdered?"

Padilla had asked him when he'd last talked to Laura but he hadn't volunteered a time of death.

"I don't know. Why?"

"What if she was murdered at the same time you were trying to protect me?"

Shit. He hadn't thought about that.

"You shouldn't be here," Angela said. "Take the day off. Let me give you some TLC."

"No thanks," he said with more of a snap than Angela deserved.

"I'm not making a pass." She offered a wan smile. "Well maybe a little, it is my nature. But I promise to behave if you come home with me and sleep this off."

Chuck couldn't muster a smile.

He wanted to sleep, but when he closed his eyes he

saw Laura standing in his kitchen, wrapped in his daughter's bathrobe, scrambling eggs and laughing at his comical attempts to get her back into his bed.

But there was more behind the refusal to accept her offer. It was open knowledge that he and Angela had a flirtatious relationship. When the cops dug into his whereabouts he didn't want to be on the defensive about their friendship. Nor did he want them jumping to the conclusion that jealousy or a threesome that went sour got Laura killed.

"Thanks for the offer but I need to get some work done."

"You're half drunk, you can't deal with tenants."

"I'm too hung-over to still be drunk."

"That is dumb logic. You really can't talk to people, not the way you look.

Chuck stood and waited until the dizziness settled.

"I don't plan to talk to anyone."

"Then what are you going to do?"

"Knock holes in a wall."

Britney walked into the club house. One wall was striped to studs. The floor and furniture were coated white with sheetrock dust. A lamp lay shattered on the floor.

"You ready to stop punishing yourself?"

"I don't need a lecture or a mother."

"I didn't think you did. When Jack died you held my hand, listened to me ramble and offered your shoulder for my tears. Without your support I'm not sure I would have survived. Let me pay back the favor. I made soup.

You can eat it or feed it to Runner, won't hurt my feelings either way. But you are going to take a couple of aspirin, stretch out on the recliner or my spare bed and try to get some sleep."

"I can't sleep."

"Then we'll talk or watch a movie."

"I'd rather…," he swung the hammer and knocked a metal vase onto the floor.

"Temper tantrums and boiling rages I understand but they don't solve anything. I'm giving you two options. You come home with me or I'm calling your friend Beny and asking him to come babysit you."

Chapter 24

"**D**etective Padilla," the man barked into the phone.

"This is Dave Uribe at central command. I have the information you called about earlier. Two cleaners were used to wash down the walls at Laura Cannon's place. Agent Green is a pine scented extra strength disinfectant. We found particles of a blue sponge, possibly from a floor mop, on the walls. Fresh Breeze is a lemon scented combination stain remover and disinfectant. The fabric softener and detergent found at the house didn't match what was found on the towel around her neck. There was a faint trace of the Fresh breeze disinfectant on the towel around the vic's neck."

"Could the disinfectant have been on the killer's hands and rubbed off onto the towel," Padilla mussed.

"Could have," Dave Uribe said. "A blue thread that didn't match the towel around Laura Cannon's neck was found in the kitchen. It had been saturated with Agent Green."

"Where in the kitchen?" Padilla asked as he wrote in his notebook.

There was a pause. "The evidence bag is marked, second drawer, left front corner, kitchen."

"You're saying a different type of towel was used to do the cleaning?" Padilla asked.

"The blue thread in the kitchen was terry cloth but it's a lower quality of thread. There's a slim chance the thread comes from the same towel manufacture, but my educated guess is that the thread found in the kitchen is from a kitchen towel or a towel of that quality."

"I've never heard of either cleaner," Padilla mused.

"No reason you would, you won't find them at the local grocery store. Both products are industrial cleaners. Two places in town sell the line."

Padilla jotted down the names.

"Before you waste time chasing your tail there are a couple of snags?" Dave said.

"Of course there are. Spit um' out."

"The product can be ordered online. The company should have a data base of sales so that's not necessarily bad. But the company's major buyer is the US government, as in military. I talked to the local sales representative. He said it's trucked by container loads to military installations."

Shit! There were four bases within a fifty mile radius of El Paso.

Padilla wasted two hours driving and talking to the owners of both businesses. Except for contracts that were held with school districts and one hospital, neither business kept records of individual buyers. And neither sold the product on a regular basis to any janitorial service. According to one store manager the product was too pricey to waste on office buildings and small businesses that wanted clean but didn't care about sterile or environmentally friendly.

He pulled to a stop in front of Laura Cannon's house, ducked under the police scene tape, and entered the house.

Bypassing the living room he entered the kitchen. The drawers, held the usual kitchen gadgets, placemats, hot pads and towels. The dishes, in sets of four, and the short supple of serving pieces indicated Laura didn't do a lot of cooking or entertaining.

The teddy bear cookie jar was filled with homemade oatmeal raisin cookies.

The five bottles of red wine were from a winery in Oregon. His wife liked the wine. It was good quality but not over the top expensive.

The can goods stacked in the pantry leaned towards soups and heat and eat staples like chili and canned vegetables. There was a half used box of instant pancake mix, two boxes of brownie mix and an opened jar of peanut butter. He pealed the lid back on canisters and found, flour, granulated sugar and brown sugar. Jars of spices, sugar sprinkles and baking ingredients were stacked in the pantry next to cookie sheets, muffin pans and spring loaded cake pans.

He stood in the middle of the small kitchen and looked around. Like the smoothie maker, juicer and large electric mixer in the pantry the combination coffee and espresso maker was top of the line quality.

He opened the refrigerator. The juicer and smoothie maker explained the celery, carrots, fresh blueberries and yogurt stacked on the shelf. She'd drink the smoothies and gulped down glasses of freshly made carrot juice to justify the handful of cookies she'd eat for lunch or a midnight snack.

Padilla understood the logic, he'd done it himself.

He looked around the dining room and stepped into the living room. Nothing jumped out, nothing said this is off.

The muffled sound of the neighborhood dogs barking penetrated the closed windows.

Padilla walked to the front window and lifted the curtain back. The street and sidewalk were empty.

The sound of the screen door opening bought Padilla's hand to his gun.

He walked around the built-in bookcase, plastered his frame against the wall and waited.

The squeak of the mailbox lid opening eased the grip on Padilla gun, but instead of holstering the 40 cal. he pointed it towards the floor.

With his left hand Padilla opened the door. Three magazines flopped onto the floor.

The mailman looked at him round eyed and startled. His mouth fell open like a wide mouthed bass on a hook.

Padilla locked the safety and slipped the gun into the holster.

"Can you speak to me for a minute?" Padilla asked.

"Don't have time," the mailman stammered.

Padilla flashed his badge. "You can either talk to me here or down at the station."

"Sorry, I didn't know who you were."

"What's your name?" Padilla asked.

"Jack Daniels."

Padilla wrote the name and time in his spiral notepad and resisted the urge to comment on the obvious. "Is this your normal route, Mr. Daniels?"

"Yes sir. Had this route for eight years, before that I

delivered for rural route one."

"What do you know about the woman that lives here?"

"Ms. Cannon?"

Padilla nodded.

"Not much. She paid her bills on time."

"How do you know that?" Padilla asked.

"Businesses aren't discrete when they want money. Envelopes will be stamped with a past due notice or final notice and collection agencies are worse. I never delivered that type of mail to Ms. Cannon."

"How many houses are on your route?" Padilla asked.

"There are two hundred and fifty three houses and the apartments on Elm."

"Can you remember what type of mail you deliver to every house?"

"At six every morning I help sort the mail. Then I take the mail for my route, and do a second check as I pack my mail cart for delivery. When I put the mail in the boxes I do a third check. It doesn't take long to get to know a person and their habits."

Padilla nodded. "What else do you know about Laura Cannon?"

"She has five magazines delivered every month. Two are photography magazines." Pointing at Padilla's feet he said, "And you have those three, travel, yoga and girly stuff."

"Anything else you can think off?"

"She didn't have many friends or relatives."

"How do you know that?"

"Very few cards and letters," Daniels said with a

shrug.

"Did you every deliver mail addressed to anyone besides Laura Cannon?"

"No, sir. I'd have remembered that."

"Why?"

"She was a good looking lady. On weekends, if she was home, she'd open the door to say hi and give me a baggy full of homemade cookies or whatever she'd just baked. Never saw anyone here but her."

"What about a pickup in the driveway?"

Daniels shook his head.

"Anything else you can tell me?"

"Every Tuesday at two, Mr. Evens, on Saxon Street entertains a hooker while his wife plays bridge downtown. Mr. Hoops on DeBeers is selling dope and uses a fake rock in his garden for payment delivery and there's a stash house two blocks over."

"Are you sure about the dope and stash house?"

"As sure as being stuck me with the name, Jack Daniels."

Padilla chuckled. "Fair enough, Mr. Daniels. You have a problem making a statement to the police?"

"My boss has already told me to mind my own business. Have them drop by the house after seven." Reaching into his back pocket, he pulled out a slightly abused card and handed it to Padilla.

"You always have your address written on the back of other people's business cards?"

"Yeah, recycling saves money. I do home repair on the side and you know, if someone needs something, I like to help."

"Did you ever do work here?"

"No sir, never did."

Padilla slipped his notepad back in his breast pocket and headed down the hallway.

He stood in the doorway of the room used as an office. The report on his desk stated that the table had been wiped clean. No fingerprints and no trace of dust or a ring where four baskets had sat.

He walked to the closet and opened the door. The closet was maybe four feet deep and empty. In the back corner there were scratch marks on the wood floor that Padilla would bet matched the footprint of a file cabinet. Would it have held information on the business Laura planned to open or personal items like snapshots of an ex-boyfriend?"

In the master bedroom he opened the nightstand drawer and stared at an unopened box of tissue. No sex toys, no condoms, no lubricants, scented candles or lotions. No indication that a man had or would be invited to spend the night. But if Taylor was telling the truth, Laura Cannon wasn't averse to spending the night with a man.

The bathroom was stripped down to girly perfumes, lotions, cosmetics and all the stuff females thought were essential.

Had the killer purged the nightstand drawer and the bathroom drawers of anything that might hold his DNA? His gut answer was yes, the bastard had done exactly that.

He retraced his steps to the living room. The house was approximately twelve hundred square feet. If you eliminated the obvious places a person wouldn't touch how long would it take a person to sterilize the place?

Two types of cleaners could mean two people did the work and cut the time in half. Half a day, maybe a little longer? He'd ask his wife, she'd have a better understanding of the time.

If the killer knew Laura's schedule he wouldn't have worried about being caught. They could take their time. If done in the morning and with a couple of back windows left open the cleaners aroma would have faded significantly by the time she arrived home after work. Tired and distracted Laura could have missed the faint scent of cleaners masked by the mint perfumed candle.

He walked to the back door and stepped onto a small cement porch. The sides of the property were lined by six foot high wood fences. The single car garage took up almost half of the backyard. At the back of the L shaped plot of grass was a row of thick lilac bushes and beyond that was an alley.

Towards the northeast corner he found what he was looking for.

He punched a number and waited.

"Detective Padilla here, can you send CSU back to my location."

Blessed silence greeted Padilla when he stepped into the morgue.

Lang Yin sat in front of a microscope. Her pink smock was starched and clean. No rubber gloves covered in blood adorned her hands. Instead of being tucked inside a pink surgical cap her black hair, peppered with streaks of silver, framed her face in a shoulder length bob.

Padilla had trained himself to handle the blood and sight of empty body crevices and hearts being weighed on a scale like a bag of apples, but he was thankful that today he'd gotten lucky and could forgo the experience.

"You called?"

"The report on Laura Cannon is on my desk."

"You could have emailed it to me."

"I did but decided I wanted to see your face when you learned what I found."

Crap, don't tell me Laura was pregnant, he thought.

"Cause of death was a severed spinal cord caused by a broken neck. Not easy to do unless you've been trained or had a lot of practice."

"Which scenario do you think fits?"

Lang smiled. "You're the detective you figure it out. What I can tell you is that in the five years I've been here I've seen three similar deaths."

"You think she was killed by a serial killer?"

"No. But my curiosity wanted answers so I called Al Klein at records and asked him to check the files. All three cases involve John Does. Their bruised and battered bodies were left in the desert. None of the cases have been solved."

"The men were beaten before their neck was broken?"

Lang nodded.

"How do their deaths connect to Laura Cannon's death?"

"I found traces of Ketamine and alcohol in her blood."

"Isn't that a date rape drug?"

"It's been used for that purpose but it's not the drug of choice."

The knot in Padilla's stomach twisted tighter. "Why?"

"A dose ingested with alcohol has a faster reaction time then Rohypnol and GHB."

"What type of side effects?" Padilla asked.

"Dizziness, paralysis, slurred speech and unconsciousness are the most common side effects."

Padilla's thoughts went back to Laura's kitchen, four water and beer glasses but only three wine glasses. The wine rack had held five bottles of wine, leaving a place for a sixth bottle. Living alone, an open bottle of wine in the refrigerator wouldn't be unusual. If the killer knew Laura's habits he could have doctored the wine and hid in a closet and waited. When done, he makes a call to be picked up. *Son of a bitch!*

"How fast would the reaction time be?"

"Body weight and the amount ingested, all contribute but my best guess, ten to fifteen minutes," Lang Yin said.

Time for her to drink the wine, strip off her clothes and take a shower, Padilla thought. "Why the hell would he put a towel around her neck?"

Padilla hadn't realized he'd spoken aloud until Yin asked, "Hand towel or bath towel?"

"A large hand towel."

"Where was the bath towel?"

"Still on the towel rack," Padilla said.

"So she stepped out of the shower and didn't reach for the towel before she stretched out on the floor."

"She didn't fall or get knocked down?" Padilla

couldn't hide his surprise.

"The only bruising is on her neck. A fall would have left bruising to the knees, hands, head or possibly a hip or leg. Same would be true if someone knocked her down. I can get the file but do you have a picture of her in the bathroom?"

Padilla pulled four pictures out of a pocket and spread them on the counter.

"She's lying with her legs extended straight out and arms by her side. My memory could be fuzzy…"

Padilla snorted.

"And my name could be Sue but it isn't. Your memories impeccable, tell me the rest."

She smiled at the compliment.

"The three male victims were laid out in the same position."

"You think he beat the crap out of the men and drugged Laura Cannons to incapacitate them before snapping their necks?"

"I do."

"Why?"

"It takes strength and leverage to snap a neck. Unless a person has special training the ability to severer the spinal cord in one swift snap takes a person taller than the victim. In all four murders, the victims are between five-six and five-eight. For good leverage the murderer would need to be at least five ten."

"Unless they're lying on the ground," Padilla murmured.

"Unless they're lying on the ground," Lang agreed.

"There's one more similarity between the four murders. The killer did a twist and snap, not a clean one move snap," Lang Yin said.

"Could be he did that because he needed to position the head."

"Or," Ling said, "It could mean the killer has some medical training."

"What type of medical training?"

"A chiropractor or perhaps a medical student that flunked out of school," Lang said.

Or someone who after a few drinks bragged and demonstrated how easy it would be to snap someone's neck and leave them for dead or paralyzed. And the sick evil in someone else paid attention, Padilla thought.

"Want to offer an opinion on the hand towel around her neck?"

She shrugged.

"Maybe he didn't want to get his hands wet."

Chapter 25

"**D**etective Padilla, this is Chuck Taylor. It's been two days. Can you give me any information on Laura Cannon's murder?" Chuck heard laughter, a cash register bell and a gruff, 'thanks" in the background.

"Where are you?" Padilla asked.

"I'm headed to my office."

"You close to the Donut Hole on Mesa Street?"

"Close enough."

"I'll be sitting in a black Lincoln town car."

"Nice car." Chuck said as he slid into the Lincoln's gray leather passenger seat.

"One of the perks confiscated from a punk selling drugs to ten year olds."

Padilla jutted his square chin towards the cup holder.

"Coffee's yours. Help yourself to a donut."

"Thanks." Chuck let a jolt of the caffeine settle his nerves.

"I've run into a brick wall on Laura's background," Padilla said. "What do you know about her family?"

"Her mother died years ago. An aunt passed recently."

Padilla thought about the black and white framed

pictures Laura hung on the walls.

"What about the father?"

"The mother had Laura when she was nineteen. The father was married and had two sons."

"Did Laura meet him or his other family?"

"He was a doctor. Until his death Laura's mom was his office manager."

"Cause of death?"

"If you mean the father, I don't know. Her mother died of cancer. Laura wasn't told the truth about her parentage until after the father's death. When she told me the story, she called the doctor Uncle Walt."

"If the old man had family who just found out the truth they could be pissed."

"Could be," Chuck said.

"Did she receive money from the doctor's estate?"

"She didn't say. Laura was fourteen when he died. A college fund was started when she was born. There's a good chance the father footed the tab." Chuck said.

"If the mother continued to work for the man, could be the relationship continued." Padilla stated.

"You read the script without a prompt," Chuck said. "Several times a year, Laura's aunt spent a long weekend with her. While the aunt visited, Laura's mother went New York City for medical conventions. And once a year, she took a weeklong vacation without Laura."

"Business mixed with pleasure away from the prying eyes of people looking for gossip."

"That was my take and Laura's."

"Shortly before her death, Laura deposited a nice chunk of change into a bank CD. She also filed for a business loan. Could be she pushed the family for an inheritance."

Chuck chugged coffee and watched a woman juggle a toddler, a box of donuts and tray with three cups of coffee.

"Not my take. She liked nice things but she wasn't money hungry."

"You have experience with money hungry?"

Chuck thought of Angela and bit back a smile. "Some. I helped write the business plan to submit for the loan. She told me about the CDs, but not the amount. She planned to use the interest from the CDs to put a deposit on a house if the business succeeded."

"Doesn't sound like a woman looking for financial support." Padilla admitted. "Did Laura own a computer?"

Chuck shifted in the seat.

"She had a fifteen inch HP laptop. When she brought it to my place it was inside a dark green leather satchel. You wouldn't ask if you'd found it at the house."

"Do you know if she owned a printer or scanner?"

"She used the ones at her office."

Padilla thought about the empty desk in the small bedroom. Fixing a room for a small laptop didn't make sense. "Are you positive?"

"Yes. We discussed costs for both items when they were listed on the business proposal as items that would need to be purchased."

Chuck finished his donut and washed it down with coffee.

"Did you look through her photos for pictures of the ex?"

"We didn't find an album or photos."

"What about her camera's?"

"How many?" Padilla asked.

"I know about three cameras but there could have been more. She carried a small digital in her purse. A larger digital with half a dozen lenses and a tripod was always in the car."

Damn, the killer hadn't been looking for money, he'd wanted the camera he knew would be in the purse, Padilla thought.

"What about the third camera?"

"I never saw it. When we wrote the business plan she told me that when the business she'd worked for bellied up, they owed her a month's salary. There was no cash available so she agreed to accept a professional camera, tripods, and lighting fixtures as payment. Laura said, she lucked out because what the owner gave her was worth triple her salary."

"While you stew over the missing camera's I'm getting a refill on the coffee. You want one?" Chuck asked.

"How do you know the cameras are missing?"

"For half a second your poker face slipped. You are royally pissed."

Padilla was pissed, but at himself for not seeing what was staring in his face. Laura wanted to open a glamour photography studio. Two photography magazines were delivered monthly. Cameras were a big part of her life but the lack of them hadn't registered.

Chuck handed him a cup of coffee and closed the door.

"I can tell you that both the cameras I saw were

Cannons. How many pawn shops you think there are in this town?"

"I'll be able to tell you by the end of the day."

"Are you going to personally visit everyone?"

"It's why I get paid the big bucks."

"While you're earning that paycheck, you might want to add photography studios to your call list. If they were in the market they'd pay better than a pawn shop."

Not a bad idea, Padilla thought.

"Where was your relationship headed?"

"Don't know. We enjoyed each other's company, but we weren't crowding each other. The former boyfriend's deception left Laura vulnerable and unsure if she could trust her judgment of men."

"You said the ex was calling her. What did he want?"

"He wanted a television he'd given her as a gift."

"Sounds like a cheap bastard," Padilla muttered louder then he'd intended.

"I won't argue that. I told Laure he had no claim over the television, but she played it different. She told him the television was payment for a loan she'd given him."

"How much was the loan?"

"Not sure, but not more than a few hundred dollars. The money was to pay for four new tires."

"Do you know where the television was purchased?" Padilla asked.

"No and neither did Laura. The warranty is registered in her name. No bells went off when she gave them the serial number, but that doesn't mean it wasn't stolen."

"Did he accept her decision to swap the TV for the loan?" Padilla asked.

"Laura didn't say what was said, but he wasn't happy."

"Is that the television you bought from her?"

"It is."

'Why did you buy the set?" Padilla asked.

"I thought if it was no longer at her place he might leave her alone."

"Makes sense," Padilla said.

"Do you want the serial number?"

"That might help."

"Your e-mail address is on your business card. I'll send you the number this evening," Chuck said.

"Did he want anything else?"

"If he did she never said."

"Did you know Laura was planning a trip?"

"First I heard of it, where to?"

"Richmond, Virginia."

"That's where she was raised."

"It was a one way ticket."

"I don't know what to tell you. But I know this; she didn't plan to stay gone forever."

"You sure about that or is that wishful thinking?"

"Laura was taking the necessary steps to build a dream here in El Paso. The plans for the business were coming along and she was thinking ahead to the purchase of a house. She wouldn't walk away from that."

"What about you. Would she walk away from you?" Padilla asked.

"I can't answer for the lady, but I like to think we

were walking towards something better than a summer fling."

Padilla finished his coffee and checked his watch.

"When will Laura's body be release from the coroner's office?" Chuck asked.

"Why?"

"If her half-brothers don't want to give her a proper burial, the fact that we were sleeping with each other makes me responsible for her."

"Taylor, you're a strange duck."

"I'll accept that appraisal."

"I need to make some phone calls. I'll call you later."

"I wasn't expecting you." Chuck unlocked the screen door and stepped back to allow Angela to enter.

"Where's George?" He asked and looked past her shoulder.

"He's at the golf course with my brother-in-law. We need to talk."

She walked to the couch, sat and crossed her legs. The short tight skirt on her red spandex dress exposed a sliver of black panties.

"Would you like a beer or glass of wine?"

"No thanks."

"This afternoon a Detective Padilla came to the house and asked a lot of questions."

"What kind of questions?"

"He asked about our relationship."

Chuck frowned.

"Why would he question you about us?"

"No silly, he asked about George and me."

Chuck nodded but couldn't imagine where this was headed.

"What type of questions?"

"He wanted to know about our marriage."

What did you tell him?"

"I told him we had a few problems, but mostly we're happy."

"Why lie?"

"The cops don't need to know everything."

"Did the detective offer a reason as to why he was questioning you about your marriage?"

"It had something to do with an investigation."

"What investigation?" Chuck said losing patience.

"He wouldn't say and I tried all my tricks to get him to talk. He didn't even notice."

"Were you wearing that dress?"

Angela smiled and nodded.

"You're lucky you didn't get arrested for propositioning an officer of the law."

"I didn't go that far, but maybe close," she said and laughed. "He didn't mention the murdered girl at the apartments or your woman friend, so whatever he wanted couldn't be related to you."

Chuck sucked in a breath and let his impatience cool.

"Did the detective ask about me?"

"Your name was never mentioned."

"What questions did he ask?"

"First he asked where George worked and how long we'd been married. Then he asked if I'd mind showing him my bath towels."

"Bath towels, what the hell?"

"The towels are from a mail order catalog, monogrammed with an S."

"And?"

"Nothing. I own sets in two shades of blue and one in white. I showed them the towels and they left."

Chuck rubbed the back of his neck and realized it had become a bad habit.

"Do you know if he spoke to George?"

"If the police talked to George he would whimper like a baby."

She looked at her watch and stood.

"I need to leave I'm late meeting my parents for dinner."

Chapter 26

"**D**etective, are you following me?"

Padilla slid onto the worn wooden bench across from Chuck and lifted a finger towards the waitress.

"Don't flatter yourself, Taylor. Ten Seven Café is owned by a retired cop. Half the people in here are police or related to police."

"Hi handsome, you want the usual?" The cute strawberry blonde squeezed Padilla's shoulder and poured him a mug of coffee.

"I do. How's the kid?"

"He started walking last week. He's terrorizing everything he can reach and growing like a weed." She turned to Chuck. "Do you need a menu?"

"What's the usual?"

"Two eggs, bacon and a short stack. Two bucks and a nice tip."

"Works for me," Chuck said.

He watched her ass as she walked away. "Nice view."

"She's married to a cop."

"Only an observation. Did you find anything interesting at the Pawn Shops?"

"I bought a fishing reel. One owner tried to sell me a gun with a filed off serial number."

"Was he high or stupid?"

"Is there a difference?"

"Guess not. What about the photographer studio's?"

"A woman called one owner asking for price values, when he asked for her name and the serial number on the camera she hung up."

"Sounds like you've had four unproductive days."

"Do you watch college ball?" Padilla asked.

"I follow the Major league, Miners."

"They have potential." Padilla said with a nod.

"I heard that promise from the coach."

"He's overpaid and overrated."

"That's possible."

"Investigating a crime is sort of like football."

Chuck sipped his coffee. Padilla's starched white shirt was fresh from the cleaners. His tie, navy blue with thin diagonal stripes of red held a perfect Winsor knot. Padilla was smart, he didn't carry the hard edged cop persona to extreme and he wasn't the cunning, bumbling Colombo type.

"How do you figure that?"

"Fans buy a ticket to watch a good game, but when they leave the stadium not everyone will be happy with the ending."

"Do you know how this game will end?"

"The bad guy doesn't win."

"Or girl?"

Padilla nodded, his smile held no humor.

The waitress arrived with their meals and set a thermos of hot coffee on the table.

"Good point. Did Laura mention girlfriends or a difficult tenant at the apartments?"

"The only female friend Laura mentioned was a woman who moved just before Laura connected with the ex-boyfriend. As for difficult tenants she didn't mention anything but the normal run of the mill problems. Am I still on your list as a suspect?"

"I haven't ruled you out."

"Should I have a lawyer present?"

"Only if you plan to sue the restaurant for undercooked eggs."

"They're edible." Chuck slipped the eggs between the pancakes and covered the mound with a river of maple syrup.

"I didn't ask the other night. I'm asking now, how was Laura murdered?"

"Her neck was broken."

"Jesus!" Chuck sucked in air and blinked. A jolt of coffee settled the unsteady skitter of his heart rate.

"I thought you were going to say she was strangled?"

"Why would you think that?"

"You interviewed Angela Summerland. Her husband works for me."

"I talked to her late yesterday. How did you hear about that already?"

Crap, he thought. "You made Angela nervous. She wanted to know if I knew why you'd want to count her blue towels. I'll ask again, are there any leads you can talk about?"

"Nothing that points to you."

"I told you I didn't do it, not my kind of game."

"Don't get too cocky. I didn't have my heart set on making you the primary suspect anyway."

"Are there too many players on the field?"

"No players have been identified. But you don't fit the type."

"Nice to know. What about that moment of insanity when rage overrules common sense?"

"You had any of those urges?" Padilla asked.

"Two nights ago, two a.m., got a phone call that a dumbass fifteen year old invited a few friends over while his parents were out of town. When I pulled into the parking lot the first thing I see is a couple screwing on the hood of a car. A couple dozen naked kids are in the pool. The place smelled like dope, booze, and puke. Yeah, I've had them."

"Why did the tenant call you instead of the cops?"

"The teen lives next door to her. She didn't want to get him in trouble with the cops or his parents."

"What did she want you to do?"

"She used to be a high dollar call girl in Vegas. She had no problem with them having fun but she wanted them to lower the volume because they were disrupting her business."

"The gal's still soliciting?"

"That depends on your definition of sex. She owns 'Hello Darling.' It's a phone sex company."

"I heard that's a profitable business. How much does she pull down?"

"She told me that after taxes, she banks between five and six thousand a month."

"You really think the lady pays taxes?"

"The business is advertised in major newspapers and

two websites. She registered the name and has employees. Calls are answered twenty-four hours a day. She also accepts PayPal payments. Like every other business she's required to file quarterly reports."

"I'm in the wrong line of work."

"She's looking for a guy to take female clients," Chuck said over the rim of his coffee mug.

"My wife would cut my balls off if I suggested moonlighting as a talking gigolo. Any reason you haven't applied for the job?"

"Yeah, I blush."

Padilla snorted.

"You thought of killing anyone else?"

"If pressed, I could probably come up with a time or two."

"You think about it and let me know. I'll be at the police station waiting for your confession. Dumbass, remember you're talking to a cop."

Chuck rubbed the back of his neck. "You're saying that was a stupid admission?"

"It made my day."

Chuck left the café and headed to a park.

Runner ran the leash out to its full twenty feet, chased his share of squirrels and marked half the trees.

When Chuck pulled into his parking space, Kelly Lutz stood guard at the office door.

"What can I help you with?" He asked as he unlocked the door.

Runner skirted around Kelly and headed straight to

his bed.

"I'm tired of my apartment. I want you to paint the walls something besides ghost white and put down new carpet that doesn't look like dusty dog hair." She glanced at Runner and smirked.

"You can paint the walls any color you want. When you move, the cost of painting them white will be deducted from your deposit. As for the carpet, it was new when you moved from your old unit into the renovated unit. If you want more color, buy a rug. But like the paint you purchase it with your money."

Her smile reminded Chuck of a picture he'd seen of a barracuda, big and toothy.

"You look tired. Why don't you come to my place? I'll fix you breakfast and help you relax."

"Sorry, in ten minutes I have a meeting."

"You could come to my place after the meeting." Her full lips parted and her tongue did a slow left to right slide.

Kelly made the gesture look like a cobra getting ready to strike.

"I have reports to finish."

"A few hours won't hurt. Besides, I know how to type. When we're done relaxing I'll help you finish the reports."

"If you want a quickie ask Hector or Frank. If you're trolling for business and plan to take John's to your apartment, I'm giving you a thirty day's notice."

"That wasn't nice. You used to visit me."

"You tried to blackmail me into lowering your rent."

"That was a joke."

"Kelly, you wrote a letter to the owner and

insinuated that you were a sixteen year old virgin, and I was a dirty old man."

"The owner told you about that?"

"A copy of the letter is in your file. Now tell me what you really want?"

"I don't have an agenda."

"You always have an agenda. You turned the refrigerator off on purpose. You don't give a damn about the color of the carpet or the walls. Spit out what you're after or leave."

"You used to stop by for coffee. No reason you can't do that now."

"Have you heard the saying, once burned twice shy?" He opened the door and gestured for her to leave.

"I was hurt because you dumped me."

"I'm flattered. I didn't know a ten minute nail pounder could be mistaken for a marriage proposal."

She sat on the edge of his desk, crossed her long legs and offered a smile. "You've done a good job cleaning up the complex."

He allowed a thread of his temper to flare. "Are you referring to major renovations or evicting the riffraff and whores?"

"I'm not a whore."

That depended on ones definition of the word, Chuck thought.

"Don't believe I insinuated that you were. Jenna Jones stopped by the office after you showed her through your place. She said she'd be by to sign a lease next week. What did you think of her?"

"She's pushy."

"You're familiar with that trait. Anything else?"

"She was interested in you."

"I'm flattered, but not interested."

"She thinks she can change your mind."

"So do you, but it's not going to happen."

"We'll see," Kelly said. "She mentioned that without a job, she can't afford to live here for long. I seriously doubt that singing for your supper pays that well."

He had an idea how Kelly paid the rent, and kept herself in expensive perfume and three hundred dollar shoes. As long she didn't bring her business home, he didn't care, and the same would go for Jenna.

"I want to talk to you about Hector," Kelly said.

"If you're going to tell me you're screwing him, I really don't care and neither will the owner."

"I don't trust him and neither should you."

Chuck walked to the counter, poured a cup of coffee and sat at his desk.

"Why's that?"

"He's always plotting."

"You're wasting my time. If you have a complaint spit it out."

"He's a scammer. He gets ahead by taking advantage of others."

"I could point out the obvious, but go on."

"I'm not like Hector. You prettied up the place, and got rid of the human waste. But with the good came a steep increase in rent. Trying to get a break was business; it had nothing to do with you and me."

And pigs wore purple hats and flew. Hector had been sniffing her heels for months, so why the sudden back stab? Chuck took a sip of coffee and waited.

"Hector wants your job."

"Being such a cushy job, I don't blame him. You have any idea how he plans to accomplish his goal?"

"If I tell you, what do I get in return?"

"A thank you."

"I could have my ass shot for telling you anything. What I know is worth a free year's rent or more."

"You tell me what you know and I'll pass it on to the owner. If he feels it's worth anything, he could decide to lower your rent, but first you hand over the information."

"How do I know he won't screw me over?"

"You don't. But you could be lying through you pretty capped teeth. If you have worthwhile information the owner will be fair, if not," Chuck shrugged and let the silence between them simmer.

George opened the door and walked into the office.

"Sorry Boss, am I interrupting?"

"Kelly, you have anything else to say before you leave?"

"Screw you." The window pane rattled when she slammed the door.

"Booty call?" George asked as he headed to the coffee pot.

"Could be, but screwing a rattlesnake would be safer."

"Anything I need to get started on?"

"Not yet. Who was on call last night?"

"Roberto." George answered after his first slurp of coffee.

Chuck reached for Roberto's clipboard and scanned the top sheet.

"He didn't receive any calls. How's Angela?"

"Her moods change by the second. She was pissed when she dropped me off."

"Why?"

"Don't know and frankly I've stopped caring."

"Why?" Chuck asked and regretted the question before the word faded.

"I don't know. We used to be good, solid, but after…but she's changed. Hell I have too, but it takes two to make a marriage work."

George had dodged the subject. And Chuck realized that pauses and lapses in George's conversation weren't unusual.

"You both changed, so you decided to chase tail?"

George shrugged. "I was one hundred percent faithful."

"You forget I was there when you bragged about Angela's cousin giving you a blow job."

"That was after Angela started the merry-go-round."

Chuck had wondered, now he knew and didn't feel any better for the knowing.

"So, your answer was to do the same with Angela's cousin?"

"It didn't happen that way. Her cousin lived with us for a while. One night Angela was gone, we had too much to drink. Things happened."

"Angela caught you?"

"Might have been better if she had, instead the guilt eats away and we both get angrier."

Chapter 27

Padilla stepped inside Radio Shack and sized up a green haired teen weighing the odds on sticking a game down his pants and walking out of the store without getting stopped.

At the cashier counter, an older man with salt and pepper hair stood with his hands braced on the counter.

Padilla walked to the counter, angled his stance so he could watch the teen, pulled out his badge and flipped it open. "I'm Detective Padilla, El Paso Police Department. I'd like to speak to the store manager."

The kids head whipped around. His green eyes flashed with fear. His face flushed crimson when Padilla offered an, I dare you smile and a curt nod. The kid turned his back to them, fumbled through the pockets of his pants and a minute later shuffled out of the store with empty pockets and empty handed.

"Thanks, for that. I'm Todd Shelf, manager, window washer, and janitor. What can I do for you?"

"I'm following up on a case. Chuck Taylor claims he purchased a scanner from this Radio Shack. Did you sell him the scanner?"

"Show me a warrant and I'll be glad to help you."

"Everyone thinks they know the law," Padilla muttered. "Look, I'm trying to help. All I need to know is if, when and what you sold to Chuck Taylor."

"Name doesn't sound familiar."

"You want to make a lie believable look me in the face. Before you embarrass yourself again think about this, if Taylor hadn't told me about this place I wouldn't be here."

Todd sucked in a breath, stuck his hands in his pants pockets and looked Padilla in the eyes. "Chuck's been in the store a few times."

"And purchased what?"

"The day of the bank robbery he came into the store to purchase a car radio. He left with the Bearcat handheld scanner and a frequency manual."

"Why buy a scanner when he came in for a radio?"

"I convinced him to purchase the scanner."

"Why?"

"I'm a damn good salesman." Shelf sucked in his gut and puffed out his chest.

"The scanner can eavesdrop on 911 calls and cops responding?"

"They can, but it isn't eavesdropping. The calls are on basic open bands. Reporters and eager lawyers used the devices for years before they became popular with the general population."

"You said basic open bands. Are there radio bands that are off limit?"

"Are you going to arrest me?"

"Not for revealing what's saving me time researching on the internet." Padilla snapped.

"You can listen to any radio wave sound."

"Does that include cellphone conversations?"

Todd Shelf nodded.

"Taylor purchased the scanner the day of the bank robbery. But you just referred to him as Chuck. Is he a personal friend?"

"Not personal, but I like to call regular customers by their first name."

"How many times has he been in the store?"

"A few."

"Can you be more specific?" Padilla asked.

"Not really."

"Was anyone with him?"

"He's brought the dog into the store, Runner I believe he called him. But I suppose you're asking about human companion's so the answer would be no."

"After the initial purchase has Taylor returned to browse or purchase?"

"Purchase."

"Being a hotshot salesman do you remember what you sold him?"

Todd grinned. "He got a home charger, a case and stand, microphone, recorder, and a cable to connect the scanner to a computer."

"Would you say he's a frequent customer?"

"I don't remember seeing him in the store before he purchased the scanner, but since then he's been in the store several times. By the way, we have a lot of merchandise at half off right now."

"Thanks, I'll keep that in mind. Did Taylor pay cash or charge his purchases?"

"Charged."

"Can you look up the dates you sold him the charger

and the other items?”

"I could while you find something to purchase to say thanks to a caring citizen taking time to answer questions without a warrant.”

"All I need are the dates of purchase.”

Todd Shelf picked up a micro led flashlight. "Everyone needs a flashlight. This one will run 24/7 for six weeks before needing a new battery.”

"Six weeks, huh, ah, would you look up the dates, please.”

Todd handed Padilla the flashlight and smiled. "Give me a minute to access the credit card account.”

Padilla roamed the store and stopped in front of a cellphone display.

"Two year contract and you can take that new Razor home today. With a couple phone calls I can even arrange for you to keep your current phone number.” Todd said as he punched a couple of keys.

"Anyone ever tell you you're pushy?”

"My wife, but she married me anyway.” Todd walked across the room and handed Padilla a piece of paper. "I did you one better, this is a printout of the receipts. Dates and times are at the bottom of each receipt. So, who's your current provider?”

"Verizon.”

Todd Shelf nodded. "Let me see your phone.”

Padilla reached into his pocket and handed it over.

"You've got to be kidding. I haven' seen one of these in years.”

"It works and I like it.”

"It's a dinosaur and the case is cracked. May I ask what Chuck did to grab your attention?”

"I don't know that he did anything other than be in the wrong place at the wrong time."

"And this has something to do with the scanner?"

"It might," Padilla hedged.

Todd glanced at the card Padilla had left on the counter. "Homicide detectives only work murder cases?"

"Unless it's a slow day. I appreciate you answering my questions. This printout helps."

"I appreciate you buying a cellphone." Todd walked to the counter and scanned the box before Padilla could form an objection. "That will be ninety three dollars. Cash or charge?"

Padilla shook his head and reached for his wallet. "What happened to free with a two year contract?"

"The phone's free. You're paying for the case, desk stand, car charger and screen cover."

"You should have been a used car salesman."

"I was." Todd glanced at the credit card Padilla handed him, "Jim."

Padilla looked at the thread bare carpet, walls in need of a couple of coats of fresh paint and tired display units. "Why give that up to manage this dump?"

"My wife inherited this dump." He nodded towards the flashlight still in Padilla's hand. "You want two or three flashlights?"

Chapter 28

Runner was asleep on his bed. Periodically his back legs twitched and he whimpered through a dream. No doubt, one that involved squirrels or the blue ball he chased without ever tiring, Chuck thought.

Chuck shifted in the recliner and went back to reading the David Baldacci novel in his hands until the scanner beeped and familiar voices caught his attention.

"I want my money."

Chuck reached across a plate holding what was left of his dinner, an inch of cream cheese icing that had topped a three layer triple chocolate cake, and punched record on the tape recorder.

"I told you we would need to move slow, let the heat die down. A couple more weeks you'll get your money."

"A couple of weeks my ass. I need the money now."

"The cops are still asking questions. We go as planned."

"You better not forget about me."

"As if that were possible! I told you how it would be. I got things to do."

The scanner beeped, a dial tone, and then the distinct sound of a phone number being punched into a cellphone filled the void.

"*Hey girly, what's going on?*" Chuck recognized the voice as the same man who had demanded payment.

"*Nothing worth repeating. I want to head to a hot tropical island and have someone fulfill my dreams.*"

"*Not much longer and you'll be able to do that. I'm just waiting for my money.*"

"*Why can't you just get it?*"

"*I told you, it's not that simple. Things have to go in order.*"

"*It better not be too much longer. It wouldn't be hard to find someone else to appreciate me.*"

"*It will be soon, I promise.*"

The scanner beeped and a dial tone filled the void.

Hungry and tired of his own company Chuck left Runner in the backyard to chase shadows and headed to the garage.

Fifteen miles out of town, he pulled into the parking lot of The Texas Ranch House. The original two story red brick ranch house sat on the southeast corner of a working cattle ranch. On the other side of a split rail fence, turned silver gray with age, several hundred head of cattle roamed the fields.

Chuck pushed through black saloon style doors and stepped into a western saloon setting that would make Wyatt Earp and Billy the Kid feel right at home.

"Howdy. How many in your party, sir?"

The man's faded jeans were pressed. The heels on his gray snakeskin cowboy boots were worn down. A crisp white western cut shirt was pulled taut across his shoulders.

"Unless you know something I don't, just me."

Chuck's smile didn't reach to his eyes.

The man nodded. "We have a full house. If you don't mind hugging the bar for a while, a table should be available in thirty minutes."

"Works for me." Chuck gave the man his name and ambled into the bar. He found an empty stool in the back corner, ordered a Jack and Coke and leaned back to take in the scene. The long mahogany bar and back bar had been purchased from an old bar in Houston that was being torn down.

Above a double row of liquor bottles hung an oil painting of a semi clad redheaded beauty cozying up to a cowboy playing poker. The woman was a famous local madam who became the second wife of the man who homesteaded the ranch.

Chuck took a sip of his drink and followed the man making his way through the crowd.

Padilla settled onto the stool next to him and ordered a long neck Miller.

"Small world, Detective Padilla?" Chuck said.

"The names pronounced Padeeah."

"Touché."

"Well Detective Padeeah, should I be flattered that you choose to sit next to me?"

"You should. I'm off duty. The name's Jim."

"You could have picked a different stool to set your sorry ass on, Jim."

"Could have, but I prefer the company here."

"I did too until you showed up." Chuck took a drink and nodded at a guy he knew that sat halfway down the bar.

"Are you always a hard ass or just being

difficult?"

Chuck rubbed his neck and muttered to himself.

"Difficult. I'm licking my wounds and wondering how to shut off my feelings and crawl back into the hole where life was simple."

Confessionals weren't something Chuck did willingly; to do so with the detective surprised him. From the look on Padilla's face he'd been caught off guard too.

Jim tipped his beer, took a long pull and stared at a scantily clad woman draped over a half drunk companion.

"That would explain burying the ownership of the apartments under a corporation. And working there as the manager."

Chuck set his drink down.

"What do you want?"

"A couple of beers and a medium rare steak."

"Never knew a cop that wasn't working," Chuck said with a snort.

"Could be true, but the wife claims I should be more like you."

"Smart woman to know I've got you beat in the handsome and charming department."

"The people I work with aren't impressed by charm. But we do have several things in common."

"Yeah, do tell?"

"We both got suckered into purchases by Todd Shelf."

One corner of Chuck's mouth lifted. "What did he tap you for?"

"New cellphone and enough extras to fill the front

seat of my car. Then he talked me into four flashlights, and a remote control police car."

Chuck grinned.

"The flashlight guaranteed to run six weeks?"

"That's the one."

"You play with remote control cars?"

"Stress relief at the office."

"I got caught up in the excitement of the police chase. What's your excuse?"

"I'm a sucker for new gadgets."

Jim drained his beer and tipped the empty bottle towards the bartender.

"We both got lucky and married good women. We both have daughters who believe they know how to run our life better than we do. And we both know where to find a damn good steak."

"You've been doing your homework."

"My job," Jim replied.

In the background noise Chuck heard his name called and signaled to the waiter. He pulled two bills from his pocket and tossed them on the bar.

"You know so much about me you might as well be my date."

Jim cut a laugh short and stood. "I was hoping you'd ask."

A short thin waiter with a swagger that defied his bowed legs and a slight limp, led them to a table in the center of a square room that held forty tables.

"We'll both have the house special; steaks medium rare, baked potatoes fully loaded and the salad bar." Chuck told the waiter before he could walk away.

Companionably, they walked to the salad bar, loaded their plates and headed back to their table.

A votive candle, in the center of each table, set an inviting atmosphere and cast shadows in the far corners of the room.

"Cozy." Jim said as he sat. "You're not the prettiest date but at least you won't expect a goodnight kiss."

"There is that." Chuck leaned back in the seat. For the first time since he'd seen Laura's name splashed in big bold letters across the front page of the newspaper the knot in the back of his neck uncoiled.

"I didn't kill Laura." Chuck said before he could swallow the words.

"I wouldn't be sitting here if I thought you did, but for the record, you're still a person of interest."

Chuck took a bite of salad and thought about the list of possible suspects. It was short, and like Padilla he'd put his name on the list.

"Have you checked out the half-brothers raised by Laura's father and his wife?"

"Dead-end. The wife died a year after her husband. Oldest son's a corporate attorney. The younger son's a GP. After his internship the doc set up practice in upper New York. At the time of his father's death he was going through a nasty divorce. He decided to cut his losses, move back to Virginia and take over his father's practice."

Chuck frowned. "Laura never mentioned that."

"Laura was fourteen. The attorney and Laura's mother were the same age."

"Good Lord, I never thought about the age

difference between her parents."

"Did the father confess his sins to the son?"

"No need. Apparently, Laura was a dead ringer for her paternal grandmother."

"So the sons knew. What about the wife?"

"The sons were ten and eleven, when their mother was diagnosed with MS. The disease deteriorated her long and short term memory. By the time the boys left for college, she believed her sons were her bothers and her husband was her father. According to the doctor, they liked Laura's mom and had no problem with their father finding happiness where he could."

"At fourteen, how would you have reacted if you learned your honorary uncle was really your father and you had two half-brothers old enough to be your father?" Chuck asked.

"I'd have been pissed and probably would have raised hell."

"I thought the same," Chuck admitted.

"My daughter is into high drama, so I found Laura's reaction puzzling," Jim said.

"Meaning?" Chuck asked.

"Laura called a meeting with her half-brothers and her mother. She told them she didn't want the truth made public as it was no one's business. And she wanted assurance that her mother would be allowed to continue to work at the clinic."

"Did they comply with her requests?"

"They did." Jim answered.

"When was the last time the men talked to her?"

"The day after her mother's funeral the three of them met for lunch."

"Did the doctor provide for Laura and her mother in his will?" Chuck asked.

"Besides the salary from the clinic the mother was given a generous monthly allowance that covered raising Laura. After Laura's mother died the brother's offered to pay Laura the monthly allowance. She declined the offer."

"So the family angle's a dead end," Chuck said.

They ate in silence for a few minutes. Not an uncomfortable silence, but one filled with unanswered questions.

"Have you read the report Laura filed about the kittens and cat that were killed."

Jim set his fork down and pushed his empty salad plate away. He'd run Laura's name through the computer, there'd been no hits.

"Tell me what happened." His voiced snapped with frustration.

"A tenant moved out and left a cat and a litter of kittens. Laura couldn't bring herself to take them to the animal shelter so she took them home and used a packing box to make a shelter for them under a tree in the backyard. One morning, after she'd spent the night at my place, she found them on the back doorstep. Their necks had been snapped."

Shit. A bone jarring chill ran down Jim's back.

"Are you positive Laura filed a report?"

"I talked to her right after she'd hung up from the call. She was still irritated that the woman who took the report didn't sound interested." Chuck paused and swore quietly.

"I asked her if she'd given the woman the ex-boyfriends name. She admitted she had but she'd been uncomfortable with the idea that she'd been involved with someone who could be that heartless."

"Do you remember the date?"

"No, but she hadn't planned to tell me about the cats. She called to thank me for the flowers I'd sent. The date would be on my credit card and the florist would have a record of delivery."

Padilla stood, pulled the cellphone out of the inside pocket of his jacket and indicated with a finger that he'd be right back.

When he returned a bottle of red wine and two filled glasses were on the table.

"I've ordered a search for the complaint. Are you sure she never referred to him by name, even a nickname?"

"Not unless jerk is a term of endearment. It made her mad that he kept calling and that he didn't believe he needed to repay the money he'd borrowed, but she didn't sit and bitch about him."

"Did Laura say why they split?"

"She didn't go into details, but he took her to a Memorial Day party. The people there made her uncomfortable. They came to an impasse over the situation and she told him they were through. Laura's secretary might know what happened."

Jim shook his head.

"Laura kept her private life separate from work."

"Same as I try to do. It makes the job less complicated if you're forced to reprimand or fire someone," Chuck stated.

"But you haven't been totally successful," Jim

said.

"You think you know something, spit it out."

"Heard you had a thing going with George Summerland's wife," Jim said.

"Where'd you hear that?"

"Cop mentioned finding the two of you playing patty ass out by the airport."

"Cop has a dirty mind. Angela and I are friends, end of story."

"You want to make it more?"

"I don't tango with married women."

"Does her husband know that?"

"He does. You got something else sticking in your craw?"

"During the investigation for Anna Marie I heard that you and George are chummy."

"George and I meet at the shooting range by the dump a few times a month. Why would someone mention that?"

"No one knew how Anna Marie died. George found her body. It was mentioned that you and George are sharp shooters."

"You mind telling me who volunteered that information?"

"Frank Hansen."

Chuck frowned.

"Did he say how he came by that opinion?"

"Said Angela invited him to the range."

Chuck shook his head. "Angela will drive George to the range but she won't touch a gun. The night Frank showed up I'd picked George up. Angela wasn't there. When Frank arrived he fumbled around and then claimed he'd left his ammo at home. When I volunteered my gun he didn't seem happy."

"Is he a good shot?"

"Better then he led us to believe."

"What makes you say that?"

"He was a sharp shooter in the service, but at the range, just before he pulled the trigger he'd move the barrel a fraction to the left."

"You call him on that?"

"I didn't, but it's given me food for thought."

"Look, I'll lay it out for you. A cop saw you pulled over on the highway to help Laura. He wrote down both your license plate numbers and the date and time in his log."

"He rolled down his window and asked if everything was okay," Chuck said with a nod.

"Your business card was in her office desk. A florist card with your name on it saying, 'thanks for a lovely evening,' was taped to her computer screen. None of them are a motive but they connect the two of you. I also found something at the crime scene and it's being checked for possible matches. Off the record, I'd be looking for a damn good attorney. On the record, I'll work my ass off to find out who killed Laura."

"What did you find?"

Padilla shook his head. "I can't tell you yet."

"Find a match?"

"Not yet, but it's still early in the game."

Padilla pulled his phone out and looked at the caller ID. Without a word he stood and walked towards the men's room.

Five minutes later he returned.

"They found the complaint Laura filed. They'd spelled her last name wrong. And instead of a name, the person who took the complaint wrote, woman pissed at ex-boyfriend, blaming him for dead pussy, ha ha."

"You got a cop with some anger issues," Chuck said.

"Don't get me started," Padilla said and reached for his drink.

Chuck buttered a warm yeast roll. "You found my fingerprints in the house. Surely you found others?"

"The house was stripped clean. The walls were washed down. We couldn't even find a print of Laura's."

"What type of cleaner was used?"

"Two were used, Agent Green and Fresh Breeze. Why do you ask?"

Padilla didn't blink as Chuck processed the information.

"I told you about the theft and vandalism problems at the apartments."

"You use Agent Green or Fresh Breeze?"

"The product is good but there are less expensive cleaners that do just as good of a job. So no, I listened to the sales reps pitch and declined."

"Did they leave samples?"

"He tried. I didn't want to waste time turning him down a second time, so I refused the samples. How long was the bastard in the house?"

"Hours would be my guess. But the walls could have been washed down weeks ago."

"Or the night the kittens were killed," Chuck stated.

"Not a bad idea," Jim said. "Fresh traces of the cleaner were found on the door handles and in the bathroom, probably done as he entered and left the house."

"Where'd you find my prints?"

"They were on the underside of a long narrow table in the living room."

"Must have been when I pulled the table out to untangle the television and speaker cords," Chuck offered. "Do you think the ex-boyfriend washed the walls to eliminate his DNA or eliminate fingerprints that are on file with the national data base?"

"My take is both, but there are those who disagree."

"Those who disagree are hoping to hang me."

Jim blinked.

"Open and shut cases make us look like we're good at doing our job."

"Does your boss find it difficult to breathe when he's got his nose stuck up some newsman's ass?" Chuck asked.

Padilla grinned and toasted Chuck with a tip of his wine glass.

"Besides an irritating ex, what was going on in Laura's life?"

"You know she was going through the preliminary steps to open a business."

"How long had she worked on that?"

"I think it had been in the back of her mind since the company she worked for folded. She didn't follow through with the idea until recently because she wasn't sure she wanted to stay in El Paso."

"The ex could have wanted the money she was going to siphon into a business, or put into the CD." Jim said as he stabbed a green olive and dunked it in a bowl he'd filled with French dressing.

"That's possible, but Laura didn't brag about her finances and never asked me about mine. I can't imagine her sharing that type of information with him."

"They'd known each other longer than the two of you. You don't know what was disclosed during late night pillow talk."

As if the salad Chuck was eating had turned bitter he winced at the blunt truth.

"What type of collateral was Laura going to use to get a business loan?"

"According to a banker friend, being female and single was enough."

"Humph. For what it's worth, you don't fit a killer's profile."

"You said that once before. Next I know I'm admitting to wanting to kill a few dozen kids. This time I'll say I didn't realize there was a type," Chuck said.

"The heads claim its nonsense, but after a few years on the job you can look at someone and tell if they have the instinct to kill. Even if it's accidental, killing someone changes you."

With years of military discipline to rely on, Chuck kept his features neutral.

"Have you killed someone?"

The waiter arrived with their steaks and waited until they told him they were properly cooked before he left them alone.

"I've killed." Jim said after he'd eaten a couple of bites. "Sometimes they leave you no choice, but let's save that for another beer."

"You mentioned a daughter?" Chuck prompted.

"Amy. She's a sweetheart and a constant pain in my ass."

"That sounds typical. How old is she?"

"Nineteen. The same age as your daughter."

"Is she in college?"

"She is, but unlike the free ride your daughter has, Amy works for a law office and goes to college part-time."

Chuck stiffened.

Tipped in frost his voice dropped a notch. "Trapped in a space half the size of a coffin Carrie held her mother's hand while she died from internal injuries. Then she spent three months in a hospital and another year before she could talk above a crocked whisper. Given a choice Carrie would work her way through college."

"I was out of line." Padilla started to rise.

Chuck shook off the anger with a toss of his head.

"Sit down. I don't offend that easily. Frankly, I'm surprised you dug that deep into my past."

"Rules of the game; dig under every rock that looks like it's hiding something."

"The facts are buried under five layers of bullshit. What lie did you decide to believe?"

"A small newspaper in the company's hometown

named you as the recipient of an out of court settlement. They alleged that people were fired, but everything was written in a way that the paper couldn't be sued for libel."

"No other details?"

"None."

"So you jumped to conclusions?"

"Guilty. I assumed it was one of those dumb shit lawsuits. Like the ones filed by the klutz who spilled hot coffee or the idiot who stood on a metal ladder to move a live electrical wire."

"Not an unreasonable assumption." Chuck delivered the comment with a nod.

"Do you want to relay the facts or brush this under the table and move on?"

"Are you collecting data to fill a line in your daily report or genuinely interested?"

"What you say goes no further than this table."

Chuck ate a piece of steak and sipped his wine before clearing his throat. His voice was low, the words matter of fact. His face and eyes wore an emotionless mask.

"A winter storm shutdown a three hundred mile stretch of I-80 through Wyoming and Nebraska. When the roads opened, the corporate office told their drivers to make up the lost time. Twenty hours later, a driver dozed off. When the tires hit the rumble strip he awoke, but exhaustion disoriented him. He jerked on the wheel. The back load stated weaving and the rig went into a slide, he over corrected and lost control. Before the double load jackknifed two cars were pushed through a guardrail. The almost vertical drop ended at the bottom of a narrow rocky ravine."

"Mother of God, I'm sorry."

"So am I. Two weeks after the accident a cop handed me a copy of the email from the company instructing the drivers to make up the lost time or lose their jobs."

"How did the police get a copy of the email?"

"The driver had printed a hard copy and stuffed the paper in his personal belongings. It was insurance in case he got stopped at a weigh station and fined for ignoring the government regulated time limits set for commercial truckers."

"First rule of business, cover your ass," Jim said with a nod.

"The doctor's didn't expect the driver to survive his injuries, so the company lawyers hung their hat on that and used him as their, sacrificial lamb. When the driver survived, and heard he'd been labeled a reneged with disciplinary reports in his file for not following rules, he blew the whistle."

"Did the company try to publically smear the driver's reputation?"

"They tried and might have succeeded, but five other drivers stepped forward and handed over copies of their emails. My wife's death and my daughter's injuries were caused by greed. It was a bitter pill to swallow and yes, I seriously thought about killing someone."

"Understandable, I'd have done the same. Why didn't you go public with what happened?"

"Given time I might have, but when the police filed their final report, I had a daughter in ICU and a wife in the morgue. Four days after the police report was filed three company lawyers arrived at the hospital."

Chuck took a bite of steak and swallowed. "Have you ever watched the Three Stooges and paid attention to their perfectly executed timing?"

"When I was a rookie two old time cops played the parts to perfection."

"Then you understand when I say they executed the sympathy act, we want to help proposal, and protect our ass offer with perfect timing. While they talked, I swear melodrama music swelled as they reached the climax." Chuck paused and took a sip of water.

"The high point was a financial incentive to forget the company's part in implementing your wife's death?" Jim asked.

"It was, but I didn't buy the sympathy act. I tore up the check, stuffed it in the most obnoxious lawyers pocket and kicked them out. During three subsequent visits they doubled the previous day's offer."

"Makes you wonder how long they would have gloated if you'd accepted the original offer," Jim said.

"During the fourth visit, one of the lawyers made a remark about a driver killing someone in an accident being no different than military personnel killing a civilian during battle—it was just the price of doing business."

"Did you rearrange his face?"

"Before I could take a swing a couple of military buddies stepped between us."

"You ever see the man again?"

"Nope."

For several minutes they concentrated on their meals.

"Do you believe in dreams or spirits?" Chuck asked when his plate was empty.

"I believe in gut instincts that warn me to watch my back, or pay attention to a certain person, or piece of evidence."

"Close enough. After the lawyers left, a doctor pushed me into my daughter's room and told the ICU nurse I could stay as long as I wanted. I sat in the chair and held Carries hand. I don't know how much time elapsed before my wife's favorite perfume overshadowed the hospitals antiseptic cleaners. When I looked up, Meg stood on the other side of the hospital bed. She wore the same dress she'd worn on our first date."

Chuck drained his wine glass and cleared his throat.

"She said she'd heard the lawyer and made me smile when she said she'd kicked him in the balls just like I taught her to do if she ever needed to defend herself. Then she sobered and told me to take the money. I told her I wasn't interested. Like other arguments we'd had, she calmly listed the reasons I was wrong. I'd need to retire and become Carries caregiver during therapy. Military doctors wouldn't be able to provide the specialized treatments Carrie needed. Medical care would be expensive, and my stubbornness would force me to spend the rest of my life paying off medical bills, and possibly deprive Carrie of living a normal life."

"Sound advice."

"It was, but that didn't mean I wanted to take what I thought of as blood money."

"In the long run, stubborn pride isn't beneficial," Padilla said.

"So I've heard. Nick Patterson, a friend who joined the Navy and became a lawyer for JAG told me Meg was right. I needed to think of Carrie and myself because in the end the company would weather the bad publicity and continue to thrive."

"JAG is the Navy's Judge Advocate General's Corps?"

Chuck nodded. "Three days after the last encounter, two new lawyers called and asked if I'd meet them in the hospital coffee shop. After feigning interest in Carrie's condition they doubled the last offer. The amount was enough to buy a small country, but in their arrogance they made it sound like pocket change that meant nothing."

"You accepted that offer?"

"No, because their egotism pissed me off I stuck to the plan Nick suggested. I told them to double the offer, deposit the settlements in two accounts and sign an agreement that Carrie's health insurance would be paid-in-full for life. Employees in the chain of command responsible for the email sent to the driver were to be fired and not given letters of recommendation. And a letter of apology to the driver was to be posted in the driver's hometown paper."

"They agreed?"

"The only bulk was the apology to the driver. When I stood to leave they changed their mind."

Jim lifted his brow. "Hell of a lot of money."

Chuck nodded.

"How's your daughter?"

"Better than the doctor's ever thought would be possible. Last year we ran in the Boston Marathon. Are you close to your daughter?"

"Wife says we're too much alike—stubborn to the core. I'm a cop, I'm naturally suspicious. Amy claims I never trust her."

Chuck nodded. "After my wife's death I became over protective. One day Carrie told me to stop smothering her. It was the first time since her vocal cords healed that she projected her voice loud enough to say she yelled. I had to fight back the tears. Her latest campaign was a dog. You've met Runner so you know who won."

"We got stuck with a mutt Amy found in a parking lot. The thing pees on the floor when it's happy."

"Your daughter lives at home?"

"Amy claims my screening her boyfriends killed her social life. She and two cousins share an apartment and shop for groceries out of our pantry."

"Did you screen the boys?"

"Damn right and still do."

Chapter 29

"Taste these and tell me what you think." Britney placed a plate on his desk and handed Runner a homemade dog biscuit.

"You're spoiling my dog and my men. They come in every morning looking for your samples."

"You want me to stop?"

"Just saying you're spoiling us. I'm running an extra half mile to work off the extra calories."

Chuck eyed the four squares on the plate. Each square had been cut into quarters.

"They look like frosted brownies. What are they really?"

"Not saying. Taste each one and give me your opinion."

He took a bite, drank some coffee and repeated the process.

"They all taste good, but I like the second one the best."

"Why?"

"Do I have to have a reason?"

"Try."

He took another piece of the second brownie.

"The texture. The second one has more texture, like a cake."

"I agree, but your opinion helps, thanks."

"What are you trying to make?"

"A birthday cake, but the birthday boy is gluten intolerant and his wife is diabetic. Trying to make a sugar free chocolate cake with no flour that tastes good has been a challenge."

"Happy to help."

George walked into the office, poured a cup of coffee and looked at the plate like a starving waif.

"Help yourself," Britney said.

"Thanks, I've never had fudge with frosting but that was great," he said after eating the pieces left.

"Fudge." Britney picked up the plate and left.

"I'm giving you my two week notice. My last day will be a week from Friday."

Chuck tossed his pen on the desk, leaned back in the chair and crossed his arms.

"Where are you headed?"

"North. It's time to cut the losses and get out."

"Who offered you a job?"

"A relative who lives outside of Chicago won a contract to build a golf course. I'll manage the project."

"Congratulations. How does Angela feel about the move?"

"I haven't told her. When I leave I'm making a clean break."

"Jesus George, that's a real kick in the ass. You're married to the woman. Don't you think she deserves to know what you plan to do?"

"Could be, but I'd appreciate it if you didn't mention this conversation to her."

"Then why did you tell me?"

"Despite my acting like an asshole once in a while, you haven't fired me. If I'd been in your position, I wouldn't have been as generous. I appreciate that and the times you've covered my ass over work hours."

"What about Angela?"

"We're not good for each other." At the door he turned. "Angela's not subtle. If you're interested wink and she'll fall in your lap."

Chuck reached for his coffee and wished it were laced with a shot of whiskey.

He was missing signals, information or both.

Laura's observation that he didn't fit into the beer gut, baseball cap mentality had been right. But maybe while playing the part of the easy going country bumpkin who lived paycheck to paycheck, he'd shut off his ability to accurately read people and situations.

The door opened and Detective Jim Padilla strolled in like he had a chip on his shoulder and was looking for a fight.

Chuck didn't need a gut feeling to know trouble had landed on his doorstep.

"Detective, coffee's fresh, help yourself."

Padilla looked around the room before stepping up to the counter that held a mini refrigerator, sink, and coffee pot. "You got janitorial service?"

"I have an arrangement with one of the tenant's teenage son's. What can I do for you?"

Padilla added three packages of sugar and a slug of creamer to his coffee. He sat across from Chuck, balanced an ankle on his knee and took a sip of the coffee.

"How can you drink that crap?"

"I just left a place that smelled like a rotten sewer. My sense of taste and smell are numb.

"You mentioned a tape. I'd like to listen to it today."

"It's at my house. Anything new you can tell me."

"Not yet. The cops did another search of Laura's place. They found this in a junk drawer in the kitchen." He reached into his jacket pocket, pulled out a business card and tossed it onto the desk.

Chuck studied the card and flipped it. There were two red smudges, like something had rubbed against the card but no writing.

"This was the card used by the former owner. I didn't like the pea green color or the logo, still don't. Why does the card have your hackles up?" He pushed it back across the desk and watched Padilla slip it in his breast pocket.

"It doesn't fit the story that you only met Laura a couple months ago."

"My name is printed on my business cards. The one in your pocket was generic. L & L Printing Company designed the card I've used for the last two years."

"You're saying you didn't give that card to Laura?"

"Can't give out what isn't in stock."

"How many nights did she spend at your place?"

"I don't have them notched on my bedpost. Why is that important?"

Padilla looked like he was debating something.

Whatever it was made him edgy.

"Give me a ballpark figure."

"A dozen where she spent the night and maybe another half dozen evenings," Chuck said.

"Could Laura have picked up the card in your truck or at your house?"

"If a copy of that card was in my house, it would have been in my daughter's room buried in a drawer."

"Did she spend time in that room?"

"Not that I saw."

"Was she ever alone in the house?"

"No."

Chuck paused. "Laure borrowed one of Carrie's bathrobes, but I got it out of the room."

"How do you think she came across the card?" Padilla asked.

"I have absolutely no idea."

"Can I use your restroom?"

"Right down the hall."

Padilla returned to the office holding a blue hand towel with the initial S embroidered on one end.

"Nice towel. Do you have the full set?"

"They weren't sold as sets. They were sold in packages of six. I bought four packages."

"Where?"

"Sam's Club."

"All the same color?"

"That was the only color they had."

"You mind if we go to your house, have a look around and pick up the tape?"

Chuck felt the edge of Padilla's discomfort dig into his shoulder blades.

"When?"

"Now. May I have the towel?"

"There are clean ones at the house, but suit yourself."

Chuck clipped the leash on Runner and turned to Padilla. "Who's driving?"

"I am."

Padilla headed to a black Crown Victoria. The starter growled, the air conditioner was lukewarm and the recycled air smelled like yesterday's belch.

"What happened to the town car?" Runner sat on the floor between Chuck's legs and looked back and forth between them.

"Captain doesn't like my attitude. This is my punishment."

A white city patrol unit and an unmarked black Ford sedan were parked at the curb. Padilla pulled into the empty driveway.

Chuck unlocked the front door and stepped inside.

Five officers followed and fanned out through the house.

Padilla walked into the kitchen, checked out the backyard, and strolled down the hall before joining Chuck in the living room. "Nice little house. Who did the remodel?"

"I did."

"Who cleans the place?"

"Leia Stewart. She lives next door. She comes over a couple of times a week to clean and watch the movie channel."

Padilla wrote a note in a small spiral notepad.

"Thanks for cooperating. I don't have a warrant so

you didn't have to allow us in here."

"I don't have anything to hide."

Padilla picked up the scanner and turned it on. It beeped and static filled the room.

"Is this the scanner?"

"Yes."

"I talked to the officers who answered the domestic across the street. Heard how you tried to play hero and got punched in the face instead."

"When I walked over my thought was to distract him until the cops arrived. It never crossed my mind that he'd turn on me."

"Never trust a bully," Padilla said.

"I'll keep that in mind."

"Is this the recorder?" Padilla picked up the machine but didn't press play.

"It is." Something about the question and the tone was off. Chuck took a closer look at Padilla. Last night's friendly dinner conversation had been replaced with a buttoned down, rigidness that was as friendly as a wolf that hadn't eaten lunch.

"Do you record all the conversations you hear?" Padilla asked.

"I recorded the ones I told you about and calls from two tenants."

"Why would you do that?"

"Some tenants call at odd hours to complain. If they become a problem a recording of threats can be used to evict them."

"Is someone threatening you?"

"A redhead is pushing the lets be friendly button. And a guy who moved out objects to not receiving his deposit back."

"Could the guy turn nasty?"

"Already has."

"Why aren't you returning his deposit?"

"He drilled holes in the floor and a wall in one of the bedrooms."

"Why the hell would he do that?"

"Sex, Padilla. He was into bondage and S & M."

Padilla ran a hand down his face. "You said you use the scanner to keep informed. But if I remember correctly, you said you didn't know about Laura's death until you read it in the paper."

"After Laura and I left The Kitchen, I went to the grocery store. I got home around eight-thirty, put the groceries away and took Runner for a walk. I never had the scanner on during that time. Shortly after that, I left and didn't take the scanner with me."

"Where did you go?"

"I drove to George Summerland's place. He wasn't home, but I talked to his wife Angela."

"What time was that?"

"A little after eleven."

"Isn't that late for a drop by visit?"

An older officer walked into the living room carrying a box.

"We found a gun. It's been fired recently."

"Is the gun registered in your name?" Padilla asked.

"It is. The last time it was shot was the week before Laura was killed. At the target range by the dump, George was with me."

"We need to take the gun with us. Do you have any other guns or rifles in the house?"

"My grandfather's old Colt is in a safe in the closet," he said. "Why, I'm not aware of anyone being shot."

"Routine check, would you open the safe for us?" Padilla asked.

Chuck walked into the bedroom, opened the closet and pushed a row of shirts aside. When the safe was open he stepped aside.

Padilla retrieved the Colt and the box of ammo and closed the safe.

"If you don't mind, I'd appreciate you coming to the stationhouse with me?"

"Am I under arrest?"

"Did you kill Laura Cannon?"

"No."

"Then unless proven otherwise, you're a free man."

"When will you return my guns?" Chuck asked as they entered the living room.

"You should be able to take them with you when you leave the stationhouse. You mentioned having more blue towels at the house. What do you use them for?" Padilla asked.

"They're rags. Lately they've been used for puppy accidents."

"Where do you keep them?" An officer stepped out of the kitchen to ask.

"There's a stack under the kitchen sink and two or three in the garage."

"Do you keep a towel in your truck?"

"One's tossed behind the seat."

"Mind if we check out your truck?"

"Suit yourself. Are the towels under arrest?"

"Smartass." Padilla shot a glance at the two cops

standing in the doorway.

"On your way to the station stop by the Superior Apartments and get the towel in Mr. Taylor's truck."

He turned back to Chuck.

"Is the truck locked?"

"You've seen the truck. Can you think of anyone who'd want to steal it?"

"No."

"Neither can I. It's unlocked and the windows are rolled down." He said to the officers as they exited the house.

Chapter 30

"**S**trange, isn't it?" Detective Padilla sat behind a large rectangular desk with drawers running down both sides. With the chair pushed slightly back he stretched out his long legs and crossed his ankles.

"What's strange?" Chuck braced an ankle on his knee.

Hours before he'd thought his survival instincts had rusted into worthless dust. He'd been wrong; they'd just been dormant until needed.

The mirror on the wall looked innocent enough, but Chuck would bet the bottom line on his portfolio that they were being watched and recorded.

What had happened that put Padilla at cross wires with his boss and him on the hot seat and the number one contender as Laura's murderer?

"When my wife tells me about sending a guy to ER to get a tetanus shot from a man hating nurse I didn't know you from Adam. Then days later, one of your employees discovers a girl's body in one of your apartment units. And then you stroll into the precinct offering information on a woman who's been murdered, a woman you picked up on the side of the road and have been dating. Next thing you know we're bumping into each other all over town."

Padilla pulled a pencil out of the desks slim center drawer and tapped it on the desk like a drumstick.

"It's not unusual for a killer to offer information in exchange for inside knowledge on what's happening with a case."

"I didn't kill Laura."

The pencil got tossed, rolled across the desk and stopped just short of the edge.

Padilla flipped open his pocket size notebook and glanced at his notes.

"You told me that after watching Laura leave The Kitchen parking lot you got in your truck and drove to Albertson's grocery store."

"That's right."

"Laura called while you were pulling into the parking lot?"

"She did. Have you checked Verizon for the call log?"

Padilla didn't move his head, but his eyes darted towards the two way mirror.

"How long were you inside the store?"

"Not sure."

"Give it a good guess," Padilla said.

"Around forty-five minutes."

"What did you do next?"

"Drove home, put the groceries away, and took Runner for a walk."

"What did you do after that?"

"Shortly before eleven I drove to George Summerland's house."

"What would you say if I told you George denies that?"

"He wasn't there. I told you that."

Padilla slid the note pad across the desk.

"I want you to take that pencil and paper, and write down exactly where the hell you were when Laura was killed. What you were doing, and who, if anyone, can vouch for you."

"I told you where I was. Check the security camera's at the grocery store."

"The cameras were down that night for maintenance," Padilla said.

"You claim you haven't used the business card we found in Laura's desk for two years. Is that correct?"

"Yes."

"The printing companies verified that you had a new card designed two years ago. George claims you use the old business cards when you run low and are waiting for an order of the other card."

"That's a lie." Chuck spit out.

"Ask Laura. She knows we don't use those cards anymore."

"Laura's dead."

"I meant Angela." Chuck ran his fingers though his hair. "In fact, I gave all the cards away."

"Who did you give the cards too?"

"Shit, I know who the killer is."

"First you don't know shit, now you can identify the killer. Taylor, your comments are starting to make me think you are the killer. Why don't you tell me what happened. Write it there on the paper and quit fucking around."

"I'm not fucking around. Look, I know why George didn't know I was at his house. I also think I know why you found an old business card at Laura's."

"Was it a lovers spat? Did Laura dump you or did you want more than she wanted to give? That's it isn't it? You met her, wanted to get into her pants and she blew you off. So you killed her."

"Didn't happen."

"Then tell me what did happen."

"I don't know, but I think I know who killed her."

"Tell me Mr. Detective, who do you think killed Laura?"

"George. Or at least George had her killed."

"Why do you think George Summerland killed your girlfriend?"

"I don't know the why, but I think I heard him plan the murder."

"You heard George kill Laura?"

"Yes. No." Chuck rubbed the back of his head. Padilla was pushing, hammering the point to get him to trip up. He knew the routine but why, what lie did someone say to put the pressure on him?

"George has a habitual phrase that he uses. He begins or ends sentences with, one-hundred percent. I've never heard anyone else use that phrase. One of the guys I heard on the scanner used it several times, just like George would have answered. I have some conversations on tape."

"You mean like someone who ends every sentence's with, you know or trust me?"

"Exactly."

"How did George kill Laura when he was at home

with his wife?"

"He wasn't home with Angela."

"That's not what Angela Summerland said in a statement."

"That's a damn lie."

The door opened and one of the officers who'd searched Chuck's house motioned that he needed to talk to Padilla.

Chuck couldn't believe Angela would sell him out. But the pithy look on Padilla's face said otherwise.

Long minutes later Padilla returned, closed the door to the interrogation room and sat on the corner of the table.

"There was no towel in your truck. What do you think happened to the towel?"

"I have no idea. Last time I remember using it was when I worked on the battery in Laura's BMW."

"Does anyone else have access to your truck?"

"I told you, the trucks never locked, so what do you think?" Chuck shot back.

Padilla nodded.

"Here's the deal. Your gun didn't match the one we're looking for."

"Laura wasn't shot. What the hell is this about?"

"We got a call, said you had a gun that would match an unsolved murder. We were also told that the gun that belonged to a dead bank guard would be found at your house."

Holy Shit. Only George and Angela knew about the gun. Why would one of them be trying to frame him?

"So you jumped to conclusions and decide to act like the tough detective and prove I'm guilty. The answer is no, I don't have any other guns. Is anyone behind that two-way mirror?" Chuck asked.

"Not now. Look I got orders to push you. Right now my opinion isn't worth two plug nickels. Watch your back and don't talk to anyone."

"Which cop at my house is reporting your actions to the brass?"

Padilla winced.

"I'm not sure, but someone saw us at the restaurant last night. And it was reported that we talked over breakfast at the Ten Seven Café."

"What about the conversations I recorded?"

"Do you have proof it was George?"

Chuck tilted his head back and stared at the water stained ceiling.

"Shit. Patterns of speech and lying about the business cards fall under circumstantial evidence. I recognized the phrase as George's favorite but no matter how hard I've tried I can't totally convince myself it was him talking."

"You're free to go, but don't leave town. If you come across something be careful. Someone is trying to pin a murder on you."

"Five minutes ago your boss had me branded as the killer. What changed his mind?"

Padilla opened the door.

"Call if you think of anything that would help."

"What about the towels?"

"Consider them under arrest."

Outside Chuck took a couple of deep breaths and pulled the cellphone out of his breast pocket.

"Angela, can you pick me up? I'm at the North East

Police Station."

He nodded to a couple of cops as they passed him.

"Twenty minutes. Thanks, I'll be out front."

They were seated in his living room before Chuck broke his silence.

"Why the hell did you tell the police that George was with you the night Laura was killed?"

"What are you talking about? A police officer questioned me about my marriage and asked to count my monogrammed towels. You were never mentioned. Nor was I asked if George was home the night of the murders. I told you that."

"According to Detective Padilla, you gave George an alibi for the time of the murder."

"Chuck, I swear, I haven't talked to any detective or been questioned about a murder or you."

"Why should I believe you? Tell me why?"

"Because if I wanted to screw you over, I could have told George we were screwing like bunny rabbits. Why would I give my cheating husband an alibi?"

Chuck sank into the recliner and closed his eyes until his temper cooled.

"Do you believe me?" Angela sat on the couch with her knees drawn up to her chest. She looked ready to cry.

"I believe you." Padilla's warning that someone was setting him up for a fall made more sense. Padilla knew something. The question was what.

"You took the companies old business cards home to

make flash cards to teach your niece her multiplication tables. Do you have any of them lying around the house?"

"A few, they're in my craft room. Why?"

"One of the old cards was found at Laura's house. She managed the Westlake apartments for two years. The time frame is close to when I changed cards. It's possible she applied for a job at Superior, but I think I would have remembered that."

"She could have picked up a job application when you were out of the office. The business cards are attached to the application."

"Padilla won't accept that simple of an answer."

"Why not?"

"There weren't any staple holes on the card."

"You think George met her at a bar, handed her a card and gave her a line about being the apartment manager?"

"The thought crossed my mind."

"You really think George is involved in murder?"

"I honestly don't know what to think. George gave notice this morning."

"He told me last night that he'd found another job."

"Then why tell me you didn't know?"

"I don't know."

"You don't seem upset about him accepting a job in Illinois."

"He told me the job was here. What a prick. He set you up to tell me that part. I won't go with him. I suppose he knows that."

Chuck decided not to offer that George planned to make the move solo.

He looked at his watch and swore.

"Angela I'm sorry, but I need to get back to the office."

"Do you believe me when I say the detective lied? I wouldn't hurt you."

"I believe you."

Chapter 31

Detective Padilla pulled his unmarked police car to a stop.

It was two in the afternoon. Kids were at school and parents at work. The neighborhood looked deserted.

He took the sidewalk that bisected a freshly mowed lawn.

The house was painted celery green with a forest green and white trim. Flowers lined the flowerbed and fresh mulch kept the weeds out.

His knuckles rapped the forest green door.

The female who answered the door was five-five and slim. Except for laugh lines fanning out from the corners of her eyes her skin was smooth and makeup free. Her light brown hair was braided and pinned up like a crown on her head. She wore black leggings and a loose fitting golden yellow top that stopped at mid-thigh.

Her smile was genuine and her cinnamon brown eyes danced with mischief as she took him in.

"Hi, I'm Princess Leia. Who are you?"

"I'm Detective Padilla. I'm a friend of Chuck Taylor's."

"I don't know anyone by that name."

Jim frowned.

"Your neighbor in the white house."

"Oh you mean my brother Luke Skywalker. Chuck Taylor is an alias he uses. Has he gotten himself in trouble, again?"

"Again? When was the last time?"

"Luke commands a fighter squadron for the Rebel Alliance. A few weeks ago he had a nasty encounter with a Wampa. He was lucky to walk away with only a black eye and a swollen nose."

"Do you live here alone?"

"I live with my parents Bail and Breha Organa."

"Are they home?"

"They went to Holt to do some shopping."

"Do you have a key to C...Luke's house?"

"Is Luke in trouble?" She asked without answering the question.

"Not at all. How often do you visit Luke's house?"

"Whenever I want. He bought a new television so I could watch movies on a large screen. It's like sitting in a theater."

"Do you do anything besides watch movies?"

"I make sure my brother is comfortable. Please don't tell Luke that, it would embarrass him if he knew I fussed over his creature comforts."

"Do you mind telling me what you do to help make his life comfortable?"

"I straighten things around the house. Put fresh flowers from the garden in the vase on the table. Sometimes I cook and set it in the oven so he has a hot meal when he comes home, just little things."

"Your secret is safe with me. Thank you for talking

to me Princess Leia."

Padilla pulled a business card out of his breast pocket and handed it to Leia. "When your parents return would you please ask them to call me?" He stepped off the porch and headed down the sidewalk.

"Detective."

Padilla turned.

"Yes."

"You remind me of my husband, Han Solo. Have you met him?"

"No Princess Leia I haven't had the pleasure."

The squeal of kids playing in the pool drifted through the office window.

The tantalizing aroma of a barbeque grill made Chuck's stomach rumble.

Hunched over the computer, he finished entering the rent payments. He'd just shut down the computer when the office door opened and Roberto entered.

"Why are you still here?"

"There's water damage in J-6."

Chuck frowned.

"That's the vacant unit?"

"It is. Mr. Jenkins in J-5 was on his way here when he saw Frank and told him the door to J-6 was open."

Shit. "Anyone inside?" Chuck asked.

"No."

"Did you see anyone near the unit?"

"No."

"How bad is the damage?"

"Not bad. Someone plugged the kitchen sink and turned the faucet on. We got the water mopped up. The kitchen and dining room will need a little touch-up paint and maybe new baseboards."

The empty unit had been cleaned and rented. He expected the couple to start moving in over the weekend.

It wasn't an accident, but why, it didn't make sense.

"Thanks, for taking care of the mess. You and Frank headed home?"

"Frank said something about talking to Kelly. I'm headed home."

Chuck finished the bank deposit, and put the late payments received in the small safe bolted to the floor inside a cabinet in the storage room. He still didn't understand why people insisted on paying cash.

Chapter 32

Chuck opened a glass door and stepped into the North East Police station. It was a different station then the one he was interrogated at.

The foyer was cramped and smelled of disinfectant and floor polish. If someone wanted to sit and stare at the black and white wanted posters tacked to dingy gray walls, two wire framed blue chairs filled the need.

A large black lady with frizzy hair and inch long Christmas red fingernails sat behind a glass partition. A cell phone was pressed to her ear.

He stood at the window and listened to her gripe about a no good husband.

"Do you mind?"

"Mind what?" Chuck asked.

"I'm on the phone."

"So I heard. Since your soliciting advice, here's mine, kick the lazy bum out and your problems will be solved."

The ladies nostrils flared. "Look, Dear Abby, you want to file a report take a number or get online." He placed his hand on the glass so she couldn't shut the sliding window.

"The number dispenser is empty and I don't have a computer." The lie easily slipped off his tongue.

"Borrow your neighbors or go to the library."

"Since when can't you file a report at the Police station?"

"Sir, I don't make the policies."

"You're telling me that an agency that is supposed to serve the public has a policy to refuse service to people unless they file a report online?"

"You heard correctly."

"Are you shitin' me because you'd rather talk about a deadbeat husband than actually do the work you're being paid to do?"

"Sir, remove your hand from the window."

"I'm not here to file a report. I need to talk to Detective Padilla. I was told he was here."

"You can contact him online or call the non-emergency number and leave a contact number."

"This is the address on his business card. Does he work here or not?"

"I'm not allowed to release that information."

"So if you can't do anything why are you here? A sign that reads 'no service, go online and don't hold your breath while you wait for a call' would save the tax payers money."

"Sir, I don't like your attitude. I'll have an officer meet you outside."

"Are you going to e-mail him?" Chuck was halfway to the door when two officers entered.

"Is there a problem here?" The officer was young, a tough looking blonde with a cocky smile. His name tag said Fletcher.

TMI   Grindstaff & Plummer

"No problem. I want to talk to Detective Padilla. You want to let him know I'm here?" Chuck shot back.

"Why don't you come to the back and we'll discuss the problem?"

Fletcher opened a thick metal door that led into a wide hallway. The floors service brown industrial linoleum was worn and chipped at the edges. The lower half of the walls, were painted lime green. The upper half was white. Like family photos documenting a life time, eight-by-ten missing children bulletins lined the wall.

Fletcher ushered him into a small oblong room with a sturdy oak table and four straight-back oak chairs.

"Look, I came in to talk to Detective Padilla. The office bulldog won't let him know I'm here. End of story."

"You think causing a disturbance will get you in to see Detective Padilla?" Fletcher said.

"What disturbance. The bulldog was using work time to make a personal call and got testy when she had to cut her conversation short. All I want to do is talk to Detective Padilla."

"Do you have a driver's license or another form of ID on you?" The second cop, a lanky Hispanic asked. His name tag said Rodriquez.

Chuck started to reach for his back pocket.

Rodriquez grabbed his arm. "Sir, don't reach into your pockets."

"What the hell?"

"Sir, you need to cooperate," Fletcher sneered and rested the palm of his hand on the butt of gun clipped to his belt.

"I am cooperating. You asked for ID. Unless you plan to cop a feel, I need to use my hand to remove the wallet from the pocket."

Rodriquez jutted out his chin towards Fletcher. "Have a seat and keep your hands out of your pockets. Do you have a gun, knives or needles on your person?"

Chuck sat. "Why the hell would I? If you treat everyone that walks in like this, I'm surprised there aren't more letters to the editor complaints about police stupidity. Do us both a favor, get Detective Padilla."

"Sir, this is for your safety," Rodriquez said.

"Safety? You guys are nuts. If I'm not under arrest, I'm leaving."

"Sir, remain seated," Fletcher warned.

Rodriquez gave his partner a look that stopped Fletcher cold. They walked into the hall and left the door open.

The chair was hard and cold, but not as chilly as the atmosphere and the attitudes of the officers and the receptionist.

Padilla walked past the open door, did a double take and stopped.

"What the hell are you doing here?"

"Good question."

Chuck stuck his head out the door and looked down the hall.

"Ask the blonde bozo with the attitude talking to the bulldog at the front desk. You'd think it was a crime to ask to speak to you."

"You should have called or sent me an email."

"What the hell happened to serve and protect?"

Fletcher walked into the room and folded his arms

across his chest.

"He was causing a disturbance. Mouthed off to Madeline and threatened us."

"Threatened you with what?"

Padilla cleared his throat.

Chuck followed the order and fell silent.

"What did he threaten you with?" Padilla demanded.

Fletcher stewed.

Rodriquez didn't comment.

"Chuck, follow me." Madeline stood in the hall. Her fat fleshy arms crossed under a heavy bosom that heaved with each breath.

"Madeline, Chuck's a friend. Next time buzz him through."

"After that damned interrogation you put me through, I'm delighted to know we're now bosom buddies." Chuck hissed as he followed Padilla down the poorly lit hall.

"Don't push your luck. I can leave you with the bozos and let them book you."

"I appreciate you intervention, friend."

"What brought you here this morning?"

"I heard something that I thought you needed to hear."

"On the scanner?" Padilla asked with little interest.

"Yeah."

"About Laura's murder?" Padilla asked.

"No, I imagine the chance of hearing someone confess to murder would be listed under, fat chance in hell or in your dreams," Chuck said.

"But you taped someone planning a murder."

"But no murders occurred." Chuck said.

"You don't know that for certain."

That made Chuck pause.

"You think the men hid their real agenda under a subterfuge of words, but they weren't smart enough not to talk about a murder on a phone that could be listened to on a scanner?"

"No one said a murderer is smart."

Padilla opened a scuffed white door and they stepped into a small cluttered, windowless office. The walls were gray or maybe dingy blue. A scratched and dented metal desk looked ready to collapse under the weight of neatly stacked files and an outdated computer.

"How the hell do you get any work done in here?"

"I don't." Padilla answered with a grin. "What was so important that you battled with Madeline to talk to me?"

"I heard talk about a stash house."

"They actually called it a stash house?"

Chuck rubbed the back of his neck. "Not exactly."

"Did you ever think that ninety-nine percent of what you hear on the scanner could be bullshit?"

"I'll keep that in mind the next time I hear a gal have a dozen orgasms during phone sex."

"Sounds like overkill." Padilla said with a straight face. "Tell me about the call."

"Two men talked about a drop, said the cash would be available on delivery and gave an address. I decided to check the place out."

"Of course you did!"

Chuck chuckled.

"You sound like my old commanding officer."

"What was the address?" Padilla asked.

Chuck handed him a piece of paper with the address.

"The yard's full of old newspapers, mailbox is stuffed full of junk mail. The place looks unoccupied but there's a path worn through the weeds to the front door."

"That doesn't mean it's a stash house."

"True, but I decided to do a little surveillance work."

"Did the shiner teach you anything?"

"Yeah, it was a reminder to stay out of striking distance unless I'm prepared to do battle."

"Chuck if this is a stash house the guys won't use fists they'll use guns, fit with silencers."

"You're full of cheery opinions, but you have a point."

"Did you enter the house or stay in your truck?"

"I parked three doors down from the house, between pickups that were as beat-up as mine."

"That's hard to believe," Padilla said.

"At half past two this morning, a black extended cab Ford truck with a custom made shell parked at the curb in front of the house. The driver and a passenger dragged seven large black plastic wrapped bundles into the house. I took pictures with a digital camera." He reached into his pants pocket. "Here's the memory stick."

Padilla slipped the disc into his breast pocket.

"One of your tech boys will be able to lighten the shots and get a good ID and the license plate of the truck."

"That was dangerous and stupid but thanks."

"Not near as dangerous as walking in here." Chuck said as they left the office.

Chapter 33

"All units in the area, five, zero, zero Dyer, shots fired robbery in progress. Unit responding?

"North 34, North 17 two blocks away, North 22 from station, Chief 4 from station, Constable 2 from Dyer and McCombs.

"All units responding, be advised, rp states suspect down.

"Chief 4, did you say suspect down?

"Affirmative, suspect down."

Chuck slipped into his jogging shoes, pocketed the scanner, clipped the leash on Runner and headed down the street at a slow jog.

Taking side streets and cutting through a small park they'd jogged about a mile when a line of police cars and emergency vehicles came into view.

Chuck slowed to a walk, caught his breath and shortened Runners leash.

He spotted Padilla's battered, half dead Ford double parked next to a four door silver Escalade. Leaning against the Ford's passenger door he crossed his arms and watched.

Minutes later Detective Padilla, with hands jammed

into his pockets, glared at Chuck.

"You just happened to be out for a walk and come across the scene of a murder?"

The scanner in Chucks pocket spit out a request for assistance at the scene of a three vehicle accident.

"That scanner isn't good for your health."

"The jog here was healthy."

"Why the hell are you here?"

"We're buddies." Chuck said with a devilish smile.

"Think of this as show and tell, I wanted to see you at work."

"I'm touched. Now get the hell out of my sight Luke Skywalker."

"You upset that Princess Leia didn't mistake you for Hans Solo?"

"How do you know she didn't?"

"She told me a powerful Jedi Knight visited and asked questions about me. She described you, right down to the crescent shaped scar on your left hand."

"You could have warned me."

"You have to experience Leia to understand her. Don't you need to get back to work," Chuck asked.

"He's not going anywhere. When Leia introduced herself, I thought she was pulling my leg."

Chuck nodded. "You wouldn't be the first to think that."

"How long has she lived in her own world?"

"That's hard to pinpoint. Leia's a year younger than me. As a kid she had a phenomenal imagination that got us in a lot of trouble because I never could tell her no. She was comfortable at my house, but she wouldn't play with other kids on the block. In public she'd stare at her feet and refused to talk. Her parents put it down to extreme shyness."

"Is her name really Leia?"

"It's Marsha, but she won't answer to that name."

"Did she attend school?"

"Within days of starting kindergarten she stopped talking and drew into herself. The diagnosis was autism, which she probably had all along."

"But she's educated," Padilla insisted.

"Until I reached high school my grandmother home schooled both of us. Leia has a high school diploma and a couple hundred credits from online college courses."

"What type of college classes?" Padilla asked.

"Mainly astrology, mythology, and political science classes," Chuck said.

"What caused her to retreat into her own world?"

"No one knows. She got a cold that turned into pneumonia. Her temperature spiked, and she spent a month in a coma. When she came out of the coma she became fixated on the Star Wars movies."

"When did Leia decide you were Luke Skywalker?"

"When we came home for my mother's funeral, Leia called me Skywalker. My wife was Queen Padme. Carrie is Leia's daughter Janie."

"Wasn't Queen Padme the mother of Luke and Leia?"

"She was, but that type of logic isn't a part of Leia's world. If she doesn't accept you, you don't exist, or you become one of the evil forces traveling the universe."

"She asked me if I knew her husband. Who has she selected as Hans Solo?"

"One of her doctors," Chuck said.

"I talked to Leia's parents." Padilla said. "They're not sure she has enough focus with reality to be questioned. Do you agree with that?"

"Questioned about what?"

"A week ago a woman with Princess Leia's distinct earmuff hairstyle was sighted in a car outside a liquor store."

"Bob mentioned that after Leia had been to a doctor appointment they stopped at the deli. He said they parked directly in front of the store so Leia could see them through the window, and not panic at being left alone in the car. He told me they'd been lucky and left minutes before the shooting."

"A witness and her four year old daughter saw Leia as they cut through two cars to get to the sidewalk. The woman placed her order then sat at a table by the deli's front window. Her daughter distracted her, but she saw a black guy look in Leia's direction. Her daughter and Leia waved at each other as the car pulled out of the parking place. Less than a minute later the first shotgun blast was heard."

"Did you ask Bob and Cathy to let you interview Leia?"

"Before I talked to them, I wanted to ask you if it would be a waste of time."

Chuck watched a gurney holding a black body bag get loaded into the back of a coroner's wagon and pull away from the curb.

"Leia isn't retarded, mentally slow, emotionally unstable, or any other label society wants to use for different. She is highly intelligent, articulate and under the gloss of fantasy Leia can discuss what happens in her life. But to get that information she can't be pressured."

"Is that a warning to back off, or I'll see what I can do to help you?"

"Both," Chuck answered.

"When you had me at the station you said someone told you I had a gun that could be traced to a murder. Is that the murder you meant?"

"No, they mentioned an open case from early last year.

"Did the caller leave a name or was the tip anonymous?"

"Anonymous," Padilla said.

"Can you tell me about the murder?"

"Not much. A female body found by the shooting range."

"I remember that. Angela refused to go near the place for a couple of months. How old was the woman?"

"Twenty-three years old, with two priors for selling drugs."

"Did you get the name of her pimp?"

"She wasn't hooking and wasn't a user."

"Are you saying she was connected to a drug lord?"

"That's a possible. Also possible she was a girlfriend to someone with connections."

"Someone who knows me?" Chuck said.

"That thought crossed my mind," Padilla said. "Tell me again about your employees."

"What I know or what I suspect?"

"Let's start with facts," Padilla said.

"George Summerland, age forty-four, married to Angela Summerland, no children. Two years employment. Steady worker. He resents working for anyone. Former Army MP. If I was under fire I'd want him covering my back."

"I thought George was in the Air Force," Padilla said.

"No. Maybe he did a detail at the Air Base, but he was Army."

"Interesting." Padilla made a note and nodded." Okay, continue."

"Hector Gomez, age thirty-six, married to Ilene Gomez, three daughters between the age of five and ten. Two years employment. Steady worker, has a temper but knows how to control it.

"Roberto Sanchez, age twenty-two. Hired a little over a year. Has a warped sense of humor that gets him in trouble. Comes from a large family and no matter what, he doesn't cross his mother. Damn good at his job, but unless he learns to keep his mouth shut he'll never hold a job with a future.

"Frank Hanson, age forty-nine, divorced. Hired two months ago. Does his job. Not a big talker, he works to fit in with the crew. Retired Army."

"Now tell me about George and his wife," Padilla said.

"Put that way, I'm not sure what to say."

"Try," Padilla ground out.

"Angela is a flirt. We met about three years ago. No hanky-panky, but from some of the flirting anyone not knowing the situation could jump to a different conclusion."

"George knows the truth?"

"You asked that once before. He knows. I've made that very clear. If George got upset at every guy Angela flirts with, he'd suspect she was sleeping with every guy in town."

"How's the marriage holding up?"

"It's not. George just gave notice. He's moving to Illinois. Angela say's she's staying here. For a time I thought George was physically abusing her. But I think that's wrong."

"What made you change your mind?"

"Bits of conversations and the way George withdraws rather than becoming violent when his temper flares. Could be wrong, but I think Angela is the aggressor. If my theory is correct, while trying to calm her George leaves bruises that make it look like he's the abuser."

"How out of hand is his drinking?"

"I've never seen George drunk or arrive at work with a hangover. I'm not saying he doesn't have a problem, but the only one who mentions his drinking is Angela."

"You said you thought George killed Laura or had her killed. You still think that?"

"No, it doesn't add up. I can't imagine anyone copying George's habit of saying, one hundred percent, but the only other possibility would be someone trying to set him up. Trying to setup both of us makes less sense."

"The person who pointed a finger at you called the police. It could be that the people making the phone calls hope you'll point a finger at George."

"That would mean the first conversations weren't staged and they know I overheard them talk."

"It would. Who knows you heard the conversations?"

"I told the guys the morning after I heard the men talk a second time. George told Angela. Roberto probably told everyone in his family. So a few hundred people; give or take."

"Why'd you shoot off your mouth?"

"I was teetering between what I heard being a joke or fact. I wanted someone else's impression before I played Chicken Little and called the cops."

"What was the consensus?"

"Wait. Call the cops only if I heard another conversation. Which I did. The cop who took the call acted like I was an idiot and said to call back when the murder was fact not fiction."

"How many conversations had the talker using the phrase, one hundred percent?"

"I don't know. Not every conversation was recorded, but the phrase wasn't used every time."

"Have you discussed every conversation you overheard?"

Chuck let the leash out so Runner could sniff some bushes.

"I didn't mention every one and haven't mentioned any of them since Laura was killed."

"Keep it that way," Padilla said.

"I talked to Angela. She used the old business cards for a family project. There are some leftover but they're stored in a craft room that I seriously doubt George has ever stepped inside. You questioned Angela about monogrammed towels. What was that about?"

"Can't answer that," Padilla said.

"Angela denies telling you or any other cop that George was home the night of the murder."

"Can't discuss that, either," Padilla said.

"You ever think your job sucks?"

"I've had that impression a few times."

"I searched online for information on matching voice waves. The new technology is impressive. Can you use the tape to match it with a suspect?"

"The costs are too high. After an arrest we can run the test to help nail a conviction. Tell me your impressions on Hector?"

"I believe he knows more about Anna Marie's death then he claims."

"Was he ever in a gang?"

"Not that I know. Might mean nothing, but he's vocal about the stupidity of scarring the body with tattoos."

"Have you ever seen him naked?"

"He's not my type."

Padilla snorted.

"He keeps swim trunks in his truck so he can cool off in the pool. Unless there's something on his ass, his body's clean."

"Okay what else?"

"I've overheard a few conversations that make me think he has connections in Mexico that go beyond family. Nothing specific; just a gut feeling. Last year I was invited to his house for a Day of the Dead Celebration. The place was clean and nicely furnished, but nothing beyond what he can afford on his pay."

"Is he green card or citizen?"

"He's mentioned being the third generation to be born here. His wife has an aunt and uncle, and several nieces, just over the border that they visit regularly."

"Okay, tell me your impressions of Frank."

"Not much. He's quiet, but he sees everything. He was laid off from a computer company that had a contract with one of the bases. He's a good handy man, but he's never done any construction. He's sniffing around one of the tenants, but from comments Hector's made, I get the impression he makes the rounds to some of the tit and ass bars."

"What's his connection with Hector?"

"At some point in the past they were neighbors and frequented the same bar. The story I got was they ran into each other, Frank mentioned looking for work and Hector told me. I think if he gets offered a job in the computer field, he'll be gone the next day."

"Have you fire anyone recently?"

"A doper walked before he had a chance to donate a sample of blood. That was over a year ago."

Padilla nodded to a uniformed officer who had stepped out of the house and looked their way.

"You think of anything else. Give me a call," Padilla called over his shoulder.

Chapter 34

Leia stood beside a picnic table painted grass green. Her brown eyes, filled with mischief, mirrored those of the older gentleman with steel gray hair that stood next to her.

"Detective Padilla, how nice to see you again." Leia extended her hand for a firm handshake. "Who is the lovely woman with you?"

"Nancy, my wife."

When Chuck finished the formal introductions for Leia's parents, and Nancy and Jim Padilla, Nancy turned to Leia and her mother. "Thank you for inviting us to join your Sunday afternoon barbeque."

"It's always nice to meet friends of Luke's." Leia said pleasantly but with a hint of reserve.

The meal of grilled chicken and corn on the cob was accompanied by two salads and brownies covered with a thick layer of cream cheese frosting.

The men gravitated towards discussions about baseball and the latest trades and merits of paying million dollar salaries to football players.

But Jim kept half an ear tuned to his wife as Nancy coaxed Leia into a discussion about her favorite subject, politics. As the leader and administrator of the New Rebel Alliance Base Leia had strong opinions about what constituted sound decisions and what would lead to war. The names she used for the players were real, at times her descriptions of political personalities were comical and insightful. The political arenas, in Leia's mind, were worlds scattered across a star studded galaxy.

"On my last visit into town, on market day, I was disheartened to see two Sith Warriors openly carry light sabers," Leia said.

"Did you lecture the men, like you do me when you think I'm stepping out of line?" Chuck asked into the sudden silence.

"No." Leia said with a haughty huff. "I was in no mood to confront cocky hoodlums."

"You have fun confronting me," Chuck said and gave her a wink.

"You I know how to handle. Besides if you don't listen to reason, when Hans returns he can be persuaded to knock reason into your thick skull."

What makes you think they were cocky?" Instead of his normal snarly cop tone, Padilla tried to make his voice sound merely curious.

"The way they walked down the sidewalk, like they owned the world."

"That's not cocky, that's confidence. If you could see yourself when you enter a room, you'd see the same confidence."

Chuck spoke as if this was something they'd discussed in the past, Padilla thought.

"When I enter a chamber to attend a meeting, I need

to show confidence. These men were different."

She paused, and Padilla feared that would be the end of the conversation.

"Were the men well-dressed handsome warriors?" Chuck asked.

"I'm a married woman," Leia stammered.

"So are Nancy and Breha, but if I walked down the street, and they didn't know me, they'd take a second look at my handsome face," Chuck said.

Leia giggled.

"Promise not to tell Hans what I say?"

"We promise," Leia's father answered.

"The men were like salt and pepper; one darkly handsome next to the buttermilk complexion of his companion. That is what made me look and then I couldn't tear my eyes away."

"Were they tall or short?" Chuck asked.

"They were a little taller then you. The light skinned warrior had blue eyes, the same shade as yours. The other warrior's eyes were black as a moonless night. Both of them had wide square shoulders like Hans."

"Leia, how could you see the color of the warrior's eyes?" Leia's father asked.

"They ambled down the center of the sidewalk like they would knock down anyone in their way. When they reached the transport vehicle next to ours they stopped and slowly turned full circles like they were expecting to see someone."

Or doing surveillance to see if they needed to take out witnesses, Padilla thought.

"Did they see you?" Padilla asked.

"Oh yes. The pale skinned warrior bent over the

window and looked at me. I smiled and waved." She wiggled four fingers to demonstrate.

"Leia the men were Silt Warriors, why would you wave?" Chuck asked.

"When I was captured and enslaved, I learned not to show fear in the face of the enemy."

"Very smart and quick thinking," Padilla said, and shot Chuck a warning shake of his head. "After you waved to the man what did he do?"

"He walked back to the dark warrior. They stood facing each other and talked. A few times they glanced at our transport vehicle. The dark skinned man looked mad, but the blonde shrugged and walked away."

"Where did the light skinned warrior go?"

"He walked to the door of the store and waited until his friend joined him. Then they walked inside."

"What type of clothing does a Sith Warrior wear?" Padilla asked.

"They were dressed in black and wore light weight black jackets that brushed their thighs. The letters SWAT were on the back of the jackets in white."

All three men sucked in a breath.

"Besides the color of their skin can you describe the men?" Chuck asked.

Leia cocked her head.

"The dark warrior had short black hair, a high forehead, thick brows, deep set large eyes, a long straight nose and full lips. His face was round and his neck was thick. A scar, like a bolt of lightning, was just above his right ear."

"Did you see any jewelry?" Padilla asked.

"Not on the dark warrior. The fair skinned warrior

wore a ring on his right hand. I saw it when he leaned on the window."

Padilla swallowed his excitement. "The fair skinned warrior, did he place his hand on the window?"

Leia nodded. "Like this," She spread her fingers and placed her hand flat on the picnic table. "That's why I saw the silver band. It was a snake or a dragon with a forked tongue and a red stone in the eye. It winked, the stone winked at me."

Light reflection, Padilla thought, and filed the information. "Can you describe the pale skinned warrior?"

"His hair was pale yellow and short like the dark skinned warrior. The forehead had long worry lines and more lines fanned out from his eyes. His nose was long and narrow at the nostrils. High cheekbones, a square jaw and a dent right here." She placed her finger in the center of her chin. "His eyes were beautiful, like a clear blue morning sky."

"Leia, you mentioned light sabers. When did you see them?" Chuck asked to break the silence that had fallen.

"When the light skinned warrior leaned over the window his jacket fell open. The light saber was under his jacket. Are you looking for the warriors?"

"Yes, we would like to talk to the warriors," Padilla said. "Your descriptions are a great help. Thank you."

"I am happy to help the Alliance. Now can you answer a question for me?"

"I'll try," Padilla said. He looked at Chuck and got a shrug.

"The two Sith Warriors I saw. Would it be reasonable to assume that you don't know what they look like?"

"It would."

"Excuse me please. I will return shortly." Leia stood and walked into the house.

Padilla looked at Leia's father. "Please make my day and say you haven't washed the car's windshield."

"I haven't," he said.

"You know who the men are?" Chuck asked.

"There have been a string of similar robberies in four states. No witnesses lived, but in one case a woman driving by saw two men enter a liquor store. Two things caught the woman's attention. They were wearing black coats with white letters on the back and one man was black and one so fair.

"SWAT is special weapons and tactics team. What are the chances the men are renegades?" Leia's father asked.

"Anything's possible. The letters could also be nothing more than tape put on the jackets in case something went wrong and they needed an excuse for being in the vicinity. What was said today goes no further. Later today I'll return with a fingerprint kit. No matter what, I promise you that Leia's name will never be written in any report."

"Thank you, for that," Leia's mother said.

Leia returned and offered a shy hesitant smile.

"The men I told you about were bold and intimidating. I don't like admitting that I was attracted to warriors, but their beauty intrigued me. There's a computer program that creates faces by selecting features and putting them together. One night, when I couldn't sleep, I did this. She placed the sheets of paper on the picnic table. These are not exact, but they are very close."

Chapter 35

Chuck opened the door and stepped aside.

"You look like hell. Is the news good or bad?"

"I just stopped next door to thank Leia again for her help and let them know the men have left the state," Padilla said.

"You know that how?"

"They left three dead in Enid, Oklahoma."

"Shit. When I think how close Leia was to those bastards my skin crawls. You want a beer?"

"Thanks, but I need to get back to the station."

"What can you tell me?"

"The pictures Leia created were almost dead on; it only took the computer a few hours to make a match. With the fingerprints we lifted from the handprint left on the window the case busted open. The men are brothers, same father, but different mothers. They applied and were accepted into the SWAT training. Halfway through the program they were kicked out."

"Who figured out they were loose cannons?"

"Don't have that information." Padilla glanced at his watch and swore.

"Tomorrow night Nancy and Amy are having a girl's

only night. If you're in the mood for a steak, I'll be at the Ranch House around seven."

Chuck sat at the kitchen table. Absently eating a ham and cheese sandwich and chips, he caught up on e-mails and paid the utility bills.

The quiet, that at one time had relaxed him, now made him feel isolated.

Since Laura's death, he'd been sucked back into life instead of sitting on the fringe watching others live their lives. Conversations with Padilla reminded him that people talked without using fuck as a possessive noun. And women wore sexy dresses and stilettos for Saturday night dates instead of Saturday night jobs.

He put a stamp on the phone bill and stood to get a beer.

The scanner beeped.

"This is one-hundred percent the last thing I need you to do."

Chuck pressed the recorder and forced himself to breathe.

"You said that the last time."

"I'll pay. You know I'm good for it."

"You haven't paid me for the last job."

"You'll get one-hundred percent of everything I owe you. I have it covered."

"Shit, put the money in my hand, then I'll believe you."

"I made sure he was too late to deposit the rent money. I'm hitting the office safe tonight."

"Tonight is the last deal. I expect payment tonight."

The scanner beeped. Chuck heard a girly giggle and another girl describe a boy's sloppy kiss.

He turned off the recorder and muttered, "Shit."

On the way out the door he called Padilla and left a message on his voice mail.

A sliver of light slipped through the edge of the blinds.

With his legs drawn up to his chest Chuck sat on the rock hard floor, beside a file cabinet that shielded him, but gave him a clear view of the front door.

An hour passed. Chuck resisted the urge to stretch his cramped legs and ease the pressure on his tailbone.

A key slid into the doors lock and the knob turned.

The sturdy frame of a man, silhouetted from a light in the parking lot stepped into the office and turned off the security alarm.

The pen light he held drew a weak pale yellow beam on the tan tiles.

His rubber soled shoes made a slight squeak as he passed the desk and stepped into the storage room.

Chuck stood. His knees popped. He froze and counted to ten before he hugged the wall and made his way to the storage room door.

The cupboard that held the company safe was open. The pen light, set on the floor, reflected a halo of light that bounced off the safe's matte gray surface.

The man held a shiny metal bar in his left hand and a hammer in his right. Chuck watched him tap the metal into the thin line between the door and the frame.

He counted the eleven solid taps it took to puncture a hole into the corner of the door. Then watched the man grab a crowbar set on top of the cabinet and fit it into the hole. With three solid blows from the hammer, the safe's door pealed open.

From the doorway Chuck said, "You surprise and disappoint me, Hector."

Hector turned and chuckled. "You surprised me, man. I didn't see you slip in here. I was really disappointed, thinking you hadn't gotten my message."

"You were the second guy on the scanner. Who's the other guy?"

Hector shook his head. "Stupid puto, you still don't get it."

"Then explain it to me."

"Who do you think killed Laura?"

"Are you taking credit?"

"Laura wasn't' my side fuck."

"But you know who killed her."

Hector shrugged.

"It's time to go."

"Until the police arrive I'm comfortable," Chuck said.

"You're too impulsive to think ahead. I set this trap, and you took the bait, just as I expected."

The hard nudge of gun barrel poked Chuck in the small of his back.

"Give Hector the gun or I'll pull the trigger." The woman's peppermint scented breath brushed the back of his neck.

"Hello, Kelly," Chuck said.

She nudged the gun deeper into his back. "You should have taken my offer to swap information for rent," she whispered next to his ear.

"Be nice and drop the gun, or I'll pull the trigger," she said louder.

Chuck dropped the gun.

"Good boy. Now kick it towards Hector," she purred.

Hector stuffed the gun into the waistband of his black jeans. Reaching inside the safe he pulled out the bank deposit bag, tossed it in the air, and gave a soft chuckle.

"You need a new safe, Boss. You should have bought one that doesn't open like a tin can."

"I'll be sure to remember that on Monday?"

"I wouldn't worry about that, Boss. You won't be working here come Monday."

"Meaning what?"

"It's time for me to get a promotion."

"The owner's not going to hire you as a manager," Chuck said evenly.

"If not me then Kelly, she can be very persuasive."

"Why do you want to manage the complex?"

"Opportunities, man. This place makes it easy to turn money."

"Why didn't you make me a proposition?"

Hector shook his head.

"You don't take orders well, man. Just like when I told you to stop listening to the scanner. Did you listen? You should have listened, Boss."

"What happens now?" Chuck asked.

"We're going for a ride. I have a little reception

planned for you and Angela."

"You told the detective, Bill Nelson that you were George. Why?"

"Opportunity, man. He interrupted me and Kelly having a discussion."

"Is that what you call trying to get into the companies files?"

"How'd you figure that out?"

"The third time you used an illegal password you tripped the system."

"Sometimes you surprise me and don't act so stupid," Hector said. "The detective assumed I was you, and said he needed to talk to George. I told him I was George and introduced Kelly as Angela. Stupid bastard didn't ask for identification."

"What did he want?"

"He said he was doing a follow-up on information another detective received. We told him we were home the evening Laura Cannon was murdered and never saw you. When I told you listening to a scanner wasn't smart, you should have paid attention," Hector said.

"The first two conversations I overheard about the murder were real?"

Even in the darkness Chuck saw the flicker of fear that flashed in Hector eyes.

"You never mentioned the first conversation. Maybe that's good, you would have been dead before we could build a cover-up."

"Who's really pulling the strings? It's not you or Kelly."

"No one you know. Too bad you tried to be the good guy and wanted advice on what to do with the information. When you recorded the other conversations you forced me to change my plans."

"You're the one who called in the anonymous tip about guns at my house."

"Not me, Boss. A friend owed me a favor."

"Laura wasn't shot so what good did that do you?"

"It made the detective working the case look like he wasn't doing his job."

"And it took the heat off you. Did you kill the woman found at the dump last year?"

"Shooting is messy work. I don't shoot people."

"But you know who did," Chuck said.

Hector shrugged.

"Who killed Anna Marie?"

"It was an unpleasant accident," Hector said.

"Who killed her?" Chuck asked again.

"Not me, but the situation needed to be dealt with immediately."

"If you didn't kill her why get involved?"

"I'm what you might call a cleaner. I clean-up messes before they become a problem."

"You drove here and put her body in the gutted unit. Did you hope to cause me problems with the police or was it an impulse decision?"

"I hoped it would make you nervous and get you to toss the scanner away. But you didn't cooperate."

"What about the vandalism. Was that you?"

"Now why would you think that?"

"Why not?"

"Anyone ever tell you that women get pissy when a guy turns down their favors?" Kelly's breath brushed across Chuck's neck.

"You damaged the unit because I wouldn't screw you?"

"I didn't give a damn about your dick."

"Then why the hell vandalize the place?"

"If you'd cooperated, you would have had some nice pictures to remember the moment. And we would have had access to the company computer."

"I understand the blackmail, but how would sabotaging the work accomplish that?"

"I would have called the owner and told them you'd admitted to me that you'd vandalized the job. After you were fired I would have applied for the management position."

"Why would I destroy property?"

"Who knows, doesn't matter anyway. You bought the scanner and heard Hector talking to…a friend. That made them really nervous, so they came up with a different plan."

"Free rent and a possible paycheck isn't enough reward for murder," Chuck said.

Chuck felt a shudder roll through Kelly's hand and shake the pistol pressed against his back.

"True, but your boss closed down a lucrative side business. There are people who weren't happy about that."

"Kelly, shut-up," Hector growled.

"Time to go for a ride. Boss, you do anything funny Kelly will shoot you in the back and I'll kill any witnesses."

Chuck knew his best bet was to overpower them before they reached the car and drove off.

Kelly nudged the barrel of the gun in his back.

"Please don't make me pull the trigger," Kelly whispered in Chuck's ear.

Hector opened the driver's door to a black town car Chuck had never seen. With a gun at his back, and Hector aiming one at his side Chuck got into the front the passenger seat.

With Kelly sitting directly behind Chuck, Hector pulled out of the parking lot.

The night was as silent as the inside of the car.

The car sailed through green lights as if they were royalty being granted easy passage through dark deserted streets.

Finally Hector slowed and turned into a familiar subdivision.

He parked, and waited for Kelly and Chuck to exist before he left the car and opened the kitchen door at George and Angela's house.

With the barrel of the gun, Kelly nudged Chuck into a large kitchen painted beige and decked out in shades of plum.

Chuck's military training and survival instincts had kicked into overdrive. The downstairs was too quiet, void of energy. Only the three of them occupied the floor. But the upper floor held the unknown.

"Where are George and Angela?"

"George will join us shortly. Angela wasn't feeling well. She's taking a little nap." Hector laughed at his joke.

"Sit," Hector commanded. "I'm sure Angela would want you to feel at home."

From the refrigerator, Hector pulled out three beers.

"Relax," he said and placed a can on the table in

front of Chuck.

A splash of light filled the living room then moved across the walls. A silver car Chuck didn't recognize rolled past the open drapes.

Two car doors slammed.

Seconds later the back door opened and slapped against the wall.

With Frank at his heels, George stumbled into the room.

A strip of gray duct tape secured George's hands together. Another band of tape held his arms tight against his torso. Above the strip of tape covering his mouth his nostril's flared. His brown black eyes were crazed with fear.

Frank pulled out a chair and pushed George against a shoulder until he collapsed onto the seat.

"What the hell is Chuck doing here?" Frank demanded.

"Just an added bonus for you to handle," Hector replied.

"No way!" Frank shouted.

"Think of it as payback for Chuck screwing your girlfriend," Hector said.

"What girlfriend?" Chuck demanded.

"You didn't know?" Hector chuckled. "Frank dated Laura."

Chuck looked at Frank, but he'd kept his eyes locked on Hector.

"Who killed Laura?" Chuck demanded.

"Does it matter? By the way Frank wants his television back," Hector said.

"You killed Laura because of a television?"

"Laura died because she ruined our plan," Hector said.

"What plan?"

"You're the one who couldn't control your girlfriend, so you tell him, Frank." Kelly's voice was an octave higher than normal. Sitting across from Chuck she kept glancing at the door as if she were gauging her chance of making a run and not getting shot in the back.

"When Laura's aunt died she was sole beneficiary to a house and the contents," Frank said. "I couldn't believe it when Laura said she didn't care about the money. She was going to keep a few sentimental items and give everything else away. Giving away three million dollars didn't make sense. Wanting to earn your living isn't noble, it's plain stupid."

"So you told Hector and came up with a scheme to steal the money?" Chuck asked.

"Taking what she was going to give away isn't stealing. It would have been a simple transfer of funds to people who would appreciate the generosity of the dead."

"You pressured Laura to marry you?" Chuck prompted.

"That was advice I should have refused."

"What was your plan?"

"I wanted to take her to Vegas, get her drunk and marry her. My signature for a quick divorce would have been the value of the estate. It would have worked and she'd still be alive."

"When she refused marriage what was the backup plan?"

"Laura was giving the house to a friend who runs a

woman's shelter. I advised her to talk to a financial adviser. Look at long term options that would create a continuous cash flow to help the shelter. We went to a lot of trouble to set up a meeting between her and a friend of Hector's that does off-shore investments," Frank said.

"You mean he fronts a fake financial firm that would advise Laura to invest a good portion of the money off-shore. But within a few months Laura would receive a letter saying the investment went bust," Chuck said.

Frank nodded. "It was a good plan, but she didn't like the man or Hector and told me to hit the road."

"Was the man behind the investment company the same one that did the investments for the owners of the apartments?"

"Too bad you're not so dumb after all," Hector said.

"Why did you kill her?"

"If she was married, and died without a will, the grieving widower can claim the estate."

"But you weren't married."

"A small detail that could be handled for a few dollars and a creative forgery," Hector said with a shrug.

"Who did you plan to set up for Laura's murder?" Chuck asked.

"George," Kelly answered.

George whimpered and fell out of the chair. With his legs tucked into his chest, he sobbed.

"Whimpering bastard," Hector muttered as he placed his pistol at George's temple. "Adios, asshole."

Hector smiled, looked at Chuck and pulled the trigger.

Chuck flinched.

Kelly screamed, jumped out of her seat and backed against the door. "Shit, did you have to do that in front of me?" Her voice wobbled and a glassy sheen glazed her eyes.

Hector offered Kelly a twisted smile.

"You should thank me, now you won't have to pretend you like him." He walked to the sink and washed his hands.

"Damn bullets are messy," he said as he wiped his hands on a kitchen towel. With a glance at George's lifeless body he laughed like a demented hyena.

"One-hundred percent perfect, Boss," he said and laughed louder.

Kelly stood with one hand squeezing the doorknob. Her pupils were dilated and her breathing shallow. In a trance, tears rolled down her cheeks as she silently stared at George's lifeless body.

Frank leaned against a counter. His face held no expression, but his eyes were glued on Hector.

"Why involve George?" Chuck asked in a voice that didn't match the thundering tempo of his heart rate.

"Why not? With his drinking and his military background he was an easy mark. Except for work there were no ties back to us."

"When I told you about the conversation on the scanner what changed?"

"We didn't know if you'd heard the full conversation and were toying with us. Not knowing forced us to revise our plan to draw your attention away from Laura. Angela is an unfaithful tease. It wouldn't be a stretch to make you believe he want to kill her. But you talked about the calls in front of George and never picked up on the words I threw in to make you think of George. That wasn't so smart, Boss," Hector said.

Hector was wrong, for a short time he had thought George was guilty and never seriously considered that the talkers were Hector or Frank. That was his fatal mistake.

"Who helped you? I think I would have recognized Frank's voice."

"Frank's not so good at disguising his voice. But my wife she's good at impersonating people. Maybe not so good over the scanner, but she does a good John Wayne," Hector said.

"You expected the cops to conclude that instead of killing Angela, George killed Laura. Why?"

"Cause he was hot for her and after she turned him down, she started sleeping with you. Ain't that right Kelly?"

Kelly swallowed but didn't take her eyes off the finger of blood that slowly crept under the table. "That's the story George told me when he was crying in his beer and sharing my bed."

"And my part in this scheme?" Chuck asked.

"I hadn't figured on you taping the dummy conversations. I watched one of those cop shows that used voice patterns to catch a killer. I don't think you'd have the balls to tell the cops you'd listened to cellphone conversations, but you became chummy with that Detective Padilla. We couldn't be sure you would keep your mouth shut. Now you have to pay for causing that problem."

"You think killing me will solve your problems?"

"Boss, you broke into the safe at work and stole the

rent money. You and Angela were going to run off together, but George walked in and it became a three way fucking messy murder. Get it?" Hector said and laughed.

Chuck did, and because Angela openly flirted it could be a believable story.

"Why would I break into a safe that I have a key to?"

"Think man. You want it to look like a burglary, Boss."

"If I'm getting ready to run off with Angela why would I care if the cops figure me for the burglary?"

"Maybe I didn't think that right, but it don't matter," Hector said with a, who gives a damn, shrug.

"What if I hadn't turned on the scanner this evening and heard you set me up?" Chuck asked.

"I'm on call tonight. If you hadn't arrived Kelly was going to call the answer service to report a stranger walking around the office. I would have called you to come back to the office."

"Frank, how the crap did you get involved in this insanity?"

"I'm sorry…"

"Frank don't be a wimp. You don't owe him an apology. I've done you big fucking favors. You owe me, man," Hector shouted.

"After buying people's silence you'll have what two maybe two and a half million dollars, and that's only if you get premium prices for the estate. Split three ways that's not a lot of money."

"But that's just the beginning," Kelly said more to herself than Chuck.

"Meaning?"

"Kelly, shut up," Hector growled. "Frank, take Chuck upstairs to join Angela. Kelly and I are headed to Chuck's place to pick up the tape. When we get back, I expect both of them to be dead."

Chuck studied Frank until the sound of the car engine turned over.

"Who killed Laura?"

"Hector."

"And because you can't see past a fist full of bills you let him. You make me sick."

"It wasn't like that. After I got back from the Gulf War I was messed up. Before I cleaned up my act, I got involved with some people. I saw things I shouldn't have seen. Hector helped me out. I'm paying back the debt."

"Hector's not generous." Chuck said. "With what you know, do you really believe he's going to let you ever walk away? One day your usefulness will have run its course, what then? You really think he'll let you live?"

"If Laura had listened to reason I would have convinced her to invest the money and she'd still be alive."

"Don't blame Laura for your stupidity."

"It's not my fault she got bitchy when Hector pointed out Kelly at a barbeque and told her I'd been screwing her on the side. Her damn righteous attitude is what got her killed."

"Don't you think Hector did that on purpose? Hector's playing you the same way he played me with the phony kill my wife calls."

Frank shifted and darted a glance out the window. He was too far away for Chuck to rush him without getting a bullet in his gut.

"Get up. We need to go upstairs and wake up sleeping beauty," Frank said.

Chuck stood, waited, Frank took one step, two, the third brought him within striking distance.

With murderous rage Chuck kicked out, but Frank twisted and his foot hit Frank's rock hard gut instead of the arm holding the pistol.

The gun fired.

Chunks of white ceiling plaster showered them.

Frank swung his arm wide to keep from falling.

Chuck drove the butt of his hand and wrist up Frank's chin and into his nose.

Cartilage broke. Blood gushed. Frank shook his head like a wet dog. Blood and spittle sprayed the walls. He spit teeth out like they were wads of paper.

Blind with rage, Frank swung wild. His fist connected with Chuck's mid-section.

Chuck sucked air and danced out of Frank's reach.

With a twist that popped a knee, Chuck did a one-two kick.

Frank arched backwards. The first kick missed, but the second kick glanced off his shoulder.

Pain shot through Chuck's knee. Using the pain to fuel his energy, he spun and landed a blow to Frank's midsection.

Frank's knees buckled. He landed hard and rolled.

The gun in his hand clattered to the floor, slid across cream colored tile and disappeared under a plant stand.

Frank pulled a knife from his boot. The curved blade flashed in the light. In one fluid motion he rolled to a stand and swung his arm in an arc.

Chuck jumped back but his reflexes were slow. He felt the warmth of blood trickle down his chest, but didn't take his eyes off the knife.

A deafening shot vibrated the windows.

Chuck dove beneath the table.

Paralyzed, Frank watched the blossoming flower of blood spread across his chest. A soft chuckle bubbled out, and he fell to his knees. He looked at Chuck, opened his mouth to speak, and collapsed like a rag doll.

Under the table, Chuck turned his head and saw Angela at the door leading into the dining room. A smoking pistol was in her right hand. Her rounded eyes were fixated on George.

Chuck stood and positioned himself to block the view of George's faceless body lying in a pool of blood.

He removed the gun from Angela's slack hand and set it on the counter.

"What happened?" She whispered.

"George. His face. Ohmigod."

Chuck caught her as she started to collapse.

"Where's a phone," he demanded.

"In the living room…or there's one there." In a daze she pointed to the counter.

Chuck picked up the phone. "The line's been cut. Where's your cellphone?"

Angela blinked. Her lips moved but no sound passed.

"Don't fall apart. Where's your cellphone?" Chuck snapped.

"In…upstairs, in my purse. What happened? Tell me what happened," she screeched.

Chuck grabbed the gun off the counter. Hector will

be back soon. We need to get upstairs and call the cops. While we wait I'll explain what I know."

With one arm around Angela's shoulders he led her towards the stairs.

Angela's bedroom wasn't what he expected. Done in red, black and purple it reminded him of someone's warped idea of a bordello.

Headlights shot across the bedroom window.

He went to the window and looked down onto the driveway.

"Shit. Hector's back. Where the hell's your purse?"

Angela stood at the doorway. With her arms hugging her waist she held a vacant stare.

Chuck shook her. "Sweetheart, you need to concentrate. Where's your purse?"

Her eyes darted to a table draped in red silk. "It's not here."

"Who knocked you out?" Chuck demanded.

"I…Frank and Kelly knocked on the door and said they needed to talk to me about George leaving. I…we sat at the living room and I served tea and cookies. I remember feeling lightheaded. I asked them to leave so I could lie down. That's the last thing I remember. When they brought me up here they must have taken my purse."

"I'm going downstairs. Don't follow me." Chuck ordered.

"Frank, where the fuck are you?" Hector screamed.

Chuck stopped, pressed his body against the wall and leaned his head around the corner. A light from the living room cast a long shadow across the floor.

A darker bulk loomed in the shadow.

"Hector, the cops are on their way. If you want to get out you'd best leave now."

"Where the hell is Frank?"

"He's in the kitchen keeping George company."

"Not good, Boss. I was looking forward to breaking his neck."

"Sorry to disappoint you."

"Fuck, if you had minded your own business none of this would have happened. Now I got to kill you and Angela. Guns are messy, gonna cause problems," Hector muttered.

"How was it really supposed to work, Hector?"

"George would be blamed for killing Laura. Angela would have been free to find another sap to pay her bills and I would be rich."

"I don't believe you. You planned on getting rid of Frank."

"Frank was starting to have a conscious. His whining like a bitch was getting on my nerves. After he eliminated George, he would have disappeared." Disgust filled with rage shook his voice as he spat each word out.

"You want to live?" Hector asked. "We could work it out. Blame Frank for everything. I keep the take and go home, and you go home and pretend you spent the evening watching television."

"What about Angela?"

"You took away my fun so I'll have fun breaking her pretty neck. Make it look like a lover's quarrel between Frank, George and her."

"It's not going to happen that way. If you drop the gun before the police arrive, you won't be charged with attempting to kill a police officer."

"I don't think so, Boss." Hector stepped out of the shadows, raised his arm and pulled the trigger.

A chunk of plaster hit Chuck in the eye. He ducked, blindly aimed his pistol towards where Hector had stood and fired.

A second shot whizzed past and slammed into the wall across from Chuck.

On his stomach Chuck held his breath and listened, eased forward, aimed and pulled the trigger.

Sitting he braced his back against the wall and wiped his eyes with the sleeve of his shirt.

The eerie silence that surrounded him was comforting.

He counted out a full minute before poking his head around the corner to look down the stairs.

Hector lay face down on the tile floor. A finger and leg twitched.

He walked down the stairs, stepped around the pool of blood staining the white tile and checked Hector's wrist for a pulse.

Satisfied, Chuck wiped his fingerprints off the pistol in his hand, pressed Hector's fingers around the handle and set the pistol on the tile next to the lifeless body.

"It's one-hundred percent, Hector. You lose."

"Chuck? Chuck? Are you okay?" Angela's voice trembled with fear.

He'd just killed two men and watched another die. What could he say that made sense?

"I'm fine Angela. Stay where you are."

"Is he dead?" She stood at the top of the stairs and peered down.

Before he could answer the front door swung open.

Three police officers, with guns drawn, entered the foyer.

"Drop the gun and get down on the floor." One of the officers yelled.

Chuck lifted his arms.

"I'm unarmed. There's a gun on the landing at the top of the stairs."

He glanced toward the stairs.

"Angela Summerland, the owner of the house, is halfway down the stairs. She isn't armed."

Detective Padilla walked into the foyer from the living room.

"Your timing sucks," Chuck said in welcome.

"It could have been worse."

Chuck lowered his arms.

"Yeah, it could have. How did you figure out where I was?"

"I was in a meeting when you called. When I listened to your message I headed to the apartments. Before I arrived I got a call from dispatch saying Princess Leia wanted to speak to me. When I called she said a man and woman had broken into your place. The man had just left but the woman was still there."

"Leia asked if Runner could stay with her tonight. Bob and Cathy are at a bridge tournament. Is she alright?"

"Nancy's with her. She's fine.

"When we arrived we found Kelly searching your cupboards. Leia won't be happy when she sees the mess," Padilla said.

"What brought you here?"

"Besides half a dozen phone calls reporting gunfire,

Kelly told us to head here before anyone else died."

"I'm surprised Kelly told you anything," Chuck muttered.

"I was a street cop when Kelly danced at a topless bar and offered lap dances for extra money. Kelly didn't remember me, but she's memorable. When another detective stopped by the apartments to do follow-up work Kelly posed as Angela Summerland. Faced with both of us at your place, she knew she wouldn't get a walking pass. She was happy to negotiate a deal in exchange for information."

Padilla pulled a cassette player out of his pants pocket. "Is this your recorder?"

"It is."

He handed the recorder to an officer. "Bag it as evidence and make sure to list the tape on the inventory sheet."

Chuck and Angela leaned against Padilla's unmarked car parked in the driveway.

Frank, George and Hector's bodies had been transported to the morgue.

Half a dozen city police cruisers were parked along the street and yellow and black crime tape cordoned off the property.

All but a handful of neighbors had returned to their home.

The local news stations hung in the background.

"Do I look as bad as you?" Angela asked.

Chuck looked at the light weight jacket Padilla had

given him to cover his blood stained shirt.

"You look like you faced the devil and survived. From where the news cameras are set up they can't see anything but the back of our heads."

"I'd forgotten about the cameras. I was looking at the blood on your hand and wondering who it belonged to."

"Don't go there, Sweetheart. It will drive you crazy and won't change anything."

"I loved him," Angela said.

"I know."

"What am I going to do now?"

"Take one day at a time. Weigh your options and build a new life."

"You make it sound easy."

Never that, Chuck thought.

Padilla walked out of the house and approached them.

He kept his voice low and his eyes on the cameraman across the street.

"Chuck, do you know where Hector was the day the bank was robbed?"

"He reported to work before I left for a meeting. He was working on an empty unit. If he needed supplies he could have left for awhile. Why?"

"The gun that belonged to the security guard at the bank had a horseshoe carved in the handle. The gun was next to Hector's body."

"Hector bragged that his cousin was one of the robbers," Chuck said.

Padilla nodded.

"Angela, I'm sorry about your husband. I know

you've given a statement, but tomorrow you'll need to give a taped statement. Is there someplace we can take you for what remains of the night?"

"Thank you. My parents are waiting across the street."

Chapter 36

Chuck watched an officer push a dolly into the backroom. After a few grunts, the dolly, loaded with the safe, was wheeled to a waiting van.

He'd given a formal statement to the police and a brief statement to the news media that clogged the street and hounded every person entering or leaving the complex.

His eyes were bloodshot and he'd drunk enough coffee to wire his nerves for the next round of questions from tenants and reporters.

Sitting at his desk he listened to an officer question Roberto.

Roberto kept shaking his head, but he was answering the officer's questions with a quiet reserve that impressed Chuck.

When the officer left, Roberto pulled a beer from the mini refrigerator and sucked it dry.

"I never had a clue, never saw or heard anything but their sexual bullshit. With what they did how could that be?"

"They knew what they were doing, and played their parts well. Don't second guess or kick yourself for not knowing something was off."

"Can you shrug it off that easily?"

Chuck rubbed the back of his neck and shook his head.

"Hell no, not today, or tomorrow, but eventually you'll put this behind you."

"I can't imagine forgetting this."

"You won't forget, but the impotency you feel will fade."

"You're sure about that?"

"Yeah, I'm sure," Chuck said with a sigh. "There's nothing you can do here today. Go home and find something to do that will take your mind off this."

"I need a few days," Roberto said and left.

"We're done here," an officer said as he followed two other officers out the door.

The sudden quiet was unnerving. Runner whined and nudged Chuck's hand with his cold nose. The dog hadn't left his side since he'd arrived home and surveyed the destruction Kelly left.

Rubbing the dog behind his ear, Chuck shuffled though the bullshit curiosity calls stacked on his desk and tossed them in the trashcan.

When the office door opened he was surprised to see Angela.

Dark circles framed sad brown eyes and her clothes looked like she'd slept in them.

Chuck stood and met her in the center of the room. Her arms circled his waist and her lush body sagged against his.

"Are you okay?"

"Yes. No. I'm confused and scared."

"That's understandable, Sweetheart."

"The cops are still at the house. Daddy drove me to the police station to answer more questions. I'm tired of talking. It's a nightmare I want to forget."

"Did you drive here alone?"

She shook her head.

"The newsmen, they don't mess with Daddy. He's outside waiting."

She stepped out of the embrace and walked to the window. "Last night, or this morning after we left the house, I've done a lot of thinking."

"And?" Chuck stood behind her and rubbed her tight shoulders.

"If George had moved to Chicago I would have gone with him."

Her shoulders hopped up in a slight shrug.

"Crazy I know; we couldn't live with each other or without each other. Now, I have no choice. There are things I'd like to do, and I've been given the freedom to do them."

"If you need me, you know how to reach me."

She turned, kissed both his cheeks then lightly brushed his lips with hers.

"You are a good man. But not the right man for me."

Angela took his hand and curled his fingers around an object.

"I didn't tell the cops that you'd had the pistol with the horseshoe. Someday maybe you'll tell me how you got it. But right now, I think you need a new good luck charm."

She kissed his cheek and walked out the door.

Chuck opened his hand and looked at the rabbit's

foot that dangled from a keychain.

Chapter 37

They sat in a corner booth at Ten Seven Café.

Mugs of steaming coffee and a half empty thermos were on the table.

"What will happen to Kelly?" Chuck asked.

"She's an accomplice to murder, she deserves to get fat and old in jail," Padilla said.

"From your scowl I'd say that's not going to happen." Chuck said after a sip of hot coffee that burnt his tongue.

"She'd be dead before the next sunrise," Padilla said.

"With Hector gone who wants her dead?"

"After you purchased the apartments did any of the renters talk to you about the former manager, or how rent was paid?"

"I heard comments about him being worthless and selling drugs on the side. Only twenty percent of the renters stayed past the first sixty days, but those that did paid the rent in cash."

"Drug money needs to be laundered. The easiest way is through a legitimate business or one that looks legitimate. Ones with large cash flows work nicely," Padilla said.

The waitress set two specials, bacon, eggs, a stack of pancakes and a single plate of toast on the table.

"You guys need anything else you holler."

Chuck slathered butter over the pancakes. "Besides redistributing wealth into their pockets, is that what the phony financial company was doing, laundering money through the companies they controlled for their investors?"

"It was," Padilla said.

"If Laura had agreed to sell everything she received from her aunts estate and invested the money with them, do you think they would have let her live?"

"I don't. The man Laura met at the Memorial Day party was Kelly's beneficiary. He's too important to the organization to be identified."

"You're talking about the guy who didn't talk to Laura or the other women?"

"I am. According to Kelly, Laura insulted him when she told the guy doing the talking that she wanted references. After they left the party she pointed out contradictory comments the guy made. Trying to cover his ass, Frank told Hector that Laura saw through the scam."

"What happens to Kelly?"

"As a thank you, she no longer exists."

"She'll be a hard person to hide."

"You'd be surprised what a little plastic surgery can do."

"She's six-foot without those five inch heels she likes to wear."

"Without her larger than life breasts, the heels and the spiked bottle red hair she won't be quite as memorable."

"Could work," Chuck said.

"She asked me to pass on a message. The gun in your back wasn't personal. She's sorry about the vandalism, but you hurt her feelings. She'll miss you."

"I'm touched."

"You should be, the gun she had wasn't loaded. If Hector had found out she'd removed the ammo it would have gotten her killed."

"Okay, I'll put her name on my Christmas card list. Did she tell you she asked a friend to try to get pictures of me in a compromising position for blackmail?"

"JJ Jones. They've been friends since they danced at the same topless bar. Kelly called the plan insurance. She also told me about you dumping JJ on her doorstep. They couldn't figure out how you connected them."

"Kelly has a distinctive voice. I overheard them talking on the scanner. Why did Kelly think she needed insurance?"

"When Kelly's benefactor insisted Laura be eliminated, Frank had to abandon a plan to force Laura into a marriage. The benefactor isn't a patient man. They took Laura down before they could set the stage to target George in the killing. With Laura out of the picture, Kelly thought she had time to worm her way out of the picture. She wanted insurance that you wouldn't talk to the cops about her involvement with Hector and Frank."

Chuck nodded. "Hector had a temper and without time to work through every angle, he was making Kelly nervous?"

"That, and Hector and her benefactor were forcing her deeper into the web. When George announced that he was leaving, that put another kink in their time frame. When Kelly was told the hit was going down, she packed a bag with the intent to disappear. Someone tipped Hector off. He barged into her place, took her car keys and threatened to kill her if she didn't follow orders."

"You think it was JJ?" Chuck asked.

"Kelly believes it was Frank. He'd stopped by while she was packing. She closed her bedroom door, but after he left she found the door open. It was only half an hour later when Hector made his threat."

"That fits with his cover my back attitude. What was up with the towels you took from my place?"

"Nothing, I needed some rags, I thought you'd share."

"You stole my towels?"

"Get real. They were possible evidence."

"Evidence for what?"

"I saw a towel just like it in the back of Hectors car."

"You were already leaning towards Hector. You could have told me that."

"Couldn't and you know that. The thread in the towels matched thread found in a kitchen drawer at Laura's. The towel in the back of Hector's car was snagged and they found traces of the cleaning fluid."

"Why did you talk to Angela about her monogrammed towels?"

"They were a specialty order item and matched a towel found in Laura's bathroom."

"I can see that as a set up to George, but how would Hector or Frank know about the towels?"

"Kelly purchased the towel at a second hand store.

With the monogrammed S, Hector thought it would be easy to point to George if anyone came around asking questions."

"So, Angela having ordered the same towels was dumb luck."

"It was," Padilla said.

"You told me there was evidence or something being checked out. What was that?"

"Kelly confirmed that a filing cabinet, in the second bedroom closet, was removed from Laura house. It was taken out the backdoor and set on the ground between the lilac bushes. We also found tire tread. By tomorrow I should hear whether the tire tracks match Hector's or Frank's truck."

"Have you found the cameras, baskets or files that were on the desk?"

"The cameras were probably taken to Mexico and pawned. The rest is either burned or buried in the dump." Padilla finished his coffee.

"Yesterday, I received a registered letter from Laura's brothers. They went through the legal steps to dissolve their claim to Laura's estate, and named you as legal beneficiary."

Chuck swallowed the lump in his throat.

"Can you have her body released to a funeral home?"

"I can. The crime scene tapes and locks have been removed from the house. The owner asked that the place be cleaned out by the end of the month. You want help?"

"I'd appreciate that."

"How's your daughter?" Padilla asked.

"The shock of Laura's death is fading. While her

mother was dying they talked. She's never told me what was said, but she came away with strong opinions. Be prepared to release balloons and celebrate Laura's life with music and dancing."

"A wake without the alcohol, not a bad send off."

"After meeting you, Carrie enrolled in a criminal psychology. She told me she's got a list of question to ask you. How's Amy?" Chuck asked.

"She thinks she needs her navel pierced."

"When she says she wants stars tattooed on her face you'll have cause to worry."

"Good point."

"Are you still screening her dates?"

Padilla grinned. "The latest one has a clean record. Maybe there's hope."

"You going to drop by and say hello?" Padilla asked.

"At the police station? Hell no."

"We never got that steak the other night?"

"TRH?"

What?"

"Texas Ranch House"

"Why did you say TRH?"

"TMI?"

"What the hell are you saying?"

"Ask Todd Shelf to explain," Chuck said.

"My credit card can't afford to have me step within his clutches," Padilla said.

"Almost forgot, I have another message for you from Kelly. Since she couldn't take anything but her clothing she's leaving everything at the townhouse to JJ."

"The rents paid for the three months," Chuck said.

"Lucky you," Padilla said and laughed.

"Yeah, lucky me," Chuck said and gave Padilla a wry grin.

"What are you working on now?"

"Stolen weapons from Fort Bliss?"

"Why is a homicide detective investigating stolen weapons from Fort Bliss?"

"Well, let me tell you."

We hope you enjoyed *TMI*, the first book in the Chuck Taylor series. Please check out **twomuchinformation.net** or **irplummer.com** for the release of *NEI* the second Chuck Taylor novel.

If you enjoyed TMI please consider taking a moment to post a quick review at Amazon and Barnes and Noble. And post a comment at your favorite book club, twitter or Facebook. Word of mouth is the breath of life for an independent author–thank you.

Visit the author's website:
http://www.irplummer.com
http://www.twomuchinformation.net

NEI–Coming soon

Every time Chuck Taylor turns on his police scanner trouble follows. He's ready to toss the scanner into the trash when Detective Padilla, El Paso PD, asks for help.

The temperature is up and so is the crime rate, but the evidence in this case leads to a possible conspiracy involving every government agency in El Paso. This case is too big for Detective Padilla alone, too dangerous to share with the El Paso PD, but just right for his old friend Chuck to help with. That is until…

If I'm *Crazy*, I Am In Good Company

If I'm Crazy, I Am In Good Company is about ordinary people who use the intuitive gifts we are given at birth, in extraordinary ways.

Within each of us is the ability to connect with our soul conscious, the part of us that contains a filing cabinet of information that can answer what makes us unique, where we have been and where we are going.

Have you ever ignored a knowingness, a gut instinct of what is about to happen and regretted not listening?

Have you ever had a dream that foretold an important event?

Have you ever experienced déjà vu?

Have you ever walked into a room and instantly known if the occupants were angry or happy?

Have you ever felt the emotional or physical pain of another person?

Have you ever touched an object and had a sense about the owner?

Have you ever had a vision that showed a person's past or future?

Have you ever listened to the 'voice within' and have what you heard happen?

Have you ever thought about calling a person and then run into them at a store or had them call?

Have you ever wondered if you were psychic?

You are not crazy, you are in good company.

Based on Rhonda Plummer's experiences as an intuitive and teacher of intuitive awareness, and the experiences of individuals from around the globe who shared their life stories, *If I'm Crazy, I Am in Good Company*, offers insightful stories that explore how our intuitive senses teach and guide each of us every day.

Hot Ice by I R Plummer

Amy Darling is feisty, opinionated, nosy, and has a bad habit of stumbling over dead bodies. But that's not her fault, really! Then someone tries to kill her and the FBI informs she's been appraising stolen property for organized crime. The mob pay's well, but it's not the kind of career a girl can brag about. Playing sleuth, dodging bullets and trying not to fall for Mr. Wrong, weren't on Amy's agenda but that doesn't stop her from snooping, kicking ass and discovering that there's more to life when you don't play it safe.

HOCUS POCUS

Spellbound Series by I R Plummer

Taking his father's request to play 'I spy' seriously, Dr. Cole Young sets out to prove his over-the-hill uncle's sexy, young, vivacious fiancée uses hypnosis to swindle men out of money. Believing he's too smart to be hypnotized Cole poses as a client to uncover her scam.

Ginger Prescott, a gifted medium and hypnotherapist is used to working with clients with issues ranging from serious to sublimely ridiculous. But she has never dealt with a client whose touch short circuits her senses, has her mind wondering beyond the client/therapist relationship and who obviously isn't who she thought.

With help from a 300-year-old spell, a meddling aunt's haphazard approach to magic and mischievous spirits, Ginger and Cole discover that love does conquer all.

ABRACADABRA

Spellbound Series by I. R. Plummer

Rosemary Prescott, a feisty, intuitive psychic always walks away a winner from games of chance. Until her luck hits a brick wall or more precisely, Walker Owens the handsome, sandy haired devil who owns Dreamland Casino.

Accepting Walkers challenge to work at the casino for 30 days, Rosemary is determined to keep her independence by outwitting a 300 year-old spell, and a meddling aunt's wayward magic.

Walker is being blackmailed. The last thing he needs is an outspoken red head underfoot, but he needs to learn how she's, 'cheating'. And if he can convince himself there is nothing more to the offer to have her work beside him, he can dismiss the explosive chemistry between them as nothing more than temporary insanity, stress and some overly imaginative dreams.

With the ghostly appearances of their parents stirring up mischief, a plot to strip Walker of his inheritance, and steamy past-life dreams disrupting their nights, Walker and Rosemary learn that loving the right person doesn't mean losing your independence.

ALACAZAM

Spellbound Series by I. R. Plummer

Cinnamon Prescott has a fairy godmother with an attitude and a shoe fetish. And if that isn't enough to test Cinn's patience her absentminded, meddling aunt has cast a spell to hasten the arrival of her prince charming.

Within days of closing a major case the last thing FBI agent Jack Cutter needs is a distraction. But a chance encounter puts Cinnamon's life in danger and right in the middle of his undercover operation. Add a vengeance-seeking ghost, Cinnamon's supernatural powers and a 300-year-old spell to the mix and Jack quickly loses control of his case and his heart.

Forced to evaluate everything they thought they knew about themselves and what they saw as their future, Jack and Cinnamon discover that trust is the key to their future happiness.

DAZZLE ME

Spellbound Series by I. R. Plummer

One Spell.
More than three centuries have passed since Maria Romano cast a spell to safeguard the mystical powers that had been passed through her family from generation to generation. Now time and the universe have altered the spell.
One Fairy Godmother.
Salina, FGM Crime Buster, Destiny Inc.
FGM—Fairy Godmother with an attitude, a sexy wardrobe and a trigger happy finger.
One Man.
Lucifer Saints, thirty-three, six foot two inches tall, sandy brown hair, golden eyes.
One Woman.
Sandi Cummings, thirty, five foot ten inches tall, blonde, cobalt blue eyes.
One Destiny.
Lucifer Saints has the face of an angel and a devilish sense of humor that pits his law degree and his powers against the criminals he meets as a private investigator.

Sandi Cummings has a problem, a list of them actually. The family lawyer wants her to sign a living trust that gives the family estate to cats with six toes. The merchandise in her boutique has been transformed into a spectacular collection of designer clothes worth a king's ransom. A sexy ghost keeps popping into the store to help customers. And a dream is suddenly turning up the heat and the stakes to her future.

Sexy dreams, lies, deceit, and a spell cast hundreds of years ago collide as Lucifer and Sandi untangle the puzzle and create their destiny.

Joe Grindstaff--Bio

When someone ask me what I have done, it is possibly easier for me to just start listing the things that I haven't. I grew up on a farm in Chillicothe Missouri, played sports, played in the band, and was a member of every club I could get into. Not having enough money for college, I decided that the Air Force was a good alternative.

After seven years, experience working on all types of military aircraft, a tour of duty in Japan and an accident that made me a disabled veteran, it was time for a new adventure.

The new adventure came in the form of fireman, EMT-D, Chief of Police, and an investigator for the Missouri Rural Major Case Squad. But I wasn't done yet; I decided to be a broadcasting engineer with an NBC affiliate station in Albuquerque, an engineer for a company that made rocket engine controllers in Carlsbad NM, a riverboat pilot on the George Washington, and an investments manager for a good friend.

These days, well I had to slow down a little bit, so you may catch me serving you a drink on Southwest Airlines or in a classroom finishing my doctoral degree in business and information management. If your still not having any luck finding me, sit back and enjoy my book TMI, because I am already at home in El Paso, writing new adventures for Chuck Taylor in the upcoming books called NEI and NIR.

Rhonda (I R) Plummer—Bio

I'm proud to say I was a military brat. That said, I've visited almost every state in the union, and lived in ten states and Japan.

Between marriage, kids, moves and general chaos, I crammed in college, taught painting classes, and owned an insurance agency. When life slowed down, and there was time to explore new interests, I became a certified hypnotherapist, mediator and spent several years as a sales representative for TY. The job gave me a front row seat to Beanie mania and a new perspective on adult insanity—the stories I could write—maybe someday.

Home is 20 acres of land outside Boise, Idaho.

www.ingramcontent.com/pod-product-compliance
Lightning Source LLC
Chambersburg PA
CBHW071210250626
47159CB00001B/265